The Safety of Secrets

DeLauné Michel

AVON

An Imprint of HarperCollins*Publishers*

THE SAFETY OF SECRETS. Copyright © 2008 by DeLauné Michel. All rights reserved. Printed in the United States of America. No part of this book may be used or reproduced in any manner whatsoever without written permission except in the case of brief quotations embodied in critical articles and reviews. For information address HarperCollins Publishers, 10 East 53rd Street, New York, NY 10022.

HarperCollins books may be purchased for educational, business, or sales promotional use. For information please write: Special Markets Department, HarperCollins Publishers, 10 East 53rd Street, New York, NY 10022.

FIRST EDITION

Designed by Elizabeth M. Glover

Library of Congress Cataloging-in-Publication Data

Michel, DeLauné
    The safety of secrets / DeLaune Michel. — 1st ed.
        p. cm.
    ISBN 978-0-06-081736-7
    1. Female friendship—Fiction. 2. Hollywood (Los Angeles, Calif.)—Fiction.
I. Title.
    PS3613.I345S34 2008
    813'.6—dc22   2008004618

08 09 10 11 12 WBC/RRD 10 9 8 7 6 5 4 3 2

The Safety of Secrets

By DeLauné Michel

Aftermath of Dreaming

For my husband,
Daniel Lawrence Fried,
who keeps me safe.

Acknowledgments

I AM DEEPLY AND HAPPILY indebted to my fellow writer Beaty Reynolds for his clarity, insight, and support during the writing of this novel. My agent, Eileen Cope, gave me invaluable suggestions early on. I am grateful for her unflagging belief. Francis Dodick's counsel was instrumental. My editor, Carrie Feron's keen observations steered me gently, and her vision was indispensable. I am fortunate to have Debbie Stier's wisdom, guidance, and panache. Jennifer Richards is a blessing in my life. Charlotte Anderer and Daisy Gumin brought truth and beauty to this cover; I am honored they are on it. Tessa Woodward's help is indefatigable and good-humored, an extraordinary combination. In addition to her great friendship, Jamie Rose made me an honorary member of the redhead club—thank you for sharing its secrets. Christina Beck's encouragement sustained me when I thought nothing could. Lita Weissman at Borders Book Store in Los Angeles is God's gift to writers. Regina Su Mangum was generous with her sagacious advice. I will always appreciate the warmth and grace that Julia Bastida has given my family. Lee Garlington and Courtney Stuart kindly shared helpful information. The audiences, writers, and students of Spoken Interludes have bestowed upon me more gifts than I can enumerate here. My sisters Elizabeth Michel, Pamela Chavez, Maggi Michel, and Aimée Michel are each in their own way a perfect and safe sister to me. And finally, though certainly not least, my mother, Elizabeth Nell Dubus Michel Baldridge, whose unwavering love and support throughout my life has always been essential.

 *Chapter 1*

I THINK I MIGHT BE PREGNANT. And today is Mother's Day.

The only other time that I was pregnant, I found out last Halloween, so maybe my body is particularly fertile two weeks before a holiday. Because I read in this book that no matter how many days a woman's cycle is from ovulation to the first day of her period is exactly two weeks. Which seems kind of wonderful and yet odd to me for it to be that guaranteed. Though comforting, too, that amid all the chaos of life, inside every woman's body is this exquisite and punctual rhythm that is the same for us all. Like in that way at least, we're even.

That other pregnancy didn't work out, but I guess that is obvious or I wouldn't be wondering if I am pregnant now. Sometimes I imagine that Halloween was to blame for its ending since I found out on a day so connected with the dead—but also to my ancestry, actually.

The Irish brought the custom of Halloween to America in the mid-1840s when so many of them were fleeing their country's potato famine. Not that my relatives came then. They left Waterford, Ireland, in 1833; landed in Quebec; then made their way down to Corpus Christi, Texas, until "Indian hostilities," as my mother calls it, forced them to leave and they settled in Opelousas, Louisiana, then finally decades later, Lake Charles, where I grew up and celebrated Halloween.

The ancient origin of which was the belief that on that day disembodied spirits of those who had died in the previous year came back in search of living bodies to possess. They thought it was their only hope for an afterlife, so all laws of time and space were suspended, allowing spirits to intermingle with the living. But the living didn't want to intermingle with them, didn't want to be possessed, so they extinguished their home fires and dressed up in hideous clothes to frighten the spirits away. Neither of which my recently conceived baby was able to do, and I didn't know to do, so maybe it got possessed.

And that is as good an explanation as the one my doctor gave me, which basically was that some just don't make it. For two weeks, the ultrasound kept showing that I was five to six weeks pregnant, but a heartbeat never appeared. A missed miscarriage is what Dr. Walker called it, meaning my body didn't get the message that the pregnancy wasn't going forward, so it stayed stuck in this blossom like some frozen flower in a bowl that at first looks great, but then is sickening to see since it will never fully bloom.

Though after that pregnancy was over, Dr. Walker assured me that I am fine. "Honey, you two are where I'm trying to get most of the couples that see me to be," she said.

I was sitting in her office in the West Tower Medical Building of Cedars-Sinai Hospital in Beverly Hills for the follow-up appointment after my D & C, which I still wasn't really sure what that stood for. "Dice and cut" is all I could think of, like B & E for "breaking and entering," because that is how it felt.

I was surrounded by a swarm of baby pictures on the bookcases, on the desk, on the walls, all the successful fruits of her and her patients' labor. I looked at Dr. Walker. She looked as if she could play one on TV—that pretty. Blonde and sweet. A face you want to come to, like the Giant Casting Director in the sky had ordained her calling. And she was a real doctor, after all, renowned, even. So it was easy to believe her.

I left her office, and I was fine.

I got outside, got in my car, and was sitting stuck on Third Street, a thoroughfare that not so long ago used to be if not barely used then at least Plan C for how to get west or east, but now is almost as bad as Beverly. I wished for the thousandth time that about a million people in L.A. would leave when suddenly it hit me that the city's population was not going to increase by one next summer because of my husband and me, since we were no longer going to have this baby.

And I was sort of shocked, as if I was finally understanding that the pregnancy was over. Not that I didn't know it was over, but the appointment for the D & C had kept it alive in a (okay, major denial) sort of way since they were related to the baby. But now there weren't any more reasons to see Dr. Walker, until another pregnancy. And when would that be?

Immediately, I could hear my mother's voice in my head when I told her it was over.

"Oh, Fiona, honey. That's just terrible. How are you holding up?" Even though my mother was all the way down in Lake Charles, Louisiana, in the same home that I grew up in, she could have been phoning from inside my body. Her voice has always sounded like that to me, as if I've been carrying her around in me my whole life, like some terribly odd and inappropriate pregnancy that I'll never deliver.

"There is nothing worse than a miscarriage," my mother

went on. "Not that I ever had one. Or would have. I got my family's good Connor genes, but your father's sisters, as you know, each had multiple miscarriages. It's a wonder you have any cousins on his side at all. Well, you'll just try again; that's all. And it'll be fine. I'm sure of it. Though why you waited so long in the first place I'll never understand."

I had planned to move the phone repeatedly away from and back to my ear while she spoke the way I have for the past few years, sort of like one of the arm exercises I do at the gym, but my mother's opening lines were so promising that I got hooked in and listened to the whole goddamn thing.

"It wasn't that long, Mother, one year. We just wanted a little time to be newlyweds before—"

"You didn't have that luxury. Of course, you're seeing that now. And I don't care how many women are getting pregnant past thirty-five; that's when the trouble starts, particularly—"

"I'm still thirty-four."

"Barely."

But I don't want to think about all that right now. I am tired of thinking about that damn miscarriage, which has been following me around since last December like a gloomy ghostly presence sitting on my shoulder, talking in my ear, especially when we'd have sex, my husband and me.

The first two months after the miscarriage, we took off. Not off from sex, but off from the possibility of making a baby during sex, so in January and February, Neil used condoms, which he hated and I didn't love, but oh well, they did the job. And I would pretend to myself during sex that we were still dating and had never been pregnant, had never even thought about getting pregnant, and it would start to work. I'm an actress, after all, so if I can't convince myself that a false reality is true, then I really am in trouble. Everything would be going great and I'd be totally in and there with my husband, but him as still my boyfriend when sex was just for fun and it would feel fun, I'd be having sex-fun, until suddenly and completely and deeply I was not. The miscarriage would be back, sitting on my shoulder, whispering in my ear, and to make matters worse, a baby had entered the room. A big-bellied, pink-cheeked, flaxen-haired baby floating in the air just beyond the head of my husband, who suddenly was no longer my boyfriend but very much my husband, and I was supposed to catch this baby somehow. Somehow my rhythm and position and hopefully conception-friendly thoughts were going to form a lariat, and if I did everything right, then that baby up there would be rescued and held and ours, and that mean old miscarriage would go away and we could have sex again without a baby and a ghost in the room, because the baby would be inside me and I would know how to frighten the disembodied spirits away.

So, Jesus, I really hope that I am pregnant. Not just so Neil and I can be free from baby-lassoing sex, though that would be a plus and the tip of the iceberg, so to speak, of the—okay, I won't say daily, but pretty damn close—thoughts I've been having of "When will we get pregnant again?" and "What if we lose that one, too?" and, ultimately, "What if something is wrong with me?"

There is an old acting axiom that the best way to get people to think about elephants is to tell them not to think about elephants, and that is kind of how I've been feeling about this trying to get pregnant. Or being open to getting pregnant, which is my way of saying it in my head in the vain hope that the "la-di-da" attitude of that statement will somehow rub off and be my reality, but finally all I've been thinking about is elephants.

Fred 62 on Vermont Avenue in the Los Feliz section of Los Angeles is a traditional American coffee shop gone awry. Its soda fountain lunch counter, 24/7 hours, and diner-type fare offer comfort, while the bright green exterior, car-seat-style booths, and added special ingredients (Corn Flakes on French toast, anyone?) provide enough irony to allow the recently-transplanted-but-hoping-not-to-look-like-it and the here-so-long-they've-hidden-their-roots to feel as if they are back home while still maintaining a modicum of cool. Needless to say, it is usually packed.

Though this Tuesday, as I enter its refuge, only a few stragglers are scattered among the booths. A breakfast of eggs, pancakes, toast, hash browns, sausage, coffee, and pie is arrayed in front of a pale, black-dyed hair, black-lined eyes thin young man as he talks on his cell phone, glances through the *Los Angeles Times*, and shovels in food. All he needs is plaid pajamas to complete the picture that three in the afternoon is the start of his day. There isn't a hostess in sight, so I don't bother with asking permission to use the ladies' room, even though a sign on the bathroom door admonishes, "For Customers Only!" I figure I've eaten here enough in the two years that Neil and I have lived in this neighborhood to qualify for one free pee.

Not that I am in dire need to use the bathroom, physically, though I did just gulp down a bottle of water. But emotionally, mentally, and, I hope, maternally, the only thing I need to do right now is pee on a stick and have it turn blue—or pink. I'll have to read the instructions to see what the magic color is that means "Baby!"

As I walk through the restaurant clutching the drugstore bag with the pregnancy test inside, I feel like a dope fiend going to shoot up, illicit somehow, like I should be doing this at home. And in a way, I guess I should. In the comfort and privacy of my own home, with my husband in the next room, able to run out and share a TV commercial moment of immediate and in-person glad tidings about this life-changing news. But Neil won't be home from the studio until sevenish, and I can't wait that long.

So here I am. Bathroom door locked. Box opened. Instructions read. I follow them exactly. Then check them again. "Wait three minutes for results." That is a goddamn long time. The manufacturer probably thinks it sounds short, but I happen to know exactly how long three minutes is because that is the standard length of time for a theater audition monologue. They are constantly asking for a three-minute monologue. Or worse, two contrasting three-minute monologues meaning, for example, Portia from *The Merchant of Venice* and Darlene from *Hurly Burly*. But the problem I always have with that two contrasting monologues thing is, What exactly does that mean? That Portia is strong and intelligent and moral and Darlene is not? I know they are different roles in different times and places with different wants. But actually not different wants, because how many wants are there, once you get right down to it?

Love, power, money, property, prestige. Family.

I want a family. And I never used to. Not that I didn't love babies and children. But because of what happened that time, I decided to never have any. Until I met Neil, then everything changed. Or I changed. Or—

Oh, God. I have changed. Double pink lines are showing in the window of the test. Double pink lines instead of a solitary one, symbolic, I suppose, of the twoness I suddenly am. And have been for how many days? At least two weeks according to that book I read.

I want to run out of the bathroom and tell the first person I see, but that probably means black-dyed-and-lined breakfast man, so instead I close my eyes and try to imagine what is inside me. I can remember what the pregnancy book that I read last fall said about these early days: no heartbeat yet (please arrive, heartbeat), only cells multiplying in exquisitely ordered growth—I hope. But I'm not going to think about that right now. Everyone has said that having a miscarriage is not unusual. I've just gotten mine out of the way. But what about my aunts having had four, five, and six? Okay, I refuse to think about that while this ecstatic and influential result is staring me in the face, the first communication, in a sense, from my baby.

Hi, baby.

Though I know it's not really a baby: an embryo is all it is. But what on earth has more consequence than that?

Chapter 2

THE LATE AFTERNOON SUN is gentle on my face as I walk down the sidewalk to my car on Vermont Avenue. I pass a store window filled with coy slogan T-shirts, retro-yet-new clothes, and platform shoes that would make even a short girl six feet tall. I watch my silhouette reflecting in the glass, imagining how months from now (hooray!) it will be drastically changed.

Like I am inside. All because of one physical act, and from now on, I will never be the same. Or still sort of the same, but with another identity that is already forming way deep inside and will keep growing and expanding to alter and transform me.

A movie poster in a case at the Los Feliz 3 catches my eye, so I stop in front of it. Other than its turgid title, it is a picture of the hottest mostly-studio-but-still-does-indies film actress in a 1950s dress and a wistful glow. I met her once when I was working at a clothing store on Melrose before my acting jobs started coming in. Her second film had just come out, and while it was small, her presence in it was not, and it was clear that she had just jumped straight to the top. Her friend was trying on a slew of the floral and overly romantic dresses the store was known for and kept coming out to the three-tier mirror to hitch up the long skirts and arrange her breasts in the corset tops. I said something about how even I, with my small breasts, felt voluptuous in those dresses, and the actress pulled me aside and said, "Look," as she took from her bag two squishy, flesh-colored orbs.

"I just slip these puppies in right before an audition or shoot, and I'm good to go. Who needs surgery?" she said, with a wink and a grin. She hadn't had to ask if I was an actress, too, and her instant camaraderie pulled me into and almost made me part of her imminent fame.

As I look at her movie poster, I remember hearing that she was pregnant during the filming. I wonder how long she was able to work before she began to show—and how long will I?—when I realize that someone has walked up behind me and stopped in front of the poster.

I instinctively hold my bag tighter, as I turn my head to glance over. The man is taller than me, with sandy brown short hair and neat clothes that almost look like they were ironed both inside and out. I relax my grip a bit and am just about to turn back to the poster when he tilts his head to one side and looks down at me through his lashes. My stomach suddenly clenches and dread spreads through my body. I stand frozen before the poster, as if I have received a silent command. He is still next to me. I can barely breathe, much less move. It takes me a few seconds to understand that not only can I move, but I need to—need to get away from him and fast. It is all I can do not to break into a run.

Once I am walking on the sidewalk again amid the uninterested and anonymous pedestrians, I have to remind myself that everything is fine, but it is as if my world is about to end.

Okay, it's probably just the pregnancy hormones making me feel so nuts, but who knew they kicked in this soon? And that look of his was like someone, someone I once knew, I just can't think who. And maybe don't want to.

I reach my car, and make it inside just as weakness in the back of my legs hits me full size. My stomach drops and dips. Okay, I'm pregnant, for Christ's sake; that's all this is. I think. But the heat, when did it suddenly get so goddamn hot? I roll down my window to get some air, then remember that I can start my car and turn on the a.c. Okay, I just need to get home—that's all—and then I'll be fine. I pull into traffic and move (all right, swerve) into the left lane to turn onto Franklin.

But instead of taking a right onto my street, I keep driving by. There is no way I can be alone right now, so I head toward the one person who should know.

Chapter 3

"I'M PREGNANT."

"What? Fiona! Oh my God!"

My best friend pulls me toward her in a deep embrace as we stand on the doorstep of her home high in the hills off Mulholland Drive, a neighborhood for people who matter worldwide.

"I know; I'm kinda amazed."

Patricia stands back to look at me. She was clearly in the middle of a workout. Her newly lightened hair is in a too-tight-to-be-flattering ponytail, and she's wearing her captain of the girls' basketball team T-shirt from our high school days. Go, Wolverines.

"I started to call you," I say. "But I thought, Jesus, I can't not tell her this in person, so I—"

"Uh, yeah! This is so fabulous!" And we are hugging again, as if it is our next line of dialogue. "Come sit down," Patricia says, as we finally untangle, and she turns to go inside. "You shouldn't be standing."

"I'm fine; I'm barely—"

"I know, but it's fun. Come put your feet up." Patricia goes to the coffee table to move a large pile of magazines (every fashion, style, and gossip rag is there), as I follow her past the dining area, past the conversation pit (a round, carpeted area with a step to sit on all around the inside, like a hot tub without the water), and down three steps into the sunken living room.

Patricia lives in a house that was built in 1970 for a sitcom star. To the casual eye, it is just another groovy, yet kitschy split-level ranch, or "splanch," as Patricia has called it ever since she bought it last year and had it redone period perfect. But in a way, it may as well be on top of an Indian burial ground. The home that was knocked down to build it was one of the few remaining that were designed by Rudolf Schindler, a master of early twentieth-century modern architecture and a peer of Frank Lloyd Wright. A coffee table art book of Schindler's work came with the house. When Patricia showed the book to me, I was struck at how much more timeless and modern the original house looked than this one that replaced it almost fifty years later. I imagined the book being passed from owner to owner, an odd remembrance of a place none of them had visited, and now never could. As if the best thing that could happen to a home was to be demolished and only live on as a pristine photograph from the past—like an actress in this town over forty.

"Did you just find out?" Patricia says, as she sprawls out on a plastic molded lounger.

"Yeah, I bought a test, but couldn't wait to get home, so I popped into Fred's and—"

"You took it in their bathroom?"

"Well, it's not like I had to do that much more than I normally do in there."

"Fi, you didn't. That's hysterical. Like that time we were nine and you washed your hair under that old woman's porch—"

"Oh God, right?"

"The look on her face." Patricia jumps up and fairly aerobicizes her way across the room to a fully stocked wet bar. I always expect to hear Burt Bacharach music whenever I see it. "I thought I was never gonna stop laughing, and with her standing right there," Patricia says, as she deep knee bends down and grabs two bottles of water from a minifridge.

"And I had to bite a hole inside my lip so I wouldn't." Our giggles are the remaining sounds that we held in from way back then. "Lord," I say, shaking my head at the memory of it. I take the proffered bottle from Patricia's hand as she zips back to her chair. "But what a rotten little day that turned into."

"There's an understatement. What your mother did—"

"Yeah."

We drink our water in silence. Outside the wall of glass sliding doors, Los Angeles lies beyond Patricia's pool like its own body of water. I want to swan dive into it.

"Okay, happy thoughts. When're you due?"

"January sometime." I smile.

"Oh my God," Patricia's voice trills in the sparsely furnished space. "This is so exciting! I hope it's a girl. I mean, I'll be happy with a boy, but I hope it's a girl. Won't we have fun with a girl? And I get to be the fairy godmother!"

"Let's hope this one makes it so you can."

"Hush. That was just a fluke."

Patricia leans sideways and stretches out an arm to reach a plaster-of-paris head that is sitting on a low built-in bookcase. The head is of her, made by a makeup artist as a mold for a prosthetic face that Patricia wore in a never-saw-the-light-of-day sci-fi film. "My anti-Oscar," she calls it. With her fingertips extended full length, she brushes dust off the brows.

"Is Neil ecstatic?" Patricia says, as she focuses on her cleaning.

"I haven't told him yet. I'm waiting 'til he gets home."

My words suddenly seem more solid and real than the faddish furniture in the room. They fly through the air, landing on the shag carpet here, a circular shaped chandelier there. I look at them and they stare back at me while silently repeating their meaning. She knows; he does not.

Not that I wasn't aware as I drove up here that I was going to tell Patricia. And I did think about Neil—wanting to tell Neil, can't wait to tell Neil—but I also needed to tell someone immediately, and for almost my entire life that has been Patricia, so why shouldn't it be now? And, okay, I do know why it shouldn't be now—marital vows, it's his baby too—but it's my body that is going through this, and that's the kind of thing I tell Patricia. Okay, I tell her everything, as she does me, but this kind of girl/body/sex stuff definitely. It's almost like she was here first, in terms of loyalty. And in terms of years she was, so it's hard just suddenly to put that aside, no matter how wonderful Neil is, especially since Patricia and I know the one thing about each other that no one else ever will and that I wouldn't tell Neil, even if I wanted to, which I don't, so it doesn't matter. Then why am I suddenly feeling like it does?

"Wow, you got pregnant fast," Patricia says. One of her legs is straight out in front of her, and she is grasping her cross-trainer shoe clad foot in both of her hands. She has told me that she wants to lose enough weight to get down one size to a four. Not that I think she needs to, but every time I tell her that, she says, "But wouldn't it be fun for us to share the same clothes? And besides, the camera adds ten pounds."

Patricia pushes her torso down over her leg in a stretch that neither of us has ever been able to do. I immediately remember being in the girls' gym with her during PE and rolling our eyes at each other while waiting for that gruesome exercise to end. I am impressed that she is attempting it on her own. I'll do it in yoga class, but only because I have to.

"I guess that feng shui really worked." Her words sound smothered from the pose.

"I know, right?"

A month after my miscarriage, in a fit of wanting to expel the old and bring in a new healthy baby, I decided to hire someone to feng shui the house. Years before, Patricia and I had used a book to feng shui my apartment, which led, we think, directly to my meeting Neil, but I figured with something as delicate and tricky as pregnancy, big guns were needed. So I called a clothing designer friend of mine whose business had quadrupled after she had had her house done.

"Sisters," Rosie said. "And they're the real deal. Get ready to be rocketed to the fourth dimension. You'll definitely get whatever it is you want. I hope Neil is prepared."

He wasn't, but, in a way, I wasn't either, though the minute they walked in our front door, I knew in my gut that help had arrived. Kitty and Lucy were from China, and while Kitty walked silently around my home looking as if every bad feng shui energy was being directed personally at her, Lucy talked nonstop to me, asking about Neil and the baby we wanted and my miscarriage and career until Kitty walked back into the living room for us to begin.

We rearranged the furniture. We made a kind of altar of love (two crystal candlesticks and a Tiffany red heart paperweight) on a small table since it was in the marriage section of the room. We moved the drapes from the dining room windows (thank God for the roman shades underneath) and rehung them in the archway between the living room and dining room (where they looked better actually, their soft semiopaque red letting in a beautifully tinted light), so that the dining room table wouldn't be visible from the front door. "Otherwise, Fiona, people steal good luck when come to door," Kitty said. "Must protect. Only friends see."

She was the one with the true gift, who had studied for years and knew such intricacies as the eight-year cycles of when to renovate and when not to; that paintings of water should only be hung on east-facing walls; and what each of our lucky directions were, which meant Neil and I would have to switch sides of the bed.

I didn't think it was going to be a big deal to tell him, "Cutie, all your *Sports Illustrated* are now in the basket on the other side of the bed—here's why." But nothing could have prepared me for when Kitty pointed at the second bathroom.

"Here where problem is." She peered in from the doorway, as if entering meant contamination. "This children section of home. All efforts—" She closed her eyes and shook her head at the horror of it.

"Going down drain," Lucy finished for her.

"Well, there's a metaphor. Okay, so, what do we do?"

Kitty and Lucy turned to look at me, as if willing me to divine the information from them. Finally Kitty spoke. "Get rid of it."

"Great. How?"

"Fiona, you want baby?" Lucy took my hand as she spoke and stared into my eyes. "You never use bathroom again."

"What? Are you kidding me?"

The two sisters shared a look. I could almost hear them mind reading each other, "These American women! Want all the goodies without the hard work."

"Okay, okay, let me get this straight, I shut this door, then we pretend this bathroom doesn't exist?"

"No, no, no," Lucy said.

"Well, thank God, because I thought—"

"Have to fix energy. Take mirror down, close drains, put plants on toilet, sink, and tub," Kitty said, checking to see if I was following the plan. "You come in once a week water plants and sweep."

I stared from one to the other. They were both smiling at me, as if I had just told them about the healthy, happy baby I had delivered thanks to their elimination of not only an entire room, but also the second bathroom, the "What's the secret to a happy marriage? A second bathroom!" room. I couldn't even imagine giving Neil this lovely piece of news.

"Isn't there something else we could do? Get some major mojo feng shui object that would—"

"Fiona," Lucy said. "You want baby? My sister help you. This only way. We don't make what part of house is children energy. Kitty tell some people move: house so bad, nothing she can do. This easy fix."

Easy for you, I thought, as I looked at them. They were like two atoms, making up an essential molecule.

"Okay, plants for the never-to-be-used-bathroom, it's on the list. What's next?"

"Fiona, that is not why we had a miscarriage."

Neil and I were standing next to each other in the hall, looking into what used to be our second bathroom. He had started to walk in, but I pulled him out. Maybe his just being in that bathroom would affect our chances, just as Neil's riding a bicycle or taking a steam bath was temporarily verboten.

"Okay, maybe not completely technically exactly why we had a miscarriage." Though secretly I had decided that Kitty and Lucy were right. The whole problem was the bathroom, and now everything was going to be fine, as long as I could convince Neil. "But this is like taking vitamins; it's just a healthy, proactive thing we can do for our baby."

"Healthy? For us to have one bathroom?"

"It won't be so bad."

"Our mortgage just went up. Thanks to a couple of Chinese women, we're now paying the same amount for less space. Isn't that bad feng shui?"

"Can't we just try it, Neil?" I put my arms around him and began kissing his neck and mouth. "Please?"

"So," Patricia says, as she releases her other foot and finally straightens back up. "When are you telling your mother?"

I can't tell if it's my pregnancy, Patricia's nonstop exercising, or her bringing up my mother that suddenly exhausts me. "Oh. God. Not until it's definite this time, whenever that is.

When it's born. No, I don't know. I guess, what, after we see the heartbeat?"

"Don't ask me."

"Well, not for a good long while, at least, I'm not telling her."

"Good, you shouldn't."

"That's what I think, and I'm sure Neil will, too."

Neil's mouth still has the same smile it burst into when I told him the news, but a wariness flickers across his eyes as he says, "So, when are we due?"

"January sometime. Dr. Walker will tell us more exactly. And not to jinx it, but I have a really good feeling this time."

He has just gotten home from work, and as much as I thought I would let him get inside and put down his keys and Blackberry, I blurted out the news the minute he walked in the door. The large-pane windows of our 1920s Craftsman style house are open, and I can smell the roses in our front yard on the evening breeze.

"I do, too, but we need to be careful."

"I am. I'm taking folic acid, no more caffeine, and—"

"No, I meant I don't want to tell anyone until we see the heartbeat." Neil's absolute blue eyes look straight into mine. "Even Patricia."

"I'm not." I have a sudden impulse to cross my fingers behind my back since I have already told Patricia. "At least yet." As if "yet" hadn't just happened less than two hours ago. I immediately feel like Bill Clinton with the word *is*. There's a slippery slope. Okay, telling Patricia is not the same as committing adultery. And she's my best friend, for Christ's sake. Telling her is like telling myself. And it's not like she's going to blab it to anyone.

"Let's see the heartbeat, then only tell our families until twelve weeks."

"Twelve weeks? So my first female bonding over this is with my mother? Neil, I get to tell my best friend."

"Of course you do, but can't you wait? Let's just let it be our secret for a while. For us."

The house stays silent while Neil looks at me. Even the low distant din of traffic seems to have disappeared. I suddenly realize that he is waiting for my response.

"Yeah. I think so, too."

"We're having a baby," Neil says, smiling and pulling me close to him. Then he does a sideways dance around the coffee table to lower us onto the couch, where we proceed to do what led us to this state in the first place.

This morning, as soon as Neil left for work, his parting was filled with more kisses than normal and lots of admonitions to take it easy. I called Patricia immediately.

"Hey," I say to her voice mail, which I figured might pick up. "I know I'm seeing you later, but I just wanted to call real quick and ask you not to tell anyone that I'm pregnant. I mean, not that you would, I know that you wouldn't, but I'm just saying please don't because Neil doesn't want us to tell anyone yet, so I kind of had to pretend to him that I hadn't told you, so I'd hate for it to get around that I am. Not that it would, because I know you wouldn't tell anyone, but you know what I mean. Okay, so, see you at two, bye."

Chapter 4

PATRICIA IS LATE as I wait at Geisha Nail Salon on Melrose in West Hollywood for our manicure/pedicure finally to celebrate my birthday, which was two months ago. She has been late her whole life, as if the Earth should slow down its rotation so everyone else can get on her time. As if the Earth had it wrong from the beginning, and her birth marked the start of the new standard time—Patricia Woods Time. Even when I make allowances for her to be late, she is late, so I pick up a magazine from the pile on the chrome and smoked glass coffee table to look at houses and clothes I can't afford, and wouldn't buy even if I could afford, thereby feeling deprived and satisfied all at the same time.

It takes me a second to adjust to the way Patricia looks when she walks in the door: fabulous, coddled, and with a hundred and twenty five thousand dollars a week radiating from her skin. She has looked this way for over a year now, ever since the TV show she is on became the surprise national hit, thereby catapulting her income, career, life, and therefore looks into another realm.

Patricia is a hostess/judge on a network TV show called

Sports Giant, a reality show where ordinary—and I mean ordinary—people compete in a variety of extreme sports, none of which they are the least bit able to do. Most of the show's appeal (who are we kidding?) is the thrilling possibility that one (or more) of the contestants will seriously wipe out and end up—well, no one honestly wants that to happen. But then why were the Roman coliseums always so full? However, according to the show's promos that run ad nauseam, the whole point of *Sports Giant* is for "the common man or woman to test him or herself beyond their limits and find the 'Sports Giant' within." Oh. And when a lucky contestant finally does win, he or she has to scream, "I'm a Sports Giant! I'm a Sports Giant!" over and over while staring straight into the camera. The winners usually accompany that with some sort of physical gesture, like pumping their fists in the air or jumping up and down, which is meant to convey extreme joy and strength, but only serves to show even more clearly how out of shape they are and makes the audience marvel at how this person was able to survive what he or she endured in the first place, while fooling the viewers into believing that they would do better if they ever got on the show, which they then try to do.

When Patricia first landed the job, she brushed aside any qualms about leaving the "legit world" of scripted TV and film and was beyond ecstatic about (1) the money (who wouldn't be?) and (2) no longer doing the attractive-but-not-sexy-and-beautiful best friend roles. This was finally her big chance, she told me. Why wait around, hoping to get a breakout role in a small, but important independent film to put her on the map (like I still am) when she could make bank, have her own show (so to speak), and finally be "the Girl" as she called it; I could hear the quotation marks around the words. But once *Sports*

Giant was off and running, it quickly became apparent that her role was going to be the lone holdout for women's dignity while being treated like one of the guys.

Today, however, she does not look like one of the guys. Patricia is wearing a stunning skirt that looks easy and fabulous with her snug T-shirt and strappy high heel shoes. She clearly dressed for me. Now I realize that our mani/pedi is not the only thing on her schedule for today, but I don't know a woman on this planet, at least any of the ones in this universe known as L.A., who doesn't dress for her female friends. Any red-blooded, pussy-loving man is happy to see a woman in as little as possible, fashion trends be damned. Only a woman cares about skirt silhouette or what the new black is or which designer T-shirt is this season's must.

Not that I haven't dressed for her, too. I have. And I love the clothes I'm wearing: a little spaghetti strap top with a bias cut skirt. And while I did purchase them two weeks ago at Barney's (when I had no idea that I probably, I hope, won't be able to fit into them months from now), it is strikingly clear that they hail from the yes-expensive-but-not-insane third floor while Patricia's are from the hard-core, high-cost designer second floor.

As I stand up to hug her hello, the magazine slips from my lap, falling open to a page bearing the same skirt that Patricia is wearing, though there it is worn by another actress, a film star whose TV star husband recently left her after a supposedly (nationally, at least) secret, but actually (in L.A.) very public affair with his costar. The fashion magazine spread is clearly a publicist's orchestrated attempt to show how gorgeously and independently the rejected wife is handling that blow, though inside rumors around town have her flying to

Vegas every weekend to gamble away huge sums in the poker craze that has hit Hollywood because all the young actors here think they can bluff their way through a bad hand as if it were a bad script.

"Well, this is gonna be fun," I say. Patricia's cheek is next to mine as we embrace. She shot up two inches in eighth grade and we have looked eye-to-eye ever since.

"Why'd you think I was gonna tell someone your news?"

I pull back from her arms and sit down again on the couch. The dark eyes of the Vietnamese women glance up at Patricia and then quickly dart back to the nails they are filing, the feet they are pumicing, and the legs they are kneading. I can't tell if it is Patricia's fame or what she said that intrigued them.

"I didn't. I said that I didn't. I just don't—"

"Then why'd you call and tell me not to tell anyone? I mean, who would I tell?"

And that was stupid and weird because we only know all the same people. A small, pretty woman motions us toward two empty pedicure chairs that are padded like the La-Z-Boy loungers that my father never owned. I climb up into the throne of one of them. A small moat of water starts to bubble in front of me, as another small and dark-haired woman gently guides my feet into the swirling pool.

"And not to be ugly, but who cares?" Patricia says. "I mean, not who cares—I care—but everyone has something big going on—" I can easily imagine which particular realm of "big" Patricia is referring to. "You being pregnant is just one thing."

"Okay, good, then I don't have to worry because it's not interesting enough to tell." I start to climb out of the chair, my wet feet slipping a bit on the platform built around it.

"I forgot to pick a color," I say to the woman at my feet. "I'll be right back." Patricia, of course, has brought her own color, probably some mixed-just-for-her enamel that her makeup artist cooked up at home. I hope it stains her nails.

"First off," I say to Patricia as I settle back into my chair, the red polish I picked ready and waiting like the aftermath of a battle in a bottle. "I clearly said in my message that I didn't think you were going to tell, and I was only saying it out of respect to my husband." Ever since last summer, when Patricia's fiancé dumped her completely out of the blue, I have been careful about using the *husband* word around her, but now I don't care. "And you act like you've never told things before and that is so not true."

"What have I told?"

"How about, 'Don't tell anyone where you got it.' Does that ring a bell?"

"All right, so your name slipped out. It wasn't that big a deal," Patricia says, as a small and silent woman massages her hand.

"I got suspended. Not to even mention what my mother did to me. So, yes, in fact, you have told."

"Okay, already, but never anything that matters."

"Define matters."

"Fi," Patricia shoots me a look that is her mother all over. Her mother on the rare occasions when Vicky had managed to summon the time, energy, and information to try to take an interest in her daughter's life. "The tree house."

"Are you nuts? Especially here."

"I wasn't. Jesus."

I glance down at the women doing our nails, but neither gives any indication that she was listening. Not that they could have figured out what we were talking about anyway, but for Patricia even to mention that in this public place is a shock. Especially since they could be spies for the *National Enquirer* for all we know, making thousands of dollars on the side. Not that I think that they are, but with what they must hear, they could probably have quite a racket on the side like the maitre d's who call the paparazzi the minute stars show up at their restaurant.

"No cutting, please," Patricia says to the Vietnamese woman who is kneeling at her side and working on her nails. Patricia flashes her a grin that would not be out of place on the red carpet. I wonder if she is practicing. Or maybe her physically higher position has mentally bumped her into the Hollywood royalty role of dealing with service where the unspoken but understood agreement is that the servers are getting more out of it than the stars—supposedly.

"The cuticles, no cutting," Patricia says, grinning madly again.

The woman doing my manicure has already clipped the skin around my nails with a zealous precision that I was glad for. I imagine Patricia's makeup artist condemning the practice vehemently.

Patricia is staring raptly across the room at a soap opera playing mutely on the TV as if it is the greatest acting she has ever seen. I wonder if now that she is on a TV show, and no longer goes from guest star role to guest star role with the occasional independent film as I do, she has embraced all the series-regular actors on TV as if they are her long lost perfect family. I really hope to God she has not. Please have the same taste as before. Soap operas have always reminded me of Kabuki. Not that I have ever seen Kabuki theater, but from the

little that I know about it, the artificially heightened and artificially real emotions are the same. They should dub this soap
in Japanese.

"How's *Sports Giant*?" I say at the commercial break. The
wonderful/horrible thing about having a friend who is on the
hottest national TV show is that it must always be asked about.
Not that everyone doesn't have something that should always
be asked about, but most other people's jobs are not in everyone's living room once a week. So, Patricia's job must always
be addressed, like an insistent child that accompanies her
wherever she goes, demanding time and attention and praise. I
want to call it "Sports Brat."

"It's great," Patricia says, putting her fingers into the mini–nail
dryer that the small woman has brought out. "Karen Blake is
guest judging this week, so that's cool. She's great."

I nod my head. If I let myself speak, I will have to scream.
Then when I stop screaming, I will have to ask Patricia how
and when her conversion occurred. Patricia and I have detested Karen Blake together for a very long time. Okay, maybe
not detested, but have been equally baffled by her movie
stardom because Karen Blake is basically, we think, talent-free.
And it isn't like she has the to-die-for body of the other
talent-free-but-have-careers actresses in this town. In fact,
other girls' bodies have famously stood in for hers on the
posters for her films. And her face isn't even beautiful. At best,
it is nonthreatening in a nicely symmetrical way. Karen Blake
is the sort of girl you remember from the school bus in fifth
grade, so why she has a career Patricia and I have never understood. Not even great tongue technique can get an actress
that far.

"Ugh, I have to go," Patricia says. "I have to get all the way over to Santa Monica for a fitting. Did I tell you I'm doing a shoot for *InStyle?*

"No, that's great." I think about the rest of my day, which basically is just going to the gym, and wish we could trade. Then don't because then I'd have to have her whole life, too, i.e, no Neil and no pregnancy, but still. *In* fucking *Style.*

"Yeah. Then Zane and I are going to Vegas tomorrow for a long weekend, so—"

Zane. Whenever I hear the name of Patricia's boyfriend of six months, I imagine some woman in a lonely rural town stuck with dusty old videos of *Shane* and *Zorro* to get her through her pregnancy, then in the delirium of her labor, naming her child Zane in deference to them. In reality, he was probably named Jim.

Not that I've ever met him, and that does feel weird since she is my best friend, but he's been on a big shoot, and Patricia keeps saying, "Soon," whenever I bring it up. But I have seen a couple of the films that he's done since he retired from his professional snowboarding career and became a movie star and I never would have pictured Patricia with him. Mostly because he has a kind of "Can't decide if you want to fuck him or smack him" quality that I don't associate with Patricia because none of the guys she's ever been with were like that. They were more the brotherly type, but also because after a certain amount of time I think that that quality would automatically default into only the "smack him" part. But she seems happy. I guess.

"Well, happy late birthday! We should have had lunch." Patricia touches the arm of a Vietnamese woman walking by. "Can you take my wallet out for me? My Amex card is in there."

"No credit card," the woman says. "Cash only."

"Cash?" Patricia says, as if the concept is as foreign as the woman's accent. "Shit, I don't . . . Is there an ATM around here? Maybe I can just . . . Fuck, I don't have time to . . ."

I physically have to stop myself from shaking my head and rolling my eyes. I read somewhere once that the Kennedys never carry cash, and I wonder if Patricia is going all out in trying to be American royalty, an oxymoron if there ever was one.

"Patricia, you know this place only takes cash."

"No, I didn't." She looks hurt and confused, as if the rules were changed on purpose and just before she got there to ensure her failure at paying for my birthday celebration. I think of the hundreds of times we have met here for manicures. What black hole in her brain did the details of those experiences disappear into? Or maybe her brain has become its own black hole thanks to TV stardom.

"Here." I carefully snag my wallet out of my bag and hand it to the Vietnamese woman. "Take out sixty to pay for us both, please."

"Sorry, Fi, I'll pay you back. I mean, it is your birthday present, and all."

"Whatever. I really don't care." Because if I did, I would have to kill her. But I do, so I might.

Patricia is wearing an expression I have seen a thousand times. Her mouth is tucked in as if she is bracing against a frown while trying to smile. Her eyes are looking into mine with a searching, worried gaze. And she looks deeply disappointed, as if I am the one who has let her down. I want to slap her. And rewind this to the beginning when she walked in to see if we could do a better take, like happy best friends. Like that acting technique of working from the outside in: do the physical and the emotions will follow. Not that I ever believed in that technique, but maybe it could work this time.

"Well, I need to run," she says, standing up and stepping off the platform. I consider staying in my chair. Its thronelike cushi-ness is more embracing and comforting than my oldest and best friend. But stay for what? More conflict acted silently on the small screen? I step onto the floor and slip into my sandals.

"Oh, God, your belly! I almost forgot!" Patricia puts her hand on my stomach and rubs it a bit, which is odd because it doesn't look any different than it did last week. She's basically rubbing cells. I hate when Patricia tries hard.

"Yeah," I say, forcing a smile. One of the manicurists looks at us with an opaque gaze. I can only imagine what she is thinking.

"It's gonna get so big!"

"One hopes." I am shocked at how quickly something that felt like it would forever supersede any other emotion has already succumbed to my best friend's killjoy behavior.

"Well."

Patricia seems to be having a hard time leaving. I realize that I have no choice but to walk outside with her where there won't be manicurists and customers to chaperone us. Not that I think we will do anything untoward, but suddenly I really do not want to be alone with her, even on a sidewalk, where the distance and discomfort between us will be even more apparent. I feel like I'm in the soap opera on the TV, but can't remember my exit line, so will be stuck here for eternity. I decide to use that stupid outside-in acting technique, hoping that doing the action will imbue it with meaning, so I give Patricia a hug. She seems almost startled, then when I try to let go, she keeps holding on to me, so I stop letting go, but then she pulls away.

"Well, talk to you soon."

"Yeah. We're leaving tomorrow afternoon, so maybe in the morning," Patricia says.

I start to tell her that I have an early call for the TV movie that I booked but then don't because I'm not going to initiate our phone call anyway. And I seriously doubt that she will. Though if I did call her, I know that she would act as if she was just about to call me.

We pick up our bags and walk out the door onto Melrose Avenue, heading our separate ways in the unforgiving afternoon light.

Chapter 5

MY FRIENDSHIP WITH PATRICIA began with a pair of socks. We were in first grade together at the Sacred Heart of Jesus Elementary School in Lake Charles, Louisiana. Patricia sat in the second to last desk on the far right side of the room while I was firmly ensconced in the middle thanks to the *M* of my last name, Marshall. I knew her as the barely combed, brown haired girl who arrived late each day in a swirl. She reminded me of a stuffed animal whose fur had dried funny after being left out in the rain. A little combing and caressing was all that were needed, but that never happened.

One afternoon soon after first grade had started, I was sitting at the kitchen table in my house eating my daily snack of Chips-A-Hoy cookies and Delaware Punch. The windows and door were shut against the late August day, but its pressure lay just outside. The south Louisiana heat was a mass that accumulated each hour into a force that rendered everything stunned. The only sound I could hear was the air conditioner until my mother's sharp footsteps approached, first on the foyer's hardwood floor, then the dining room's soft rug, and finally the butler's pantry's scarred linoleum before she entered the kitchen. Their quick loud-quiet-loud was a drumroll of her impending presence.

"Fiona, darling, look at this." She put a glossy brochure on the table next to my plate. "It's for the Red Birds," Momma said, as she went to the refrigerator and took out a large bottle of Tab to refill her glass for the hundredth time of the day.

My mother's deep red hair was cut short around her angular face. Months before, when she had first come home from the beauty parlor with this new style, she had told me it was a pixie cut. I immediately begged her to let me have my similar-hued hair like hers. A pixie cut! The name alone was a ticket to join the land of fairies. I wanted to be a pixie.

There was a book I had that had belonged to my mother, *The Golden Book of Elves and Fairies with Assorted Pixies, Mermaids, Brownies, and Leprechauns.* I had found it in the attic when we went up there one day last year to bring down a lamp my momma decided to use in the den. I loved going in the attic with her and would run up the few times she pulled open the trap door and brought the ladder down. It was filled with other-worldly things. The trunk with her trousseau from her honeymoon with Daddy. My grandfather's golf clubs, inherited by my father, but never used. The bedroom set from my mother's girlhood room, back in the far corner and fully arranged almost as if, once a mattress was in place, her younger self could inhabit it again.

But the best discovery was the book of fairies and pixies and elves. I found it on a low shelf of her childhood books and took it downstairs while my mother was fussing with the lamp. I didn't know that she wouldn't let me have it, but I didn't want to find out.

The minute she left my room after saying goodnight, I slipped out of bed, went to my dresser that was built into the wall, and pulled the bottom drawer all the way out, so that my secret hiding place underneath was revealed. Lying on top of the treasures I had found in the neighborhood, a small milky blue glass bottle, an old house key, a broken watch missing its strap, was the book. I climbed back into bed, turned on my lamp, and opened the book. It didn't matter that I couldn't read the words. I didn't need any words. Here was a bold new world filled with wondrous, enchanting, and cunning wee folk who had always been all around me that I had just never seen. But not anymore. As I turned page after glorious page, I vowed to become one of them.

But when I begged my mother for that magically named haircut, all she had said was, "Then what we would do with all your pretty ribbons and barrettes?" And she picked up my long hair, then let it fall gently back down, one coral mani-cured nail scratching me a bit as she did.

I didn't ask again that afternoon, but I knew the haircut was wasted on her. Pixies and fairies had no interest in adults.

My mother was talking about how she had been a Red Bird and now I would be one, too. Then she went on about after-school meetings and nature walks and songs around a campfire. I had no idea what any of that had to do with being a Red Bird. The kids in my neighborhood and I played a game called "Owls and Blue Jays" where we'd divide into teams of the birds, then tear around with our arms outstretched, trying to capture each other's nest. A lot of running and flying, i.e, jumping from things, and squawking were involved, and we'd all end up flopped on the grass, red-faced and panting from the heat, but minutes later, ready for more. I figured this Red Birds was some sort of game like that, but with fancy rules and stuff added because adults were interested in it, too.

I picked up the brochure and turned it over. A picture of a girl about my age took up the top half of the cover. She had light brown hair and freckles and was smiling despite missing two front teeth. But it was what she was wearing that captivated me. It was an outfit of white and deep red. Momma never me let wear red because of my hair. Purple definitely, and pink maybe, but red was out of the question. But here was this uniform, which I clearly would wear: a deep red skirt, crisp white shirt, and, the best part, a deep red sash across the front like Miss America, but this one was filled with pretty, little colorful patches. If I looked closely, I could make out the pictures on some of them: a pine tree, a needle and spool of thread, a swimmer. This was even better than the Miss America contest, which was the supreme honor for women as far as my father was concerned, where the sashes bore only the name of the state. This sash was covered with tiny windows into entirely different worlds, whereas Miss America's kept them stuck at home. Being a Red Bird not only would enable me to wear the long forbidden color, but was a way to become someone else.

Momma showed me pictures of herself as a Red Bird, her uniform proud and perfect on her like an inner glory that all could see. And she let me try on my uniform when she brought it home a week before the first meeting. The sash didn't have any achievement patches on it yet, but the Nature Girls of America insignia was there, my troop number had been sewn on, and most thrilling of all was my membership pin. I was truly in. As Momma took the pin out of its little plastic case, she told me that the female Red Bird is unlike any other bird because it sings just as beautifully as the male bird while still taking care of the young. "Like women, because we can do everything," she said. "But don't ever tell that to a man. Especially your father."

I finished putting the uniform on and was looking in my mother's full-length, three-tier, gold-rimmed mirror. I had never seen myself in red before. The way Momma had always acted about it, I thought something horrible would happen if I ever put it on. But nothing did. There I was with my dark red hair above the red and white uniform. No explosion, but no glory shining through either.

Then Momma said, "Don't forget these." And she handed me a pair of official Red Bird socks. They were heaven. And so far removed from the boring old navy blue cotton ones that I had to wear to school. These were like stockings, white and opaque and tall on my legs to my knees. And on each side was a cunning little Red Bird with outstretched wings starting its own journey, like I was mine. I put them on, stepped into my shoes, and then stood up. My transformation into being a Red Bird was complete.

"Oh, Fiona! Look at you!" my mother said, clapping her hands. "I have such great memories." Then she gave me a hug, the rarity of which made it all the more intoxicating.

I had wanted to keep the uniform on for the rest of the afternoon, or at least the socks, but Momma said they were only for the meetings, like some dresses were for parties: you don't play in those either, do you? And she took all of it off me.

For an entire week, I waited for the day when I could put the uniform back on. I'd go into my room just to look at it hanging on the inside of my closet door. It was like a Christmas tree heralding promises of love and joy that were taking too long to come true. Until finally, the day arrived.

On the morning of my first Red Birds meeting, I woke up early to get dressed. I wanted to surprise my mother with the vision of me as a Red Bird when she came in to get me up. I made up my bed and brushed my teeth. Then I combed my hair as best I could, but didn't try to put on a barrette. Momma always did that for me. I tried to imagine which barrette she would pick to go with my Red Birds uniform. She was constantly bringing home new hair ornaments for me, and her deliberations over the ideal one for each outfit could take forever, but the one she picked was always perfect. And I felt secure being sent out into the world with that emblem of her care in my hair.

I dragged the chair from my pale pink dressing table that my mother had said was the focal point of my room over to the closet door and stood on it to get my Red Birds uniform down. It was like one of my Barbie doll's dresses, only bigger. It would make me a whole other person, like fairy magic. I put on the skirt and shirt, pulled on the socks, slipped on my shoes, and let the sash fall over my head. Then I looked in the mirror on the inside of my closet door and I knew. If I couldn't be a pixie, then being a Red Bird was just as good.

I sat down on the rug facing the door with my dolls and stuffed animals in a circle around me to have a Red Birds meeting, like the ones Momma had told me about from when she was a kid. A small mound of Pick-Up Stix was in the center of our campfire and we all had cups and saucers from my toy china tea set for our snack. We were just into the first verse of "You Are My Sunshine" when my mother opened the door.

"Momma!" I said, jumping up so that she could see the full effect of my Red Birds uniform and be inspired to hug me.

My mother looked at me as if I was a roach on her floor. Then her features filled with a tremulous rage that something so odious could exist in her home, and a disgusted resignation that it couldn't be made to go away.

"Come down to breakfast," she said. "Now." As she strode away, her hard-soled bedroom slippers tat-a-tat-tatted down the hall.

I stood there for a moment looking after her out the opened door. Then I turned to my stuffed animals and wished I were one of them, not alive or real. My stomach started feeling sick. I wanted to take off the Red Birds uniform and never wear it again. Or somehow wear it in the way that I had when I tried it on and Momma had been so proud of me. Maybe I had put it on wrong. I walked over to look in the mirror of the pale pink dressing table to check my reflection against the Red Birds brochure that was lying on the glass top. Everything was exactly as it was supposed to be, except I didn't have any achievement patches on my sash. Maybe that's what it was; maybe that was why Momma wasn't proud of me. I would just have to get lots of those. So many that they covered me. So many that I'd be one big achievement patch walking down the street. Then maybe she'd hug me.

When I got to school that morning, I saw five other Red Birds in my first grade class. Their faces above their bright white shirts looked radiant compared to the other girls who were wearing our navy blue and dark green plaid school uniform. But none of them had the Red Bird socks, and that made me love mine even more.

Patricia burst in just as the bell rang. She sat down at her desk, looked around, then a loud "My uniform!" escaped her lips.

"No talking during class, please, Patricia," Sister Dolores said. She was one of the younger nuns at the school and had embraced Vatican II wholeheartedly by shirking her habit and wearing below-the-knee skirts with matching open vests over high-necked cotton blouses. My father thought it was a disgrace.

I turned around toward Patricia and saw her gazing longingly at Nancy Romero's Red Birds uniform. When Patricia noticed me looking at her, she gave me a big smile and pointing at my uniform mouthed, "Me, too!" I glanced back at Sister Dolores, but she was at the blackboard printing capital and little *F*s and *G*s, so I looked at Patricia again. She was still smiling at me.

When I walked outside that morning at 10:15 for little recess, Patricia was sitting on the long, low step that led to the schoolyard from the covered walkway that all the classrooms led out onto. We weren't supposed to sit there. "Steps are for walking, not sitting," Sr. Dolores reminded us daily, but there was Patricia leaning against a pole and looking as if she was waiting for someone to read her a story.

"I'm a Red Bird, too," she said, when I got close to her. "My momma forgot the meeting was today." The wrinkles in Patricia's school uniform were obvious even despite its dark color and the polyester of its blend. You basically had to sleep in those uniforms, and fitfully, for wrinkles to show like that. It made me wonder about Patricia's house. I thought of our maid, Louise, ironing the deep red skirt and sash and bright white blouse that I was wearing. I felt like a Christmas package wrapped perfectly. Patricia looked like wrappings that have been balled up and discarded.

"Oh."

"Maybe they won't know I belong."

"My mother paid," I said.

"Mine did, too."

The last few boys and girls from our class came streaming past us, heading for the jungle gym or swings or the cafeteria to buy a carton of chocolate milk for fifteen cents. Patricia sat and I stood looking at the other children in the yard. Red Birds uniforms stood out in a sea of dark plaid like victorious flags from another country.

"Wear my socks," I said, and I sat down to take off my shoes. I tried to ignore what my mother would do to me when I came home without them.

"What?"

"Wear my socks; then you'll be a Red Bird, too." The smooth concrete was warm against my thighs as I took off my socks and handed them to her. There were marks just below my knees from where the socks' elastic had hugged my legs. I hoped the deep grooves in my skin would stay there all day long as a sign to the other Red Birds that the socks really belonged to me.

"Thanks." Patricia put them on and gave me her thick navy blue ones. They crumpled around my shoes as if they had no dignity.

My socks were taller on Patricia's legs, so she turned them down a couple of times to get them below her knees. The little Red Birds on each side still looked happy, and I suddenly worried that they would fly away, never to return, and my own wearing of them would be a small, short memory.

"Now we're just alike," Patricia said. Then she smiled at me and extended her hand toward mine as if they'd been joined together forever and the switching of our socks was only a temporary break.

We stood up, linked hands, and went down the long, low steps. My socks were in her shoes, my shoes had her socks, and our individual strides contained us both. Then we walked across the schoolyard through the clusters of children to begin our very own play.

Chapter 6

"THAT'S HORRIBLE," Sarah says over the phone. "Especially since it was for your birthday."

"I know. Not that Patricia even really seemed to care that that was two months ago."

I turn off Franklin, heading south on Gower toward Hollywood Boulevard. The streets are clamoring with wide-eyed tourists and broken-down businesses and persons made crazy from unfulfilled dreams of fame, but I still love to drive through this part of town. Most of the buildings are left over from the twenties and thirties, when Hollywood Boulevard meant something significant and grand. The men wore hats and the women wore gloves and people's lives were film noir. Sometimes when I drive around a corner, I catch myself thinking that maybe I'll stumble onto a street that is still alive from way back then. And I could join them. And live there in a parallel universe sort of way. But for that ever to happen, it would just be another movie set. And I'd have to audition to get in.

"Though I know she's insane with work," I say into my cell phone. "And one time it was my fault because I booked that *ER* guest spot, but still."

"I know."

"It was all about her being upset because I'd asked her not to tell, which is totally valid that I did. We don't want people to know. This soon, at least."

I try to ignore the fact that I have just now told a second person that I am pregnant. Neil, being a man, has told no one, I am absolutely sure. But there was no way I wasn't going to tell Patricia. And then I couldn't tell Neil what happened yesterday at the mani/pedi with Patricia because then he would know that I had already told her our news. And I have to tell someone about it, so my next-best friend Sarah is it. And that means spilling the beans about the baby, so—

Not that I don't feel bad about all this. In fact, last night when Neil asked how my mani/pedi with Patricia was, I had to lie to him again. And that felt really awful since I did take a marital vow. Not that I remember honesty being in there. I know we vowed "to love, honor, and—" Okay, we got rid of *obey*, no surprise, but I can't remember what the third one was, which is a little scary to have no memory of that. Maybe I should pull out the wedding video and check. But if honesty wasn't in there, I am sure it is implied, though it does seem odd that it isn't said directly. But maybe the "forsaking all others" part is meant to cover that. So does that mean I'm forsaking Neil for Patricia with this lie?

"We went to Geisha Nails," I said to Neil last night. We were standing in our kitchen. The sun was just starting to set through the windows, so the lights were still off. I was at the stove serving Pad Thai noodles from the wok onto our plates. My back was turned to him, and I was glad he couldn't see my face. "It was, you know, girly."

"Was Patricia being Fabulous?"

"What?" I handed him his plate, and he waited to take mine, too.

"You sound like something was up," Neil said, as he went into the dining room and flicked on the chandelier with the edge of one of the plates. "Just wondering if that TV show has put her into full-blown Fabulous mode. It will at some point."

"Not everyone gets like that." I sat down at the table, and automatically handed him the hot sauce.

"Name two."

"Neil." The shrimp in the Pad Thai suddenly looked particularly pink and smelled particularly fishy. I put down my fork. "Patricia isn't like that."

"You've got to be kidding."

"I've known her my whole life, or most that I can remember, so same thing."

"Exactly why you should know. Aren't you going to eat?"

"My stomach's weird. Maybe I'll just make some toast."

"I'll fix it. Stay here." He jumped up from his chair and gave me a kiss. "That's a great sign!" Then he disappeared into the kitchen.

"Okay," I shouted after him. "So she was being a tiny bit Fabulous." Maybe telling Neil the truth about that would minimize my lie of not telling him what a nightmare Patricia had been about my asking her not to tell anyone. And minimize my lie of already telling her. "But, you know, she had that big breakup, and, Jesus, of all things to find out about your fiancé right after he dumps you."

"Yeah, an addiction to prostitutes would not make for a happy marriage."

"You're not supposed to know that, remember."

"I'm not going to tell anyone." Neil flipped off the kitchen light, came back to the dining room table, and leaned on his chair. "Almost ready. So what other secrets aren't I supposed to know?"

"What? As if."

"There must be something."

"Yeah, we ran away when we were ten and joined a band of marauding thieves. We're wanted in five states. Is that what you want to hear?"

"I just thought with how long you two've been friends."

"Yeah, well, there aren't any secrets."

"It's okay, Fiona. I believe you." Then he turned around, and went back into the darkening room.

"Of course, you're not telling people yet," Sarah says above the din of a motorcycle revving. "Not after what happened last time. Not that that will again. I have a great feeling about this one."

"Thanks, I need to hear that. Which is another thing: She is totally ignoring the fact that I had a miscarriage. We have a reason to be nervous about this. I mean, all I want is to see that heartbeat, and I'm gonna be nervous until then."

"What is her problem?"

"I know. And now things are all weird between us and I really don't feel like dealing with it." I hear a wave of techno house music get loud and then recede over the phone. "Where are you, anyway?"

"On Melrose. I needed a hit."

I immediately know what Sarah means. One day a few years ago when we first became friends, we decided to meet for lunch. She suggested a trendy little Italian restaurant on Melrose that was known for its incredible fresh baked bread. We started going there all the time and would order small house salads to eat with lots of delicious doughy bread: life before Atkins.

That day I got there early and was waiting at the table when Sarah walked in. She looked stunning. Her long blond hair was flowing, her outfit was perfect, and all she needed was a title above her head to be a living movie poster.

"Hope you weren't waiting too long," she said, as she hugged me hello. "I needed a little hit, you know? So I went for a stroll up Melrose."

"A hit?"

"Yeah, a little brand recognition. A little 'Isn't that Sarah Bradley?' You know, when I get away from those klieg lights too long, I start wondering if I exist."

I wasn't famous like Sarah was, but I could imagine what she meant. Living in L.A. means constantly having an audience. And not just for the stars, either. The entire city is an audience that everyone is for each other. A test screening of your looks and life every time you walk out your door, or, rather, get out of your car. Your own personal daily box office gross of how much attention you got that day. It is exhilarating and exhausting like a week on cocaine, and just as horrendously and gloriously addictive.

"I just had an audition for that—were you done?" Sarah says on the phone. I can hear her car door shut and the engine starting up. "'Cause I really need to talk."

"Yeah, what?" I say, even though I don't feel done. But other than changing what happened with Patricia entirely, I don't know what Sarah could say to make me feel better, so in that case, I am done.

"It was for *Love or War* and all everyone has been saying is how perfect I am for that show, which frankly makes me a little crazy because I think so, too, but it's not like I can just make that happen all on my own; Tony Robbins or not, the Hollywood gods are still involved. But so, I finally get an audition for it, and I go straight to producers because Marcia's been casting me for years. She's who discovered me and put me in that film that totally changed my life, so that's kind of great, but also kind of depressing. But so, I walk in and there are like six of them in there, writers, producers, and the director. And the room is totally tense. You can tell even if you didn't know that it's a top ten show. It has all this we-have-to-keep-our-ratings fear stuff hanging in the air. So Marcia starts rattling off their names, and I'm shaking hands, and one of them, the director, I realize I met at a party last year. Remember that one in Malibu that the rappers and hookers showed up at?"

"Oh, God, right."

"But so, I mean, I've met the guy, so I when I get to him, I say, 'It's nice seeing you again. We met last year at Douglas Wade's beach house.' And he looks at me like I've just said that I saw him wearing a dress. I mean, it was a big A-list party. It cannot be embarrassing for it to be known he was there."

"That is so weird."

"But so he still isn't saying anything and they're all just staring at me for what feels like eternity until finally Marcia says, 'Okay, Sarah, whenever you're ready.' And I'm like, Fuck. The only thing I'm ready to do now is kill the director or disappear, but somehow I have to read two fucking scenes, and all I can think is that I blew the fucking audition before it even started."

"What a dick. This is the only town I know where people get insulted when you're not rude."

"But so, I beat myself up the whole entire studio-sized way back to my car, which, by the way, was in the visitors' parking lot, not in my own private space like I used to have there at Fox. It was like being divorced and having to visit my ex."

"I bet you did great. You always do."

"I don't know. I just really want to be on that show. I can't believe when I finally get the audition for it—and Marcia did follow me out and said what a great job I did, and how she could always count on me, and you know, she's not one to—"

"Exactly, see? You're always great. And, please, you've been working nonstop for forever. You'll totally get on that show. Fuck that director. He's just a hired gun. That either was your role or it wasn't. You know that's decided in the first four seconds you walk in the room. If this one wasn't it, it'll be another one."

"You think?"

"Yes."

"I hope so. I just—"

"I'm gonna lose you. I'm coming to a bad spot." And that is true. My phone always cuts out on Gower right when I get to Paramount, where I am heading for my first day's shoot of the movie for Lifetime, like the MOWs the networks used to do, the acronym for *Movie of the Week*, which has always reminded me of a combination of *POW* and *MIA*, as if doing one is its own kind of war, and sometimes it is. But I don't want to tell Sarah where I'm going. Not that she doesn't know I got the job, or that she was up for it too, which she wasn't. We have never gone up for the same roles, making it easier to be friends, but after her shitty morning, why rub it in? "I know you did great."

"Thanks. And congratulations! It's so exciting!" For a second, I think she read my mind and knows where I am, but then I realize what she means. "And don't give that stuff with Patricia another thought. This should be a happy time—don't let her ruin it for you."

"She's not. I mean, I won't let it."

"And don't worry—I won't tell anyone."

"I know you'd never tell." But my phone has already cut out, leaving that sentence ringing in my car, as if I am the one who needs to hear it.

Chapter 7

"I JUST DON'T UNDERSTAND WHY YOU DID IT," I say to her. "You know how I feel." A waitress rushes past us with a stack of dirty dishes. She looks like she is headed straight for a spill. First day on the job, I figure.

"I said I'm sorry."

"But you're not. You're so clearly not. That's what makes it all the worse." I look into her eyes, and for a second I almost believe her. Then I remember whom I am talking to. "I can't do this anymore."

"Oh, come on, don't."

"No." I pick up my bag, get up from my chair, and look at her one last time. But the eyes that stare back at me are blank. There is nothing left to do, so I throw some money down and turn to go. But when I close the restaurant door behind me, I stop for a moment to wait.

"Cut!" The director yells. I look back through the fake restaurant door and see the director, producer, and 1st assistant director huddled around the video monitor watching the playback of the scene. The rest of us stay poised in our places waiting for the verdict.

"Moving on," the 1st AD yells. It is as if the sound stage it-self relaxes. "Fiona's close-up. Fifteen to relight."

Instantly, the hushed and phony world that I was acting in is filled with the seemingly chaotic, but perfectly orchestrated movements of the crew preparing for the next shot.

A woman carrying a heavily annotated version of the script falls into step next to me as I walk through a horde of extras from the scene to go back to my honey wagon (a trailer divided into two dressing rooms, not the monster trailers that stars command) to relax and reprepare before we shoot again. I sig-nal to the 2nd AD where I am headed so she'll know where to find me.

"It's 'I'm not able to do this anymore,' not 'I can't do this anymore.'" Unlike a lot of the film and television I have done, the script supervisor on this MOW is making sure that every line is spoken exactly the way it is written in the script. Usu-ally, a large degree of an actor's "making it his own" is toler-ated, but not on this one. I had thought when we first started shooting that this would drive me nuts, but the strictness just ended up being oddly comfortable in a familiar way.

"Right. Anything else?"

"Not for you."

She turns to go find the other actress in the scene, who, as far as I am concerned, is Patricia. Though in reality, the ac-tress is about five years younger, rather short, and is playing my little sister, who has an Internet gambling problem.

But I am using Patricia for her. Not an out-and-out plaster-ing of Patricia's face and self and history on top of the actress. It is more of a taking the character in the script and the person in my life and mixing them together through enough rehears-als (and because this is television, that means at home on my own) that they create a whole new person that I can believe in and talk to.

Like I used to do when I was a child after I didn't believe in fairies anymore. I would take aspects of my mother that I liked (such as her fixing my hair), and the perfect mother that I wanted to have, and I'd mix them together to create a parent that made me feel safe. And I did it enough so that she became real to me whenever I walked into my room, like the fairies were real until they no longer could be.

One of my acting teachers, Julian, always used to say, "The character on the page doesn't exist. You make him real." But I never believed that. The characters are as real to me as the fairies used to be. My experiences with them are real, so how can they not be?

Julian also used to talk about using emotional memories. "It's tricky," he would say, "to use a memory less than seven years in your past because the emotions around it can change. You can't rely upon them to stay the same." I always thought that was an odd thing to say to acting students in their very early twenties; that basically only left us with events up to seventh or eighth grade. Though as Flannery O'Connor said, "If you survive your childhood, you will never run out of material." But I still never followed Julian's rule.

And I'm not following it now. The memory with Patricia that I am using for this scene not only isn't seven years old, it isn't even seven days old. The way she behaved last week at our mani/pedi is all I've been able to think about, when I'm not thinking about the baby. But then I think how I'm not able to share the happiness about the baby with my best friend, and it starts up all over again. It got to the point this weekend where I almost picked up the phone to call her to talk it out, but then I thought of her in Vegas with Zane, and I couldn't see how either of those was conducive to us patching things up. And anyway, she's the one who should call me. How she was able to say, "I mean, who cares?" about my pregnancy I will never know. Even if she did follow it up with a "I mean, not who cares, I care." That was just mean.

As I step into my dressing room, I see that the wardrobe girl has been in and hung up the costume for my next scene. It is perfectly ironed, and all of its accessories are in a large plastic bag with my character's name written on it in black Sharpie pen. A fresh bottle of water is waiting for me on my makeup table courtesy of the 2nd AD Being an actor on a film or TV set is like having the most wonderful and conscientious parents in the entire world. All of your needs are taken care of before you even think of them, so that you are free to do your best. It is no wonder that most of us who end up here come from fucked-up homes, and why the craving to be on a set is so strong and so debilitating.

I lie down on the brown plaid-covered built-in daybed, telling myself that I won't fall asleep, even though I would kill to. Thank God, they didn't need us to eat in that last scene or my secret would have been out. The nausea hit full on yesterday, and I'm having trouble eating anything except weird stuff like udon noodles or baked potatoes. I feel like hell. I didn't see how I was going to be able to work today, but having to concentrate during each take of the scene actually helped, though now I just want to sleep for the rest of the day and wake up nausea-free, not that that's going to happen.

I check the digital clock on the kitchenette stove and am figuring that I can rest for about three minutes when my cell phone rings. I grab it off the floor and depress the green button as I look at the caller's number, then immediately wish that I had checked it first.

"Hello?" I say, pretending that I don't know who it is, which is ridiculous, but I don't care.

"Hi, Fi," Patricia says.

"Hi."

Pause.

I look at the clock again. I figure I have about eleven minutes before I shoot. She can have less than one.

"Whatcha doin'?"

"Working. That TV movie I got, so I can't talk."

"Oh, right. That's great."

You don't know if it's great or not, and if it is, I don't need you to tell me.

"How is it?" Patricia continues.

"It's great. I like the director."

"Who is he?"

I knew she would ask that. As if she knows everyone now. "New guy. Cliff Young. Very collaborative. You know."

"That's good."

I almost don't say anything just to punish her some more, but I relent with an "Uh-huh."

We sit for another three seconds. She gets two more, and then I am saying good-bye and hanging up.

"So, anyway, Fi, I just wanted to tell you that I'd love to host your baby shower. If you want me to."

"Oh."

"I mean, I'd be glad to. It'd be fun."

"Oh. Well," I say, as I scramble to figure out how to respond. I am so not ready to give up my resentment at her.

"I'll dig up Paula and you can bring Jane. Not exactly babies, but—"

Paula and Jane were matching dolls that Patricia and I got at the end of first grade. Not together. My mother took me to the toy store for an end-of-the-school-year gift, and I found a fabulous doll that basically was a teenage go-go girl. Her body was soft and all of her clothes, floral miniskirt included, were sewn right onto her. Even the purple vinyl go-go boots. I loved her. And she talked. I'd pull a cord behind her neck and semiadult, fatuous things would come out, such as "I like roller rinks, don't you?" and "Let's go shopping!"

Patricia became just as insane about the doll as I was, so she begged and pleaded and wheedled Vicky until she got one. Then we named them Paula and Jane, monikers any self-respecting go-go girls would ditch in a heartbeat.

"It'll be fun," Patricia says.

I let us sit in silence. I want to say yes. I just want to say yes when I don't want to wring her neck. But saying no would be such a huge and permanent mark of no-longer-best-friends.

"And," she says, "I'm sorry about the other day. I don't know what I was thinking."

"Thanks, Patricia. I appreciate that. And I'd love for you to have my baby shower. I can't think of anything better."

"Oh, good." Patricia's relief is as palpable as what I felt on the set when the 1st AD announced we were moving on. Maybe because it is the same thing.

I immediately imagine myself in Patricia's home, sitting next to her on the couch and surrounded by presents and friends and near the end of a successful pregnancy.

"And so, anyway, I also wanted to tell you my good news, though maybe you already know 'cause it's been all over the

Internet and news, but since you haven't said anything, I guess you hadn't heard, but Zane and I got married here in Vegas last night."

"Oh, my God."

"I know! I'm so insanely happy, and I kept wishing you could've been there, but, you know, here we are in Vegas, and Zane was on this crazy nonstop winning roll, and there was the chapel, and it was like, I looked at Zane, and said, 'So, what are we waiting for?' and then there we were at the altar, and—"

"Wow, that's." The improbable image of a scantily clad show-girl officiating their ceremony pops into my head. "I mean, congratulations! I hadn't heard, but this is"—astonishing—"great! I'm so thrilled for you." And wonder if you have completely lost your mind.

"Thanks, and I know it seems kind of rushed." Compared to what? The speed of light? "But, you know, I feel like I've known Zane forever, and I'm just so happy with him. It makes me wonder how I wasted all those years on Kevin when the whole time he was, you know—"

"Yeah." Okay, so this is probably pretty definitely a complete rebound wedding, and not that I've ever even met Zane, but good for her for finding someone who rocks her world after that shit Kevin.

"And sometimes you just know immediately. I mean, you did with Neil, right? You knew when you met him, and that's how it feels with Zane. I just knew. Only I didn't have to wait a year or so because I don't need to be so cautious like you, but other than that, it's the same thing."

So cautious like you. Try: made sure that I knew the guy's goddamn middle name, much less his family, before I married him. Astonishing. And this from a woman whose fiancé had an entire secret life going on for years and she never knew.

But other than that, it's the same thing. Okay, there is no same thing about my marrying Neil and her marrying Zane. Zane MacKenzie—I'm sorry, but that is so not a real name—is not a man that any woman could "just know immediately" that she could marry. The only thing you could just know immediately about him is that he's a fake. He's just some used-to-be athlete posing as an actor, who—I suddenly realize that Patricia is waiting for me to say something when my eyes notice the clock on the stove.

"Fuck! I mean, sorry, but I have to run. I'm about to do my close-up, and—"

"Oh. Well, I'll let you go."

"But I'm so happy for you. Congratulations! And we'd love to meet him sometime." I can't believe I am saying that about my oldest and best friend's husband. It is a toss-up as to which is more depressing: that or how non-best-friends this whole thing feels.

"Yeah, we all need to have dinner. There's a—"

Someone knocks on my trailer's door with such a loud and forthright pounding that it can only be the 2nd AD. The attitude of every 2nd AD on every set I've ever been on has been the same: half guardian angel respecting your privacy while fulfilling your every need, and half prison guard who, no matter what you are doing, is there to keep you in line.

"I gotta go," I say, jumping up from the day bed and cursing myself that I even picked up the phone.

"Okay, well, have a great closeup."

Why does it suddenly feel jinxed?

"Thanks, I will. And congratulations again. We need to celebrate."

"Yeah, I'll call you later."

"Bye."

I look in the mirror for a second and let out a huge breath, a sigh, actually, though I don't want to admit it is. I cannot believe that my best friend's marital news was just told to me in a five-minute phone call. Not that I can't get more details from her later on, and—who are we kidding?—there's probably footage on the Web, but not even to have known about it before and planned it with her. Though maybe after the preparations we did for her and Kevin's wedding went up in a ball of flames like their relationship did, she was ready for something quiet and small and—

Okay, there is nothing quiet and small about getting married in Las Vegas. And I can't believe she got married without me. How many hours growing up did we talk about being in each other's wedding? Who would marry first, what our colors would be, our future husband's names. She always wanted a *Paul*, which I thought was why she named her doll *Paula*, and my future husband always had a name like *Rudy* or *Clyde*, names that could steal you away in the middle of the night.

And I haven't even met the guy. For a few months, I kept suggesting that we all have dinner, but he was busy shooting a film. Then when that finally ended, and we still didn't have dinner, I started getting the feeling that Patricia didn't want me to meet him for some reason. Like she was hiding him from me. Which is weird. It's not like I was going to steal him because, first off, I'm happily married, and second off, if a guy is into Patricia, then he isn't going to be into me, and vice versa, so that's never been an issue. So why she's been so weird about us all getting together, I have no idea. Though maybe now I'll finally find out.

But I can't think about this anymore. I have a job to do here. And now I can't even call anyone (i.e, Sarah) to talk about this crazy news until after I shoot. Jesus, Patricia's timing is fucking unbelievable.

When I open the trailer's door, I see the 2nd AD standing at the bottom of the steps. She is wearing a faded black AC/DC T-shirt in, I am sure, an ironic way and low-riding, but baggy fitting jeans. All she needs is a power tool belt, and from behind, you'd have no idea if she were a girl or boy. Self-preservation, probably, so she'll fit in with the mostly male crew. She clicks on her walkie-talkie, and says to the 1st AD, "I've got Fiona. We're heading back."

As she escorts me to the set, I start to panic because I haven't prepared one bit, so I try to concentrate on my preparation while we walk, then I realize that the phone call I just had with Patricia is better for this scene than anything my imagination could ever dream up.

Chapter 8

WHEN NEIL AND I ARRIVE at the West Tower Medical Building of Cedars-Sinai Hospital for our eight-week appointment with Dr. Walker to (please, God) see the heartbeat, the morning is warm despite the early June gloom. An elderly woman is sitting on a black marble bench in the plaza in front of the office towers. Her elephantine legs are thrust out before her as if she is a bathing beauty on a Riviera Beach, and in her mind, she probably is. I live in a city where reality can change overnight. Wrinkles can vanish. Careers can skyrocket. Marriages can be made. And people live as if their fantasy has already happened, even when it never will.

Neil and I settle ourselves on a small beige suede sofa in the reception room that Dr. Walker shares with a neurosurgeon. When I first went to her office last fall, I found it an odd pairing, but then I liked that she wasn't part of one of those renowned baby-mill practices that women are constantly telling you that you have to go to if you want to have a baby, meaning *the* baby, as in *the* bag.

A young man with a shaved and bandaged head is sitting next to an older man, who appears to be his father, on a similar sofa on the other side of the coffee table. Despite his age, the young man looks afflicted in a terrible and protracted way. His eyes are closed, his head is leaning back against the wall, and he looks more exhausted than anyone I have ever seen. Even more than I am with this pregnancy, and that is a lot.

For the last week, I have been sleeping a good two hours every afternoon. Thank God, I finished shooting my stuff for that MOW. I will be going along in my day doing okay, dealing with ever-present but not completely debilitating nausea, so basically okay, when suddenly it is as if a hammer thwacks me on the back of my head, and I have to hurry to the nearest soft surface and surrender myself to it.

Usually, it is my bed. But one day last week, it was the carpeted floor behind an overstuffed, out-of-season sales clothes rounder in a far back corner of Saks in Beverly Hills. That nap, however, did not last two hours. It lasted maybe ten minutes before a startled and disturbed saleswoman awakened me by shrieking in fright. And it's not like I look pregnant, so she probably thought I had passed out. Though I did tell her that I'm pregnant, and I think she believed me, but on a certain level, it didn't matter if she did or not, because the only thing both of us wanted was me out of her department and some place else. And for me that was the laid-down front seat of my locked and alarmed car in the parking garage where I slumbered so deeply that trying to wake up was like trying to surface from the center of the Earth with only my short and manicured fingernails as tools to escape.

And that is how all of these naps have been ending. A stumbling grogginess surrounds me, and I have to try extra hard to understand and be understood, as if I am drunk from my pregnancy.

A woman sweeps into the waiting room and lands at the receptionist's window, where Isolde, who presides over the comings and goings, sits like a princess in her castle window.

"Do you have an appointment with Dr. Schweitzer?" Isolde says, meaning the neurosurgeon. The woman not only does not look pregnant, but also is of an age at which that condition would be unlikely to occur.

"No, thank God," the woman says.

The young man on the sofa opens his eyes.

"Talk about hell," she continues in full voice. "No. I'm here to redecorate his office. I have lampshade swatches for him to see. It'll only take a second. He said I could just go right in."

Isolde glances at the young man, but his eyes are closed again. "I'll check," she says and picks up the phone.

Neil looks at me and shakes his head.

Once the decorator has left the room, the young man opens his eyes, picks up his father's left arm, looks at the worn watch on it, then shuts his eyes again, and settles himself back against the wall. I wonder if he is here because of an injury or a disease. I try to imagine a benign reason to see a neurosurgeon, but I can't think of any. Suddenly, the idea that an obstetrics doctor and a neurosurgeon share a waiting area seems oddly callous. To be faced with such a parade of nascent life when the delicate matter of one's brain is in dire circumstances seems more than one should have to bear. I wonder if the doctors have become so accustomed to the never-ending dance of birth and death that they have forgotten that the rest of us have not, particularly when we are in throes of it.

Neil strikes up a conversation with the older man about the Dodgers game last night and how unhittable Gagne is. The older man says that he is driving himself and his son all the way in from Hemet, and how the drives to and from the appointments aren't so bad now with Vin Scully on Dodger radio, but he didn't feel much like listening to the Lakers games this past winter since Chick Hearn is dead and gone. Neil nods his head in solemn agreement.

I have heard of Hemet. I know if you take the 10 freeway east out of L.A. toward Palm Springs, you'll pass near Hemet somewhere. It always sounded like a place where people don't much care about or have anything to do with Palm Springs.

The older man is deeply tanned and wears a thin cotton long-sleeved plaid shirt, like the kind the migrant workers wear in the farm fields no matter the temperature to protect them from the sun. I wonder if the son is getting radiation (can you do that on the brain?), and I wish irrationally that all he needed were long sleeves to protect him from whatever ails him. Like those heavy lead blankets they put on you when you have dental x-rays, and how women are always asked first whether they are pregnant. I wonder how many women when asked that question are pregnant but don't yet know, and how many think they still are pregnant but aren't any longer. And which one is worse?

I knew my first pregnancy was over when I woke up one morning last fall wanting to have sex. Dr. Walker called later that day with the blood test results. The HCG had dropped 5,000 points and the progesterone was finally dipping, too, but I could have told her that myself. In the six weeks or so that I had been pregnant, or that my body thought it was staying pregnant, I had not wanted to have sex—until that day. So I knew, as if my body was telling me that I needed to start again.

But I didn't want to start again. And I especially didn't want to do what I had to do to end that nonsuccessful pregnancy. I didn't want to do anything except be nauseous and exhausted and pregnant and have that baby, not any other one.

At nine a.m. on a Tuesday last December, Neil and I arrived at Dr. Walker's office to erase a life that had barely begun.

We had just settled ourselves on the sofa, when the door to Dr. Walker's office opened, and a nurse called my name. I assumed she was a nurse because she was holding my file and wearing an open white lab coat, but there the similarities ended. She looked ready for a disco. A low-cut shiny top clung to her ample and clearly real (i.e, not perky) breasts, and her painfully tight pants ended at a pair of teetering, clattering heels.

"Congratulations!" she said, as she led us to an exam room. "How many weeks are you?"

"Weeks?" I said, as we walked into the same room where I had first seen on the screen the little blur that Dr. Walker had explained was the egg sack. All I could think when she said that was of *Charlotte's Web*, and Charlotte telling Wilbur that her egg sack was her magnum opus, and how few women in this town probably feel that way, what with Oscar being the de rigueur goal.

"We're not. We're—"

"Excuse me," Neil said to her. "Can you get Dr. Walker, please? You clearly have no idea what you're doing. Read our chart."

To her credit, she looked chagrined, but I couldn't help thinking that she was just one Donna Summer song away from her only concern.

"Jesus," Neil said after she left the room, "what a fucking idiot." Then he looked at me to see how I was.

I was sitting on the exam table that faced a large wall-to-wall window. There were no curtains or shades to cover it. We were up on the tenth floor, looking west over the office tower's parking structure, the low stores lining Robertson Boulevard, the Four Seasons hotel (a tad to the south), the residential streets' tidy trees, and the hills of Beverly Hills running farther west.

At my first appointment with Dr. Walker, after I had undressed and was sitting on the table with only the paper gown covering me, therefore cold no matter the room's temperature, I asked her about the no-window-treatment choice.

"No one can see in," she said. "But does it bother you?"

"No, I'm an actress. I'm used to undressing in front of people I don't know. Though Virginia has always stayed clothed. And closed, for that matter."

"Virginia? Oh, right," she said, laughing.

"And at least this isn't New York City," I said, as I lay on my back and scooted down, "where everyone supposedly has telescopes."

Neil got up on the exam table with me and took my hand. He had only met Dr. Walker once before, and I knew that a D & C appointment was the exact opposite of what he had thought would be happening the next time he saw her.

We sat and stared out the window. It was an exquisitely clear day. L.A. in December is so crystalline as to take your breath away, as if God is only able to pull focus perfectly that time of year and out here.

But I wanted to be anywhere but here. I wanted to walk out the window, light upon the garage, step on the stores, and leap over the trees to land on the hills, then run on them all the way to the beach, where I would enter the water, which would be magically warm and I could loll in its amniotic fluid until my baby was brought back to life.

Dr. Walker entered the room, bringing me back to reality. "Hey, guys," she said.

I was almost startled that Dr. Walker looked exactly the same as she had on my previous visits. I was different—why wasn't she?

"I heard what the new nurse said. I'm really sorry."

"We're not dealing with her anymore," Neil said.

"You won't have to." Then she was quiet for a moment, looking at me. "How are you doing?" she said it with the knowledge of the answer, but with the need to say it anyway.

"We're—you know. I just want to get this over with."

"You're being inordinately brave."

I didn't feel inordinately brave. But maybe she was only saying that to make me feel better. Then I wondered what it would look like if I weren't being inordinately brave. Would I have screamed at stupid Disco Nurse? Told her to be a little fucking sensitive—my hoped-to-be baby is no longer alive? Or just fallen down on the exam table and sobbed the way I wanted to, instead of allowing myself to be led down the hall for a procedure that in my mind I couldn't stop thinking was an abortion, just an abortion where the baby was already dead.

"There it is," Dr. Walker says.

I stare at the small screen, surprised that we can actually see it: The heartbeat, the thing that we never saw before. The lines on the electronic graph showing the beats per minute are reassuringly strong and each one feels like a silent good-bye to that failed first pregnancy.

"Oh, thank God," I say, reaching for Neil's hand.

"That's amazing," he says, peering at the screen.

Dr. Walker freezes the screen and presses some buttons. "For your fridge," she says, as a small print comes whirring out of the machine. She hands it to me. "Baby's first picture. And if you ever get nervous, just come in. I remember during my second pregnancy, one Saturday night when my husband and I were at the movies, I suddenly panicked that the baby's heart had stopped and it was all I could think about. It was eleven o'clock before the movie let out, but I persuaded my husband to drive us here, so I could let us in and see the heartbeat. He thought I was nuts, but I wouldn't have slept that night if I hadn't."

"Didn't you have a doctor?" Neil says.

"Yeah, but I still self-examined sometimes. It's hard not to when all the equipment is right here, but don't tell that to anyone. I think my colleague who delivered for me would get annoyed. But when you're not showing yet, sometimes you just want reassurance, so if that happens," she says, looking at me. "come by, and I'll let you see the heartbeat real quick."

"Thanks, Dr. Walker."

Neil looks at me like he hopes I will not need to do that, but will be patient if I do.

Lying on the exam table, with the picture of my baby's heartbeat still frozen on the screen, I can't imagine that I will need to do that. It is getting through telling my mother this news that I'm not looking forward to.

Chapter 9

"WHO EATS DINNER AT SIX O'CLOCK?" Neil says, as the waiter pushes the upholstered dining room chair that I am sitting in toward the perfectly laid table. "I should still be in my office for at least another half-hour. What happened to eight in Hollywood?"

"She didn't say. I got a message on my cell to meet them here at six instead."

"It's past six. And we're in separate cars. I hate being in separate cars."

"I know, sweetie, but it's their wedding we're celebrating."

"That was not a wedding. It was a publicity stunt."

"Okay, so he's instant-husband-man, but for all we know, this could be the great union of the decade."

"The decade of minutes maybe."

"Neil. She's happy about it, so I'm being happy for her, too. I mean, how do I know who she's supposed to marry?"

Neil looks at me like I have lost my mind, then turns to the waiter, who has approached our table. While he gives our drinks order—Maker's Mark on the rocks for him, ginger ale for me, which I keep telling myself is helping combat this pregnancy nausea, but I still feel like hell—I look out the tall, single-paned windows that let on to the Santa Monica beach, as I hear Sarah's voice in my head saying the words I just spoke to Neil.

"But, come on, Sarah. How does a person marry someone after only six months? And all of a sudden on a trip to Vegas? I mean, don't those marriages automatically end in divorce? Like they get round-trip tickets to Reno along with the marriage license."

"I agree, but you don't know what makes her happy," Sarah says on the phone. I can hear her Elliptical machine churning away under each of her words, a continuous loop of miles to nowhere. "She may not even. But she gets to try, and you get to be there for her as her friend."

"Ugghh, I hate when you're right and your Agape messages start coming through." Sarah attends Agape, a church, I guess you have to call it, though it is almost more of a movement: very spiritual, very loving, very accepting of all. And, as she says, the thing that keeps her from committing hara-kiri while dealing with being an actress in this town.

"It's not for her; it's for you, so you won't have this resentment." Then Sarah's voice shifts like the whirring of her machine increasing its difficulty. "But now that we've gotten the high road that you're going to take out of the way—okay, I never told you this before because who knew how long it was going to last, but remember that assistant I had last year? The one who got fired by that movie star because she wouldn't stand in the middle of the Pacific Coast Highway to stop traffic in front of his house whenever he wanted to drive out?

Well, she told me something about Zane that I swore I'd never tell anyone."

"Okay, tell, tell, tell."

The waiter delivers our drinks; thank God, since I think Neil was about to bolt from the table and go back to his office, dragging me along with him. The Venice boardwalk lies just beyond the Casa del Mar hotel's private beach, and a steady stream of badly dressed tourists and rumpled looking locals peer in to see whether they can glimpse someone who could change their lives forever, either careerwise with a role or statuswise by the sheer act of seeing them. The beach is bright with the early June sun, as if night will never appear. Or if it does, it will only be a darkening controlled by a lighting designer, able to flood us at any time with kliegs to make the perpetual playground reappear: day for night.

"Fi, hey." Patricia is standing in front of us with one arm around Zane. I have seen him before in his films and on TV, so his looks are not a surprise, but seeing him in real life with Patricia is. They look like two separate pictures that have been photo-shopped together. His image pulled from some bacchanal fest, and hers from a network sanctioned press release, as perfect and poised as a newscaster. Zane appears almost blurry, as if the notorious partying of his life has inebriated even the outlines of his skin. I feel dizzy just looking at him. The picture of them rips in half as they move to sit down.

"Congratulations," Neil says to Zane after introductions are made all around. "Welcome to the club."

Zane looks startled, as if a membership director is about to descend upon him at any moment demanding references and dues.

"The club," Neil says, "of married men."

"Oh, dude," Zane says, looking relieved. "Right." Then a look of perplexed terror flashes across his face.

"It's all still so new," Patricia says, covering his hand with her left one. Her engagement ring—though I wonder if it can technically be called that because how long could their "engagement" have been? Fifteen minutes of fiancédom?—is a large, canary-colored heart-shaped diamond. If it weren't on her (one hundred and twenty five thousand dollars a week) hand and came from (fifteen million dollars a film) him, it would look like a favor from an eight-year-old's birthday party. I wonder how their hands are bearing up under its weight.

"Let's get some fucking Dom over here," Zane says, extricating his hand and looking around. "Where are the waiters in this place?" It is as if his entire body becomes a giant hand poised to make a loud snapping sound to summon an underling. I can feel Neil about to jump into crisis prevention mode just as a waiter materializes next to us.

"A bottle of Dom for the table, my man," Zane says.

The waiter takes the infinitesimal beats of recognizing Zane, looking to see whom he is with, displaying shock that it is Patricia mixed with "but, of course, because she is so not the obvious choice," then reverting to subordinate disinterest.

"Actually, I won't be having any," I say to the waiter.

Zane's attention suddenly focuses on me, as if I am a seriously wounded member of his team and therefore either a burden to endure or an object to discard.

"Why not?" he says.

Neil is looking at me to see what I'll say while Patricia studies her menu with great interest. In a split second, my mind rejects the easy "I'm on medication" lie because for this guy, that would be an opportunity for more of a thrill. Then I hit upon the one thing that I know he'll support and understand.

"Audition early tomorrow," I say, "don't want to be puffy."

Zane nods solemnly, as if he too has been through that particular circle of hell and admires my fortitude at staying out of it.

If I had any doubts about Patricia's keeping my secret from Zane—and I did—they are instantly dispelled. There is no way he could have acted his way through that one. I have to prevent myself from letting out an audible sigh of relief because if Zane had known I have no doubt he would have blown it, and then Neil would have known I had told and—

I glance over at Patricia and she shoots me a small smile that is so out of the side of her mouth that it is almost on the back of her head. I feel a rush of love and gratitude for her. I want to push my chair closer to hers and whisper with her about the men the way we did once in high school on the single occasion when we double dated together.

It was freshman year. Patricia had just smoked a cigarette and had managed to make it look as if she had been lighting up her whole life. I knew she was relieved, as I was, that she hadn't embarrassed us in front of the boys, so I leaned over, put my hand to her ear, and whispered, "Aren't you glad you learned how to inhale?"

I started smoking one day before Patricia did. This boy that I had just finished making out with lit a Camel, its white package shiny and crinkly in the sunlight that cut through the bleachers that we were under while the rest of the school headed home for the day. Taking a drag off his cigarette didn't seem that much more different than having his tongue in my mouth. It was another hard, illicit object that sent vapors and other invisible-but-potent things shooting down my throat and into my body. After I took a drag, I started to hand the cigarette back to him, but he was already reaching into the pack to light another one for himself, leaving me with the one that he had started. It was like when I was a child and needed our maid Louise to take the first bite of an apple for me, so I'd have a place to hook my teeth into.

We could hear the school buses pulling out of the large black-topped playground that they parked on in the mornings when they emptied themselves of the children inside, then collected them again later in the afternoons, driving and parking on the painted lines of the basketball courts and chalk-drawn hopscotch boards and the one smooth area where the younger girls played jacks.

Carl Flores was new in my ninth-grade class that year. His family had moved to Lake Charles from New Orleans, so he held all the glamour and mystery of being from that much loved and envied city. He was half an inch shorter than I was, but his pale blue knit shirt fit him in a way that the other boys' did not, as if a man's body had taken him over inside. Carl wore a St. Christopher medal on a silver chain around his neck. I had always thought that saint medals were cheesy, but suddenly whenever I saw the glint of the one he wore slipping in and out from under his open collar, I wanted to take it in my fingers and free it from the fabric that held it bound. Let it come out in the world, hard and sure in my hand, where I could hold it long and fast while his mouth found mine, just as it was doing again.

The next night, Patricia and I were in her room at her mother's apartment. Patricia's older half brother, Mike, was still at his job at the mall, and Vicky, Patricia's mother, was God knows where, as usual. So I opened the window and pulled out the small crushed pack of cigarettes that Carl had given me with five still inside.

"Maybe I just won't inhale," Patricia said, after one whole cigarette had been wasted trying to get her to pull the smoke down into her lungs.

"You have to or you'll look stupid. Or just don't smoke. I don't care."

That made her grab the pack from my hands and light one up herself, sucking it in so heavily that I could have sworn I saw smoke coming out of her ears.

Patricia and I were sitting next to each other on the shiny orange hard vinyl bench at Sal's Pizza looking at our dates on the other side of the table. Carl was French inhaling his cigarette, the smoke a continuous loop advertising his mastery of all things dangerous, while Patricia's date, Patrick Patrick, was going on and on about our upcoming final for Algebra I. Patrick Patrick's parents were both doctors. I imagined them wanting not so much more of the same, but for everything to be only one thing. One kind of job; one kind of name. Ever since he had transferred to our school in sixth grade, Patrick Patrick had always been called by both names. When the teachers called on him in class, after they said, "Patrick," we'd all say in unison under our breath, "Patrick," and said it so immediately that it was just a hushed echo that was impossible for the teachers to stop.

Patrick Patrick's other claim to fame was his ability to do a perfect pratfall. He'd be standing in line on the cafeteria's hard linoleum floor, or even on the concrete sidewalk under the walkway, and his small, frail body would suddenly just fall completely straight-limbed and without his bracing his elbows or knees or hands. He was like a needle on a gauge, shooting back to zero. After a moment on the ground, and the dependable laughs and expected gasps from those new to his game, he would spring up, brush himself off, and start talking again exactly where he left off. He was cute, but in a nerdy sort of way.

Sitting here at the table at the Casa del Mar hotel, I try to imagine Zane taking a fall on purpose. But the only thing I can imagine is him on his snowboard, swooshing on snow to eminence. The last thing this man would ever let his body be is a joke. How in God's name did Patricia get from Patrick Patrick to Zane? Then I wonder whether she wonders that, too. Or maybe marrying Zane was to prevent another Patrick Patrick that is out there waiting for her, like a predestined life that she is afraid she can't escape.

The waiter returns to our table with the chilled champagne, shows the bottle to Neil, opens it noiselessly, and then pours a taste into his flute. If Zane realizes that he is being insulted, he doesn't show it, so I can only think that he does not. From what I have seen of him so far, playing it close to the vest is not one of his traits.

Neil nods, and the waiter fills the other two flutes. Then he shoves the bottle into the waiting ice bucket, but just as he is pulling out his pen and pad, Zane thrusts the large and carefully composed menu at him.

"You can take that," he says. "We're not eating."

I look at Neil and can practically hear his silent outpouring of shock. "I left work early, and you drove all the way across town in rush hour traffic for a dinner that is two hours too early and now they're not even going to eat with us?"

"We have to leave in a little bit," Patricia says, as if she was also tuned in to Neil's inner monologue. "We're going to that charity event that *Sports Illustrated* is sponsoring. Remember? I told you in my message."

Patricia looks at me, waiting for me to jump in and agree and make her excuse palatable and true, but I'm not going to because for one thing, she didn't, and for another, I'm not conspiring with her. It's her husband she should be turning to. Neil has started watching me, too. The only one left to also demand loyalty is Zane, but he is blithely refilling his glass of precious Dom.

"No, you didn't mention that. We thought we were meeting y'all for dinner."

This is so Hollywood, the land of "But there might be something better." And the reality is that on the surface, there always is. Each day awakens more perfect and gorgeous than the last, and each wave of actors arrives younger and prettier than the ones already here. Yet the only thing that this constant "trading up" leads to is having the same experience with different people instead of different experiences with the same person. Then I wonder whether Patricia will have the same outcome with Zane that she did with Patrick Patrick.

After our double date at Sal's Pizza, the four of us walked the five blocks over to the school gym for the freshman/sophomore dance. As we got to the parking lot blacktop, dark was falling, and light was beckoning through the windows set high up on the yellow brick gym building. Carl immediately grabbed my hand to lead me toward the bleachers on the big field for a make-out session before we went in to dance, but a quick one so we wouldn't get caught. Patricia and Patrick Patrick hesitated behind us. I knew she wanted him to lead her somewhere, too. And I knew, too at least from the rumors, that Patrick Patrick had never led a girl any place for that reason and most probably wasn't going to start now.

I looked back at Patricia and saw the simultaneous shame and relief of the rejection on her face. I felt shame, too, but for a different reason. Not that I was letting it stop me. Going off with Carl felt like what I was supposed to do. Like his wanting to was a silent order that my body was responding to, and the fact that I also wanted to was beside the point. As our paths diverged, I could hear Patrick Patrick talking on and on about his little sister's hamster, and Carl and I moved toward the bleachers' silent shadows, while they entered the dance's syncopated mania.

When Carl and I walked into the gym about twenty minutes later, we found the dance floor cleared, except for one couple. The music was blaring, the lights were bright, and the kids were gathered around in a wide circle cheering on Patricia and Patrick Patrick as they danced and dipped and swirled. But instead of Patrick Patrick leading Patricia, she was leading him. As Carl and I edged our way in through the thicket of students to have a closer look, Patricia picked Patrick Patrick up and swung him around, his frail body flying out at a ninety-degree angle through the room. There was a moment of astonished silence, then the kids erupted in hoots and laughter and "Go, Patricia, go!"

Patrick Patrick had almost the same smile he would get on his face when he'd do his pratfalls, but this time there was something added to it, an "I don't like this game" grimace under the smile. At the end of the evening, he assured Patricia that he had had a great time and then never gave her the time of day again.

"No," Patricia says, looking from Neil to me. Zane may as well be at another table for all the interest he has in this. "I know I told you on my message. That's why we had to meet here. And it's close to Neil's office anyway, so I figured, what's the big deal?"

I can feel Neil physically restrain himself from going off on her as to why it is a big deal. I can feel him shift into "This person is not worth my time or energy ever again." I almost prefer for him to just cuss her out and still be willing to do something with them again. Then I wonder why I want that.

Because I can't imagine not being able to hang out as a couple with my oldest and best friend and don't want to.

Neil pushes his champagne glass away from him. I half expect him to move back his chair and reach out his hand to me for us to leave. But he pulls out his Blackberry and begins checking e-mails at the table. It is clear that he intends to do this until they leave. It is behavior that Neil finds the height of rudeness, so he never engages in it, but I guess he's decided that all bets are off.

Patricia has turned her attention to Zane, or at least she is staring at him as if that will somehow hide her from Neil and me. She still has an expression of confused, but defensive guilt on her face. Zane, however, does not see it because he is monitoring the parade of people going by, particularly a trio of rollerblading beauties whose outfits make the term *second skin* sound modest.

"Well," I say, throwing the word into the silence to see whether any of them will respond, "how about a toast?"

Neil and Patricia look at me as if I am kidding or have lost my mind or both. Only Zane takes my offer without question and after refilling his glass, holds it up expectantly as if I am about to bestow upon him the crown jewels.

"To the newlyweds," I say, and I lift up my ginger ale, a symbol to Patricia of the secret she knows and could still spill, to Neil of our increasing bond, and to Zane of the hold that vanity has on him. "For a happily ever after married life."

And the four of us clink our glasses together.

Chapter 10

"CONGRATULATIONS, DARLIN'. That is excellent news."

"Thanks, Daddy."

I switch the phone to my other ear, as the smell of Neil's take-out barbecue chicken dinner wafts toward me in the living room. He is eating at the kitchen table in deference to my nausea, but it's not making much of a difference. Any food cooking in the house is enough to send me running outside. He tried tempting me with mashed potatoes, but even they were unappealing.

"A grandson would be appreciated, but I'll be happy either way."

"I'll keep that in mind."

"Good work, Fiona."

"Thanks, Daddy."

There is a silence on the line. I listen to the ice cubes in my father's after-work drink as he takes a sip. I can imagine him in the butler's pantry, having just fixed his old-fashioned, ready to take it and his paper to the back sun porch, where he will enjoy his quietude until whatever my mother has decided will be their dinner.

"I'll put your mother back on."

"Okay."

"Don't strain yourself."

"I won't."

"Let us know."

"I will."

My father takes in a sharp breath as if he is finally going to give me that oft-imagined, but uncharted father-daughter talk, but his words are consistent with every other time. "Bye, darlin'."

"Bye, Daddy."

"Margot," my father yells into the depths of the family home. "Come take the phone."

Immediately, I hear my mother's hurried steps. They could just as well belong to a Labrador rushing to its master's call.

"Well," my mother says into the phone. "Your father is just thrilled, as you can tell."

"Yeah." I wonder if this time she hid next to the archway between the dining room and the living room to listen in on our call. Or if she merely pretended suddenly to need to draw the dining room's curtains, affording her the best possible earshot. She clearly has no compunction about my knowing that she eavesdrops on our calls. Though I doubt my father would be pleased if he ever figured it out, or if I told him. But I won't, which my mother counts on. Colluding on the secret of her breaking my privacy.

"Now, when are you due again?"

I know she has her date book with her, the leather one from Tiffany's that she keeps in her bag, that is with her no matter where she goes. Except at night at social functions with Daddy, when she also leaves wallet and keys at home, tucking only her lipstick, powder, and handkerchief into whichever small bag, so assured she is of his role in handling everything

"January 15th."

"Oh, God. I thought so."

"What?"

"That's the opening of your father's new bank building. I just looked it up and that's when it is."

"Oh." I have no idea what I am supposed to do with this information. Change my baby's due date?

"Obviously, we can't not go."

"Well, thanks, Mom, I really—"

"Your father has worked hard your whole life. That is going to be a very special weekend for him, and I am not going to let him miss it."

"Oh." A trapdoor opens up underneath the nausea in my belly, and it feels as if the entire room has moved into the space there and is starting to spin.

"That baby is not going to know if we're there or not," my mother says. "And surely Carol will be coming down from Pismo Beach; won't she?"

I grab hold of the couch's armrest, hoping that will slow down the revolving room that is my stomach.

"Yeah, Neil's mother has already said that she's coming."

"Well, then. And really, Fiona, the first few days of a baby's life are hectic enough without two more people descending upon you. You and Neil and that baby are going to need to get to know each other. When I had you, your grandparents left the next day to go see my Aunt Brigid in Corpus Christi. Why anyone thinks a new mother and baby need all that company

I will never know. So. We'll come out when it's older and you're all settled. Besides, you'd barely be able to do anything with us what with that baby being a few days old."

I finally notice that Neil is standing by the dark leather club chair looking concerned. I catch his eye and shake my head, conveying to him as much as I can the full nightmare extent of this call. I will stop myself from saying to him, "Now do you understand why I didn't want this to be my first breaking-the-news call?" Partly out of preserving marital harmony, but mostly because I know he will figure that out for himself.

"Right. No. I wouldn't be able to do that."

"So. Let me say congratulations to Neil, then I really do need to get off the phone. Your father and I are due at the Garveys' for dinner."

"Okay."

"This is wonderful news, Fiona. I know this one will make it." The evil fairy in "Sleeping Beauty" couldn't have cast a better spell.

"Thanks, Mom. Bye."

And I hand Neil the phone.

Chapter 11

I HAD NEVER STOPPED WANTING A PIXIE CUT. Even at the end of fourth grade when I was ten and had known for a long time that fairies weren't real, I still wanted a pixie cut. I would ask Momma in the car just before we went into the beauty parlor, "This time, Momma, can I have a pixie cut?" But she always said the same thing to the woman who had been doing her hair for years: "A little off her ends, Marilyn, and no bangs." And I would leave the beauty parlor looking identical to the way I had entered.

That year, when it was time for my beginning of summer trim, Momma let me ride my bike to the beauty parlor. I had already been making forays on my own to Patricia's and to Clarkson's, the neighborhood grocery store that was three blocks down and two blocks over from our home to get a for-gotten jar of bitters for Daddy's nightly old-fashioned, or Gravy Bouquet for the roast Louise was making, plus always a candy bar for me. But going to the beauty parlor was a further cementing of my bike as a car. Suddenly this object that had always been only for fun—Patricia and I would play teenage runaways and pedal around an imagined New York City, or our bikes were horses, riding hard and fast over the prairies we read about in Laura Ingalls Wilder's books—was now what enabled me to enter the real world independently.

It was a Tuesday and Patricia had spent the night. We had been spending practically every weekend at one or the other's home since that day in first grade when we exchanged our socks, but waking up on a weekday with Patricia there held a richer flavor than a Saturday or Sunday. The house was usually empty except for Louise, what with Daddy being at the bank, and Momma having her bridge and tennis games to keep up. The day, the house, the hours, the world were ours to do with as we wanted, and we would enter easily into their possibilities.

Patricia's mother, Vicky, would drive her to my house and drop her off with the air of a parent leaving her child at camp, annoyed that her daughter preferred it to home, yet thrilled with the freedom it provided. She would yank Patricia's bike out of the trunk of her white Alfa Romeo with the tan leather interior. There was only one other Alfa Romeo in all of Lake Charles, a red one that belonged to a cardiologist, of course, and they both had to be towed back to the dealership in Houston for any repairs. Patricia's mother called hers Blanche after the Tennessee Williams character. That and the fact that she drove the car at all infuriated my mother. "That Vicky—" she'd say, and her self-censorship made it all too clear what she was thinking.

My father didn't like Vicky because she had an older son, Mike, from a previous marriage who lived with Patricia and her in their smallish, but elegant apartment in the complex that butted up against our neighborhood. A divorcée was bad enough, but half-siblings were just too messy as far as my father was concerned.

"She can't very well get rid of the boy, Ed," my mother said one evening at dinner when the subject had come up. "And it's not like that awful Tom is going to take Patricia, off gallivanting the way he is in Atlanta. Let's just hope she doesn't go on to marriage and baby number three."

My father appeared mollified by my mother's remarks, so she shifted the conversation to the one I knew she was dying to begin (judging from the spate of afternoon phone calls she had had): who was going to play Santa this year at the country club's annual Christmas party. While my mother prattled on, and my father either did an astonishing imitation of a person actually listening or, for some inconceivable reason, actually was interested, I was left to let my thoughts wander, which was my usual involvement with the dinner conversation.

It had been a shock to hear what my mother said about Vicky and Patricia's situation because I knew that Patricia wanted Vicky to get rid of Mike. Not that she had ever admitted that to me, except her wish for her father to rescue her. Patricia talked about that all the time. Though she never used the word *rescue*, but I had read enough Brothers Grimm by then to know what she meant. And she didn't need to explain to me why.

One afternoon earlier that year, right after fourth grade had begun, I had ridden my bike over to Patricia's house. She hadn't known I was coming. Momma had told me to go straight home after school to help Louise get ready for a dinner party she and my father were having that night. But when I got home, Louise said, "It all done, child. Get yourself outside. You more help out of this house than in it." I loved Louise. So I jumped on my bike, yelled to her where I was headed, and took off for Patricia's.

I figured she and Mike would be inside the apartment sitting on the leopard print sofa in the cocktail lounge–like living room watching TV. Vicky had had the walls painted a deep and glossy brown with blinding white trim, and the only light was from little gold candelabras affixed to the walls. Mike was five years older than we were, in ninth grade, and seeing him in that apartment was like witnessing a hurricane that barely missed a beach shack—grateful it wasn't destroyed, but doubtful it would survive.

I knocked on the apartment door. The bell had broken long ago, but I could hear the *Gilligan's Island* episode on their TV through the door and out onto the landing. I pounded again but knew they couldn't hear me. As I turned the door handle, I wondered why the TV was on so loud. Then when I opened the door and looked inside, I immediately understood.

They were on the floor. Mike was on top of Patricia, straddling her. His long dark hair fell across his face as he moved rhythmically on her. Patricia's face was turned away from the door, and she lay immobile, like when we played "light as a feather" and the person pretended to be dead. Mike's arms had a controlled fury as they pummeled Patricia again and again. He suddenly reminded me of a mechanical bank I had on my dresser; when you put a penny in the slot, a uniformed monkey would beat a drum over and over until a click occurred, then the coin would disappear.

The front door slammed shut behind me, and Mike jerked his head around with a look of wild terror and guilt. But when he saw that it was me, he gave a snorting laugh, pushed his hands hard onto Patricia's chest for leverage to get himself up, and flicking his hair, sauntered out of the room.

Patricia curled up into a ball the minute Mike was gone.

She still hadn't looked at me. I went over, sat down next to her, and stroked her back. Her back was making those heaving motions that it did when she laughed really hard, but I knew it wasn't that this time.

I suddenly understood why she had never changed into her nightgown in front of me, and wondered how long Mike had been beating her up. I figured Vicky had no idea about it because if Patricia hadn't told me, why would she tell Vicky? And ever since I had known Patricia, she had gotten herself ready for bed, usually even put herself to bed since Vicky was more times than not, out with sales reps of clothing lines for her designer clothing boutique, or an important customer, as she called them. And even if she did tell Vicky, what horror would Mike do to her then?

Patricia got up, went to the bathroom for a long while, and when she came back said, "Come on." We left the apartment, got on our bikes, and rode far away. She never said one word about it, so neither did I.

On that morning at the end of fourth grade when I was to get my summer trim, my mother had a tennis tournament, so Patricia and I set off on our bikes for the beauty parlor. It was on a heavily trafficked commercial street, but its parking lot opened onto a residential side street, so Momma decided it was okay, though I had a feeling she wasn't going to tell Daddy. And Patricia's mother would never know. She was forever working late at her boutique or having dinner with sales reps and would show up around town in outfits that none of the other mothers would wear, even mine, who was thin and pretty and stylish and stood out in a crowd the way redheads do.

Patricia and I turned out of my driveway to go down the side street away from my house. Our house was (and still is) on a corner of Shell Beach Drive, the street that fronts Lake Charles, the lake the city was named for, and is lined with historical homes, some grand, some small, but all impeccable in design. Ours was built in the twenties. It is dark green with a high porch and deep front lawn that holds large old oak trees that I played tea under with acorn caps when I was small.

But the house next door was my favorite. It was built before the war, and where I'm from that means the Civil War, and was white with forest green trim, a huge concoction of romance and intrigue. A pavilion stood on the front lawn with a bench inside it all around, and a copper roof that had turned green with a top like a stopper on one of my mother's crystal perfume bottles on her mirrored Art Deco dressing table. Far across the lawn, in a garden only accessible through a small entrance hidden in the boxwood hedges, was a marble statue of a woman. One arm was across both her breasts, and as she leaned down, the other arm held in its hand a shell from which water ran into a small fountain with a blue painted bottom. Patricia and I had named this Paradise and would take our after-school snacks there, happy in the secrecy it provided. Or if we didn't care about being seen, we would play in the pavilion, doing ballets filled with wild leaps on the benches and pirouetting around and around. Other times we were princesses, trapped in a tower, waiting for our princes to find us. The couple who owned the house were elderly, all their children were gone, and we rarely, if ever, saw them.

Often Patricia and I would cross Shell Beach Drive and play on the lakefront land in front of our house that belonged to my parents. Directly across the water from us was a man-made beach for families to enjoy the water and breeze during the sweltering days that made up most of the year. Our side of the lake was grassy with a sharp drop to the water. Other homeowners had built small docks to take a boat out from or to make it easier to swim, but my father wasn't a water sports man, and my mother preferred a pool.

The bike ride from my house to the beauty parlor was barely ten minutes. We cut across Drew Park; past the large, screened-in clubhouse where kids were playing Ping-Pong, and younger children in summer camp were having their mid-morning snack; then headed down a side street, turned onto another, then rode into the gravel-filled parking lot, our bikes suddenly skidding and sluggish in the loose rocks.

Marilyn wasn't there. She had called in sick, the frosted and glossed receptionist sitting behind the tall, gold round desk told us. "But there's a new girl, Sally. She could take you. May's well get it done since you got all the way here."

Patricia headed to the Coke machine for us, while I went into one of the little changing rooms with the louvered double swinging doors that always managed to whack me when they swung back. As I walked to Sally's chair, I passed a row of women parked in gold vinyl molded chairs that were cranked high in the air, like cars being rebuilt. The air was choked with chemical smells, the perfumed sweetness on top not hiding the harsh reality of the oil and lacquer and paint below.

The black with bright pink polka dots cotton cape I was wearing billowed out from me as I stepped onto the beauty chair's metal footrest to sit down. The footrest always reminded me of the cold steel contraption that Mr. Arturo would guide each of my feet into to measure them for new shoes. The cape caught under me when I scooted back on the seat, choking me a bit with its small neck opening. I was half-standing up and pulling the yards of fabric loose when Patricia and Sally came over simultaneously.

"Well, I know you two aren't sisters," Sally said, as I took the pale green bottle of Coke from Patricia's hand. "Lord above, look at that red hair!"

I was used to people saying things like that to me. My whole existence pertaining to my hair was one of diabolical opposites. The boys at school had recently started calling me "Flame Head," while adult women swooned over my hair's shiny vitality. But at the beauty parlor, any attempt at civility about it seemed to fall away. On one of the many times I was there with my mother, I overheard a woman tsk-tsk-ing to the victim installed next to her under the large conical hair dryers about how awful these young mothers are nowadays dying their daughter's hair to match their own, harlots they look, the both of them. I had wanted to go over and pull up my hair so it would stand tall from its roots the way Marilyn would do when she'd show off the naturalness of my mother's hair to her other customers as if she had something to do with it, and it boded well for her coloring skills.

"So, what are we doing today? Both of you getting cut?"

"Just me," I said. "I'm Fiona. My momma wants me to have a pixie cut."

Sally was too busy stubbing out her menthol cigarette in the purple metal ashtray next to the hair spray on her station's counter to notice Patricia's eyes popping out.

"It'll be cooler for summer, she says." I shot Patricia a look that was filled with the whopping victory of pulling off the world's funniest joke and daredevil feat at the same time.

"That's for damn sure," Sally said, picking up her shears and clicking them open and shut a few times in the air, like a matador taunting the bull with his cape.

Patricia went into a paroxysm of giggles, so she quickly turned around and gulped a big swig of her Coke, which promptly came shooting out of her nose.

"Ow, Patricia, I bet that hurt. Maybe you should go blow your nose," I said, looking pointedly at her. "We rode our bikes over here too soon after breakfast," I continued to Sally. "You know how sometimes on a hot day it can come up."

"You don't have to tell me."

Sally had a large purple comb in one hand, and a steely pair of scissors in the other, as she picked up a section of my hair that was hanging down to the middle of my back. The blades were open and poised when Sally looked at Patricia, who was staring at the tableau as if she was seeing the last of me.

"The bathroom's down there to your left, sugar. Just knock before you go in. Some of these old biddies don't know how to lock a door."

And as Patricia dragged herself away, Sally turned back to me, squinted at the hunk of hair she had pulled taut above my head, and began lopping off not only my long princess hair, but also my mother's vision of a perfect daughter.

Chapter 12

I'VE BEEN HAVING FANTASIES of a son this whole time. I kept thinking that we'll have a little boy who will grow up to be like Neil. Not exactly like him, obviously. And I wasn't thinking career or name or even looks really, but more the kind of man that Neil is. Someone safe to be around. One for that side of the team. Even before I got pregnant, I just always knew I'd have a son.

I am half-sitting, half-lying on the mechanized table in the doctor's office on San Vicente Boulevard, right down from Cedars-Sinai, about to have my amnio done. I was disappointed to find out that Dr. Walker couldn't do it.

"But you don't want me to," she said at my visit the month before, after we looked at the sonogram and said hello to the baby. "They're all Dr. Little does. She's the best. And besides, I don't have the equipment to do it even if I wanted to."

Neil is holding my hand. We had had the genetic counseling, sitting in a small white room whose furniture looked at best rented and at worst like a cheap set in an after-school movie produced solely to terrify teens out of prewedlock pregnancies. Never have percentages sounded so scary. As the twenty-something genetic counselor (wedding ring on her finger, picture of her two blond and shining sons on her desk) reeled off the numbers, I kept envisioning myself in a crowd of women and all of us trying to avoid our babies being struck with defects, like some dodge ball game from hell neonatal-style. I always hated dodge ball. It's such a mean game.

"You're only thirty-five," Neil kept saying in the weeks leading up to this visit whenever he could tell that I was already worrying.

"I know, you're right. We'll be fine." But all I could hear was my mother's voice, "That's when the real trouble starts."

The nurse had already been in, swabbing my stomach with the gel that reminded me of the Dippity-Do that my mother always put in her pixie cut hair, then pressing down hard with the flat sonogram wand, scanning the baby and pointing out to us the head and toes and heart and hands.

"I'm Dr. Little," the doctor said when she walked in. Her accent practically preceded her, it was such a presence.

"I'm from the South, too." I immediately hated that I had to say it. At UCLA, I had taken the requisite speech classes to erase the diphthongs from my words. When the teacher had told us to write a paragraph using words containing short vowel sounds, I went to class empty handed. I had never spoken or heard a pure short vowel sound in my life. Who knew *pin* and *pen* didn't sound exactly the same? And weren't two syllables long?

"It's really good that you're working on this," the speech teacher told me that day. "Because otherwise, you'd be stereotyped."

As if I wasn't going to be stereotyped already just for being a woman and a redhead to boot. How many times have I heard my agent say, "They already have a redhead." As if the physical appearance of actors in TV shows and films is such an accurate portrayal of what real people look like that one additional redhead would cancel out all authenticity. Sometimes I think that the main reason it would be awful if I don't ever get to do the big gun roles that I want to do (Hedda, Masha, Mary Tyrone) is that I lost my accent in pursuit of them: vocally neutered by my own choice and hand.

Dr. Little takes the sonogram wand and, pressing on my stomach, goes over the baby exactly as the nurse did, but then stops for a moment and turns the video screen toward her. I hear Neil's breath constrict as mine does.

"Everything looks great," she says. "Do y'all want to know the sex?"

"Yes," Neil and I say together as we let out our breath. I think of the box on the form that we checked off in the waiting room indicating that we want to know the baby's gender and wonder whether she even read it.

"It's a girl," Dr. Little says, and she moves the screen in our direction. She says it as if she is giving a weather report. A weather report for an outdoor wedding, but still a weather report that you can't do a damn thing about.

"A girl," Neil says, squeezing my hand and bending down to kiss me.

"A girl," I repeat, partly from shock and partly to gain time to figure out how to react. I had almost forgotten that Neil didn't care either way.

All these months that we've been pregnant, I had never said anything to him about this. But to Patricia I had said, "How can he not care whether it's a boy or a girl? It's like that scene in *Hurlyburly* where Darlene is as happy to eat French food as she is Chinese, and Eddie nearly has a fucking heart attack because how can she not have a preference? And I had always thought that Eddie was just being a fucked-up cokehead about it, but now suddenly I understand. How can Neil not care?"

"Well, I want a girl, you want a boy, and he's fine either way," Patricia said. "So whatever it is, two out of three of us will be happy."

"I won't be unhappy if it's not a boy, I just—"

Patricia looked at me as I tried to finish my sentence. I didn't even want to go there enough mentally to try to figure out how I'd feel if it wasn't a boy, much less be able to say it. I couldn't understand how Patricia could want a girl, but I didn't have the energy for that conversation. "I really think it's a boy."

"Well," she said, "there's nothing you can do about it either way."

And that made me kind of crazy because, okay, I did realize that I can't control this. I mean, I'm not like that stupid actress who, while she had her own hit sitcom, famously told an interviewer that she was successful because she wanted it badly enough, and the only actors who aren't that successful just don't want it enough. God save me. As if the power of the mind can control every studio head in town. Of course, ever since her show went off the air, and she hasn't been able to get even one tiny role, part of me has wanted to call her up and say, "I guess you just stopped wanting it badly enough, huh?" So, I'm not that far gone out here in the land of "If you dream it, it will come" to think that I could have a hand in the gender of my offspring. But, maybe, I guess, in a small, secret-even-from-me way, I did.

I just never dreamed that my son would be a daughter.

Large, silent tears are streaming down my face as the nurse wipes off the sonogram gel and swabs iodine all over my stomach, making it look like some inside/outside version of my skin. Neil glances at me, then grabs a tissue from the counter, and dabs my face with it.

"It'll be all right," he says. "Just don't watch, if you can't. I will."

I nod my head with a smile that I hope conveys gratitude for his understanding and wonder whether he believes it. If it had been an audition, I don't think I would have gotten the job. But he is holding my hand, completely engrossed in watching Dr. Little make the final preparations for the amnio. Thank God, I can let him think that these tears are about that because they are continuing to run nonstop out of my eyes, and moving down each side of my face, filling my ears and wetting my neck with their public display of my dismay.

A girl.

It is as if I've just been shipped to a foreign country, then found out that someone dear to me back home has been killed. I'm not going to have a son. My mind immediately starts going through all of the fantasies I had of him and erasing them one by one. No mother-son bond. No name I had sort of already picked out on my own. No getting to see a world totally new to me, that of little boys. And no Gulf of Mexico blue with chocolate brown accents as the color scheme for his room.

Instead, I am getting one like me, sexwise, at least. And ideally gender will be the only similarity. Not that I think I am so despicable that I don't have even one good trait to pass along. But, Jesus, I really wanted a clean slate.

Though this baby is a whole different person, and I am not

my mother (repeat this ad nauseam). But it's also all the other stuff that I know full well can happen to a girl that makes me want to stop this ride right here and now. Not literally, but I just don't know if I can live through something like that again. I wanted a son.

Tears are still streaming silently down my face, and I am completely incapable of getting them to stop even though I feel ridiculous mourning a boy who never existed. I turn my head to wipe my cheek on the sheet, and see Dr. Little holding up an incredibly long and thin needle that she then pushes through my skin.

Neil is standing next to me, eyes riveted on the monitor. I look up at the screen and watch the needle enter my womb in the only area that is dark and empty; the baby is nestled on the other side. Suddenly, the baby sticks out her arm straight toward the needle. It is all I can do not to yell, "Get away from that thing," and yank out the needle myself.

"Uh, is that okay?" I say, looking at Dr. Little to make sure she sees what is going on, but she is calmly pulling the needle out.

"All done," Dr. Little says. "And don't you worry. That needle didn't touch her. But I gotta say, I've never seen one put her hand out for it before. I swear, they've got their personalities from the second they're formed. Here." She picks up the sonogram wand and presses it on my belly. "This'll make you feel better."

Our baby's heart appears on the screen, flashing its light of life to us. Dr. Little turns a knob and the sound of my daughter's heartbeat fills the room. I imagine it in her tiny body, a red muscle under her pale skin. I want to reach my hand in somehow and hold her. Then I realize that I am holding her closer to me now than I ever will.

"Hi, baby girl," I think to myself. And for the first time, I wonder whether she'll have red hair like mine.

Chapter 13

"I THINK IT'S CUTE."

"Does my hair look redder?"

"Uh-uh. It's less red, because there's not as much. I like it. But, Fi, what's your momma gonna do?"

The sky had become close with dark, heavy clouds. Patricia and I had just gotten on our bikes and were pushing off from the grasp of the beauty parlor's gravel-filled lot. A plastic bag with a bottle of shampoo for my mother that could only be bought at the beauty parlor was hanging from the handlebars of my bike and kept slapping my left leg everytime I pedaled. I suddenly wished that a lifetime of that bottle hitting my leg could be my punishment for getting this haircut instead of what I was going to face when I got home. I tried to imagine what horror she would think up this time.

"I don't know."

"She's gonna be mad."

"She's gonna kill me," I thought.

I reached up with my left hand and started tugging on my hair in the back while repeating in my mind, "Please get long again, please." It was so high up. A huge expanse of neck lay below it. I had never really thought about my neck before, but now here it was, open to the world like a broken window that would let in all kinds of weather, but mostly bad. I wanted to race back to the beauty parlor, scoop up my tresses off the floor, and glue them to my head somehow the way I had once glued the sequins that had fallen from one of my mother's ball gowns to my doll's fingers to give her sparkly painted nails. As I pedaled next to Patricia, I suddenly felt as if I was going to throw up.

Maybe I could spend the night at her house. Maybe Momma wouldn't be home when we got there and we could call Patricia's mother and she'd come get us, not that she ever had before, but still, and I could stay there for a few nights and my hair would grow out some by then. Hadn't Momma said that hair and nails grow faster in hot months? Though every month was hot here, so maybe that meant in a few weeks, my hair would be back to the way it was just twenty minutes ago and everything would be okay again.

But I didn't think so. I couldn't even remember my hair not being long, long, long. Princess hair, my mother called it. I loved putting on a dress for Mass, or a party, or on the wonderful days when Momma would let me go to lunch at the racquet club with her, and she'd come into my room, and pick out a ribbon or barrette for my hair, and carefully put it on me, making me turn my head this way and that in the pink dressing table's mirror to check the way it looked. I suddenly had a thought that almost made my breakfast come up: maybe Momma wouldn't consider me her daughter without my long hair.

Suddenly, the sky fractured apart, and a drenching rain

wiped out all color and form with its dense grayness. Thunder slapped, lightning flared, and Patricia shrieked.

"Let's go under that porch," I yelled above the deluge, pointing at a house just ahead and to our right. "We'll wait it out."

Our tires sluiced through the rivulets that were gushing down the street, as we turned into the broken concrete driveway that led to a small yellow brick house. The porch was really just a large aluminum canopy attached to the front. A gutter had been added on top, so the vast accumulation of rain was cascading down in one spot in the front. Patricia and I stood behind the curtain of water, looking at the world through its liquid distortion, while I tried to come up with a magic rhyme that would cancel out the last hour and the haircut it held. My stomachache had spread to the back of my knees, making them feel queasy, too.

I reached up to pull at my hair again to make it grow. I couldn't believe how short it was. Shorter even than Momma's maybe. My hair was lying in sticky wet clumps on my head. I thought of Sally and the hair spray that she crowned me with at the end of the cut. It had been fun at the time: her covering my eyes with her hand, the soft whisper sound, and the light dew droplets all around. Like Momma, I had thought. I finally have hair like Momma. And afterward, when I looked in the big mirror above her station, while Sally held up a purple plastic hand mirror so I could see the back, I even looked like Momma. My eyes were bigger, and lips fuller, but otherwise—

But standing under the porch with the muddy spokes of my bike's tire digging into my leg, I felt ugly as sin, too ugly to be seen again. Even if I had still believed in fairies and pixies,

I couldn't believe that any would want to come near me to save me now.

"Louise is gonna wonder where we are," Patricia said.

"She'll figure we stopped to get out of the rain. Probably thinks we're in the park clubhouse playing Ping-Pong."

We stared at the rain some more. The house behind us was quiet and dark. A china lamp with a dusty shade stood in the window, as fixed in its place as one of the bricks in the wall.

I wanted to wring out my long hair. Grasp it in my hands, and slowly go down the length of it, squeezing out the water, feeling each section below my hands become fuller with the liquid weight. And my back felt exposed. I was used to the heavy shield of wet hair lying against it, the hair darker and more solid than when it was dry. Sometimes I wished my hair could stay wet all the time and was always glad when it was washed.

Rain from the gutter was still showering down. The bag of shampoo was motionless against the side of my leg as I held onto the bike's handlebars. I took the bottle out and looked at it. It was pearly pink with deep gray letters spelling a name that sounded scientific. It didn't smell as good as the Clairol Herbal Essence that my mother used on me. It smelled like the beauty parlor: serious about its work, but with an air of frivolity on top to try to hide that.

Patricia was busy spinning around in circles to fling the raindrops off her skin. I had seen her do that once before. "It's like the spin cycle in the washer," she'd said. She had gotten this idea from doing the laundry in their apartment complex's communal washers and dryers.

"I'm gonna wash my hair," I said, as I put my bike's kick-stand down.

"You're what?" Patricia stopped spinning, but I could tell she was still going around and around in her head.

I took a few steps and bowed my head into the rainwater's torrent. It was cool on my neck and face. My hair falling forward did not even reach my eyes. My stomach started to jerk up, so I straightened my head and put a dollop of shampoo into my hand.

"Here." I handed the bottle to Patricia, who had started laughing hysterically, then I began rubbing the shampoo into my hair. No tangles ensued, no ends needed to be specially lathered, it was all right there on my head, a small contained mass that even I could wash.

Patricia began punctuating her laughter by shouting toward the empty street. "Free hair washes! Come get your hair washed! Rainwater shampoos!"

I stuck my head back into the pouring stream. Suds were going down the side of my face to my neck and into my shirt, and my back was getting soaked all over again.

"Do you girls need a towel?"

We hadn't heard the front door open in all the racket the rain was making on that aluminum porch roof. The thin and elderly woman stood in the entrance to her home, her pale chalky skin as dry as the yellow bricks that framed her. With the back of my hand, I tried to wipe away the shampoo suds that were dripping into my eyes. I wondered how much of them were covering my head. I wished they were all gone, and I was only wet from the rain, not from the impromptu and inappropriate hair washing I was taking on her front porch. She looked at my hair, then at the shampoo bottle in Patricia's hand.

"Let me go get you one. I'll be right back." Her narrow backside that was covered in a pale yellow plaid housedress disappeared into the dark, then behind the closing front door.

Patricia and I stared at each other.

"Do you think she's gonna tell our moms? Can we get arrested for this?"

"I don't think she knows them," I said. "She doesn't seem mad to me."

"I don't want to go to a juvenile home."

"You're not gonna go to a home." Though that suddenly sounded like a wonderful escape to me.

The old woman emerged from the dim house again. The yellow lines on her plaid housedress seemed to shoot out beyond the fabric and into the air, searching for the sun, as if to coax it out from behind the clouds. Patricia stepped behind our bikes to make room, and the woman walked toward me holding a dull avocado colored towel.

"Looks like you still got some suds in there."

I looked at her, nodding dumbly, until I realized she meant for me to finish rinsing it out. As I leaned forward into the rainwater shower, the old woman lightly draped the towel on my back. It was thin and worn from countless washings, softened probably by tumbling against trousers and undershirts and blouses and nightgowns.

"That's better," she said, helping me straighten up, then she moved the towel up until it covered my head and was in my hands. I thought of our towels at home. Thirsty, my mother called them, as if they were going to drink me up each night. I wished I could take this one home and only use it from then on.

I rubbed vigorously with the towel, and my hair swished this way and that, like a car wash for my scalp. I let the towel fall to my shoulders, and ran my fingers through to comb my hair out. The easiness of it was exhilarating, until I thought about the punishment I'd be getting.

"Thanks so much, ma'am," I said, handing the soaked towel back to her. Remembering my manners reminded me of Momma, and my stomach immediately started kicking itself full of bruises. "I'm sorry I washed my hair on your front porch."

Out of the corner of my eye, I could see that Patricia was bending down ostensibly to inspect one of her tennis shoes while she pulled at the rubber sole where it separated from the dingy white canvas, but her back was shaking lightly, and I knew what that meant.

The old woman looked at me and smiled. She was wearing pale blue glasses that made her eyes look wide and unattached to the rest of her face, as if the frames were a boundary her other features couldn't cross. "Just be careful getting on home now. People don't look where they're driving these days." Then she removed the towel from my shoulders and smoothed the top of my head, so gently and quickly that I wondered whether I had imagined it.

"Well, bye," I said.

Patricia put the shampoo bottle in the bag on my bike and then got on hers as I straddled mine. We pulled away down the driveway and turned right onto the street. When we had ridden past a few houses, I looked back over my shoulder at the yellow brick house, but the old lady had already gone inside. The last of the rainwater on her porch was now a small trickle. Its transparency was diamondlike in the sunlight.

As I hurried to catch up with Patricia, who was leading us to the last place I wanted to go, I started a chant in my head that

I had been saying silently for years, "Please don't, please don't, please don't."

Maybe this time, my mother would finally heed it.

But I didn't think so. And I knew there weren't any pixies or fairies to save me.

Chapter 14

THE FIRST THINGS I NOTICE ARE THE SWANS. They are like the mirage of a fairy tale superimposed upon the grounds of the hotel. But this is the Hotel Bel-Air, so the swans are real, as real as the customers' expectations that their dreams will be fulfilled. And I have no doubt that Patricia's dreams for her belated wedding party are huge, even though it is happening three months after the Vegas ceremony.

Patricia had wanted a full-out wedding, but Zane put the kibosh on that, relenting finally to a reexchange of the rings and vows, but without bridesmaids and groomsmen.

"I hate that you won't be standing up there with me," Patricia said when we met in June to discuss her wedding party plans at Urth Café in West Hollywood. It was a stunning day with a soft wind all the way in from the beach. The table-filled sidewalk was packed with barely dressed and supremely fit people eating, talking, and surreptitiously posing in case anyone of importance was noticing. "Especially since I was your maid of honor, and I'd already asked you to be mine, too, but if I have someone, then Zane has to, and that means picking someone, and what about the others' feelings?"

I hadn't realized that entourages had feelings.

The waiter delivered my herbal tea and Patricia's huge cup of coffee made from beans grown in a third world country on a small plantation where the pickers are part owners of the company (supposedly), or at least have smiled for the camera as if they were. I would have killed for a cup of coffee, but what with the nausea I was still battling—would it ever end?—I was sticking with my new and not so wonderful friend ginger, in all its forms, so that day it was ginger tea.

"So," Patricia continues, "he figured we should not."

"How nice for him to decide that, but what about your feelings?" I started to say, but instead said, "This is your wedding, too."

She looked at me, and for a second I could see in her eyes the Patricia from when we were young. The girl who had wanted a huge fairy princess wedding with a long row of pretty bridesmaids, and colorful confetti being thrown, and a proper receiving line, and every old-fashioned tradition in full swing. But the light in her eyes shifted, and once again she was a celebrity in L.A. marrying a pro athlete/film star, and I wondered where my best friend went as she changed the subject to her wedding dress.

I almost interrupted her and said, "And what about our friendship? Doesn't that mean anything to you? You were the maid of honor in my wedding; what about me? I've been there for you since we were six years old and this dick-wad waltzes in less than a year ago, and gets to make every goddamn rule. What the fuck is that? Where did your spine go?"

But Patricia has moved on to talking about flowers, and after all, this is her wedding, not mine. I can't very well tell her that she has to put me in it; that would be the ultimate maid of honor from hell, so I consider telling her how hurt I am that she isn't having me in her wedding, but something stops me. Almost like I don't want her to know, which is ridiculous because she is my best friend; I tell her everything. Or used to. Okay, there's a depressing thought, but true. I just feel so—pushed out, which is stupid because it's not like instant-husband-man is here planning this with us, but then why do I feel that he is here anyway controlling everything, and worse, that she is letting him?

Patricia was talking about a pair of earrings she wants us to go look at that Harry Winston is going to lend her, so we can make sure they won't clash with her ring. The sun itself clashes with that ring. Earthly objects can hardly compete.

I wondered whether they weren't going to wear their rings for a few days before the nonceremony, the way Neil and I slept in different locations the two nights before our wedding in an attempt at recapturing a precoital time. And if so, would Patricia and Zane both experience the same sensation when their rings were temporarily off, a vulnerable nakedness, reminding them that their bond could be broken easily, or the freedom of no longer being weighed down?

Neil and I are sitting on gold Charivari chairs that sank slightly into the ground when we sat down, waiting for the ceremony to begin. The great lawn of the Hotel Bel-Air has been transformed by a series of tents and screens and rented subtropical plants into the giant veranda of a mythical plantation. I expect to see Rhett Butler coming around the corner any minute now. But I figure Patricia is keeping to the theme that her wedding dress dictated.

Patricia's wedding dress has the ubiquitous strapless bodice ("That's not a wedding dress," my mother said on the phone when I answered her question about what Patricia selected. "That's a ball gown. But I guess Vicky never taught her that. Of course, most people in this country don't know that rule, so she fits right in") and a full, almost hooplike skirt that is only two yards of fabric shy of being straight out of *Gone With the Wind*. Why Patricia wanted a connection, however tenuous, to that tale of marital bliss, I will never know. But she could not be dissuaded.

Not that I felt that I could have dissuaded her. Eight weeks ago at the end of June, Patricia and I met at her stylist's studio to pick out her gown. Lawrence, her stylist, is a tall, thin man who has a penchant for wearing a porkpie hat at all times. No matter the weather, or his attire, or even whether he is inside, he ignores those normally followed (for comfort's sake, at the very least) rules and wears a porkpie hat. When he and I were introduced, it was all I could do not to stare at his hat as I wondered where on Earth he found it. Downtown L.A.? Pilfered from some studio's wardrobe warehouse? And this on the man whom all of the top actresses cower to and flirt with to curry his favor to get his fashion advice. I wanted to yell, "Hey, Larry, lose the chapeau. The fifties are over and even if they weren't, a man doesn't wear a hat inside. Have you never seen an old movie in your life?"

But I didn't. I smiled and said hello to him in his cold white loft on Santa Monica Boulevard in the bad section of Hollywood, down the street from Theatre Row. L.A.'s Theatre Row is a three-block strip of ninety-nine-seats-and-below theaters (meaning too small for Equity union contracts, ergo the actors don't get paid) where almost every actor in town, including Patricia and me, has done plays presumably because we love Williams and Miller and Inge, but really because we need a TV job to advance our career and pay the bills, and we believe the lying-their-asses-off casting directors when they tell us that they'll come, even though they never do.

But it doesn't matter because there are always new actors arriving every day for the casting directors to lie to, so Theatre Row stays busy and booked, albeit audience-free. And once every few years, a casting director actually deigns to attend a play, and some struggling actor gets a huge job out of it, and that legend is enough to keep the illusion alive for another few years that the time and hope squandered doing one of those plays will actually pay off, even though it never does.

Loud rap music was playing in Lawrence's loft. I wondered if anyone has ever listened to rap music softly. I have a feeling they have not, especially Lawrence. Patricia was trying on gown after gown. For one terrifying moment, I thought Lawrence was going to decorate her like a wedding cake. She came gliding out in a dress that had more ruffles and bows on it than every debutante dress in Texas combined. She looked like she had gotten into a fight with a notions department and lost. With that dress, I was definitely going to put my foot down, but fortunately, Patricia took one look in the mirror, caught my eye, and we both started laughing hysterically while Lawrence looked bewildered and readjusted his porkpie.

"What's the music?" Neil says, as the processional song begins to signal that the wedding is about to start.

"It's from the movie of *Much Ado About Nothing*, I say, repeating what Patricia told me.

"You're kidding me, right?"

"No, I'm—"

"That is unbelievable. Does she have any idea how Freudian that is?"

I actually had tried to ignore that glaring aspect when Patricia told me which song she had picked, arabesquing across her living room while she did as if she were Titania from *Midsummer Night's Dream*. I was so shocked that she could say it with a straight face and without any apparent understanding of how it sounded that I was struck dumb and expressionless.

I hear a rustle of commotion and turn to see that Zane has arrived at the entrance of the tent. He decided to walk down the aisle right before her, so he wouldn't have to wait very long at the altar, Patricia told me, because he didn't feel like being stared at by an audience. I bit my tongue from saying, "You mean, y'all's families and friends?" Then I realized that with over three hundred people attending, they had left that realm and were well into audienceland.

Zane is sauntering toward the altar. He doesn't actually have his hands in his tuxedo pockets; it just seems as if he does. He looks like he was sitting on the couch in his den and happened to remember an unfinished bag of Doritos in the kitchen that he has a sudden hankering for, so is moseying along to get them.

And to half of America, this man is a prize.

The music makes a slight shift, and then, clearly on cue, thousands of pale pink rose petals come wafting down onto the aisle that Patricia will promenade down. That's one way around Zane's dictum of no flower girl. I have to applaud Patricia's use of Hollywood magic and her limitless budget for that one. Too bad neither of those worked for me to be in the wedding party. Or that she didn't either.

It finally really hit me when I arrived here at the hotel earlier this afternoon. They had reserved the Presidential Suite for their wedding night before their flight tomorrow morning to Fiji, where they will be for four weeks, so I met Patricia at noon to have a leisurely afternoon of getting ready for the big night. Her makeup artist, hairstylist, and Lawrence, of course, were going to arrive later, but for the first couple of hours, it was just us.

"Do you believe this?" she shrieked, when she opened the door to the suite. "This place is like four times bigger than that studio I rented above Hollywood Boulevard, remember, when I first moved out here? Can you believe it? Look at this place," she said, as she shut the door behind me, and pulled me from room to room to room to room. "But this is the best. Come see."

Then she led me back across the gracious and spacious light-filled living room, through open french doors, which let onto a private limestone patio and lush green yard with a Jacuzzi bubbling merrily away in the corner.

I lay out on a lounge chair while Patricia indulged in the whirlpool. "Baby," I explained, when she asked why I wasn't getting in, but the massage she scheduled for each of us afterward was heavenly, and lunch divine, and I was so lulled by the beauty and luxury that I almost forgot about Zane and not being her maid of honor and everything.

Until the minions arrived and began their ministrations, and suddenly the fact that we were there for Patricia's wedding, and not just some over-the-top, totally fun, girly afternoon came crashing down, and all the hours and hours we had spent, or—hello—that I had spent, helping her with these preparations were right there in my face, and I finally understood the honor part of maid of honor that I wasn't going to be getting.

Patricia appears at the entrance of the tent. It is difficult to see her and her dress because some of the guests, probably so overtaken with the nearness of Zane, rose to their feet when he walked by. I wonder whether it is Patricia's out-of-town relatives or the Hollywoodites who committed that faux pas. But whoever it was, they should be forgiven, because what with the nonstop flashing cameras, this feels more like a movie premiere than a wedding.

Patricia looks incredible as she walks up the aisle. It is hard not to be happy for her when she is so ebullient. She catches my eye and throws me a smile that I return. She seems to float away, a small figure in a huge, billowy skirt, like an upside-down hot air balloon, and as loosely tethered down. I want to follow her up the aisle, fix her skirt when she reaches her spot, and stand next to her for support. I suddenly understand why the bridal couple is always accompanied at the altar. She looks so alone up there with Zane: no friends or family for her to fall back on should the need arise during the ceremony or during life.

I tell myself that I am being silly. It's a Hollywood marriage: no better, no worse. They might even stick out the odds like—um—okay, Susan Sarandon and Tim Robbins, there's one. Or they'll get a divorce like tons of other people have and they usually end up okay. I shouldn't be thinking like this on her nonceremony wedding day. She's going to be fine.

I guess.

Chapter 15

"WELL, THAT WAS A FIASCO," Neil whispers in my ear, as the crowd presses up against us in line for one of the four bars. Ceiling fans are whirring lazily above us, a band is playing Dixieland jazz, and huge blooming azalea bushes (God only knows how they made that happen in late August) line the outsides of the tents next to the fake porch railings that were put up. The South, obviously, has risen again. We have been in this crush for the bar for a good fifteen minutes, and I still haven't seen one friend of Patricia's and mine. Who are these people that they, or I guess, Zane invited?

"Neil." I start to try to defend Patricia, but am at a loss. The nonceremony—and if ever there was a nonceremony then this one was it—was conducted by Zane's best friend, Gil, a hold-over/flunky from Zane's snowboarding days. Since Patricia and Zane already had a legal wedding, then this one could be done by anyone really, Patricia had explained to me, so Zane's best bud got a certificate online as a minister from some virtual church and presto, Gil was ordained.

Patricia laughed while she said it and had the same look on her face she had after she had gone around to everyone in our eleventh-grade class, begging for donations to pay for a parking ticket she had gotten, and then ended up making a tidy profit.

"It's not like they can't afford it, anyway," she'd said, after she saw the look on my face when she told me about the twenty-plus extra dollars she'd made. "And they gave, what, a dollar or two each; who cares?"

"Patricia, you have to give that back."

"To who? How am I supposed to pick who to give it to?"

"How about the last bunch of people you bilked?"

"Fi," Patricia said, trying, and not succeeding, to level me with a look. "Every kid at this school gets tons of money from their parents. I am not walking around and handing a dollar back to them. And anyway, for all they know," she said, starting to laugh, but clearly in an attempt to get me to join in, "it's a down payment on my next ticket."

The bell rang for class. As I walked away from Patricia, I thought, "Whatever." Patricia had always been sensitive about growing up with just one parent, in an apartment, and without the kind of money most of the other kids at this school had. I didn't need to protect them.

But this time I wanted to say, "This is your wedding. Is nothing sacred?"

But what stopped me in that instant was the fear of her answer. The look she would get in her eyes, and I knew exactly which one it would be, the hurt and confused look, as if I were betraying her somehow by finally telling her the truth. And maybe I would be. Maybe her truth, like her life, had changed so drastically that it no longer had anything to do with mine. Or with me.

Patricia and Zane waited at the altar for a full minute—Patricia flashing smiles and giggling lightly; Zane scanning the crowd and mouthing, "Dude!" whenever he saw a friend—before Gil finally slipped into place looking as if he had just finished a good solid bong hit. He was sporting a tuxedo with a pair of rubber flip-flops that looked as if he kept them in his trunk for après-surf. From my vantage point at the end of the row, I could see that his toenails were painted bright purple and gold, clearly in deference to the home team. Then I remembered that Zane and Gil had been known to hang out with Kobe.

Gil cleared his throat. "Family and friends," he said. "We are gathered together tonight to celebrate a totally awesome dude—"

Zane and Patricia swung their heads in unison to look at Gil.

"What? Bro, you are. And his rockin' bit—uh, chick—who are reofficiafying what they already made official. The big *M*."

Neil practically keeled over next to me.

"And did I miss something?" Neil is saying, as we take our drinks to go find a place to sit down. "But where were the vows? I heard the commercial that Brad did for their careers. Zane's new action film out this fall, and the day, time, and channel of Patricia's show, as if any of us needed that info, but what exactly did they say 'I do' to?"

"There were vows, they were just—" I try to remember exactly what Patricia and Zane said "I do" to, but the only thing I can recall is Gil's going on and on about their careers.

I kept looking around while it was happening, hoping to catch someone's eye besides Neil's, who I already knew was beyond shocked, as a reality check that this was the most nonnuptials wedding we'd ever seen. But everyone was staring straight ahead, gazing upon them as if Patricia and Zane were the rapture, and they, too, could join their privileged, transcendent state if only they believed hard enough. Then I realized that, in a way, this might be the most honest Hollywood marriage ceremony of all time. Because thanks to Gil, there was no pretense that this union ever would have happened if both people were not exactly where they are, i.e., famous and with beaucoup bank.

Immediately, I hear Sarah's voice in my head. "There are all sorts of marriages. Especially in this town. It's not for you to judge. She's your oldest friend. Your job is to be there for her, and if you're right, which you probably are, then she'll have you to turn to when it falls apart."

"But why should I have to do that? I've been there for her already my entire life. Maybe I'm done."

"Well, that's another option," Sarah said with the impartial equanimity of a bank officer discussing loans.

Then we were both quiet on the phone while I thought about what that would feel like: Like divorcing a sister, no, worse, a part of myself. Because without Patricia in my life, where would all those memories and experiences and mess that we shared and lived through go? They would be completely and irretrievably gone. My death before I die, and I'd have to live the rest of my life walking around with all those years gone. They would still be a memory, but a memory that I shared only with myself, and that is too dangerous because how would I know that they really did happen and were really true without Patricia to turn to? There is too much that no one else knows. Some of it big, yes, some of it huge, but lots of it small and otherwise forgettable, but, for us, deeply, deeply known.

I just wish I didn't feel so pushed out.

Neil is in front of me fighting out a path for us through the ever thickening wedding reception crowd. The air is heavy with the scent of magnolias being piped in every twenty minutes. Patricia was particularly ecstatic over this detail. "So it will be just like a New Orleans summer night," she told me. I refrained from saying that most summer nights in New Orleans smell like the shrimp tails in restaurant garbage Dumpsters that have been boiling in the sun all day long.

This reception feels like Mardi Gras after the tourists discovered it and drained away its original meaning by their sheer presence. It is clear that more people are here than were invited or that the tent can comfortably hold, but I guess it couldn't be a hot Hollywood event without the attendant gate crashers.

Neil has almost gotten us to the refuge of a table when I see Vicky and Mike for the first time tonight. I had looked for them during the ceremony, but they weren't seated in the first row, or even anywhere near the front. They are standing silently at the edge of the tent, shoulder to shoulder, watching everyone in the room. I get the sense that they would let their jaws drop if they could. Vicky is wearing a dark green very fitted silk dress with a low sweetheart neckline and matching high heels. I love that she dressed as Mother of the Bride even though nothing in the ceremony treated her as such. She was always too glamorous for Lake Charles. Other than the fact that her dress has that timeless (therefore not stylish) look that "dressy" dresses from small towns have, she would have fit right in here. I can imagine her as an aspiring actress in 1930s Hollywood, probably palling around with Elizabeth Short, and then thanking God that the Black Dahlia's fate wasn't her own, but staying on anyway, only to end up a wardrobe mistress on big studio films and glad for that outcome all the same.

Mike looks diminished. His dark hair has a barbershop (short on the sides, long on top) haircut and the navy blue suit he is wearing looks as if it would fit a much more imposing man. I try to determine whether my memory of him when I last saw him twenty years ago when Patricia and I were freshmen in high school and he was leaving Lake Charles made him more of a giant than he ever was, or whether these more sophisticated (okay, Gil is in flip-flops, but still, this is L.A.) surroundings have put into bas relief the old belief that inside every bully, a coward is hiding.

Then I figured that maybe life did this to him. I had heard from Patricia, in the rare moments when she mentioned him, that he floundered around in Miami doing bartending jobs before selling boats for a while ("No regulations in that business," I can hear my father saying about boating enthusiasts. "Let the buyer, or the fool, beware"), married and divorced in quick succession, and, last I remember, was selling cooling equipment to large hotels, two items in as constant demand as you can get in Florida: hotel rooms to cool and tourists who want them.

I start to nudge Neil for us to try to make our way over to them, but we have finally reached the table, and I realize that I don't have the energy to push through more "messy, but groomed" hairstyles in front of us.

"Wait here," Neil says. "I'll go get food."

I stand behind the chair and watch Neil get swept up into the crowd as he heads toward one of the heaping buffet tables. I suddenly have the odd, illogical thought that I will never see him again. I have been getting these since I got pregnant. Terrible, full-blown fantasies that seem to spring up completely unbidden by me of losing Neil and being left on my own with our baby: having to sell our house, and get an apartment, and living in terror of going under. But we are at a wedding, I remind myself, at the Hotel Bel-Air. Nothing bad is going to happen here other than the depressing ceremony that I just endured and having to pretend to my best friend when I finally see her again tonight that it was wonderful, an acting job if there ever was one.

I reach down and put my clutch bag on the chair next to me to save it for Neil. Not that there is a stampede for people to sit down; there is much too much gawking to be done, but still. Then I turn to look over at Vicky and raise my arm to wave at her for them to join us, but their attention is elsewhere. Mike is enraptured by a former stripper who gained a speck of respectability and a ton of fame when she married a rock star last year and Vicky is looking everywhere at once except at me.

Suddenly, Vicky's eyes stop roving the crowd, and in a move as fluid and unconscious as a sleepwalker, she steps sideways and grabs onto the tent pole disguised as an Ionic column, wrapping her right arm around it and holding on with her left hand. She looks like a woman who is in desperate need of a lifeboat but is making due with driftwood. I follow her gaze and see Tom, Patricia's father, barreling through the crowd. His once-thick blond hair is losing its battle with baldness, but the same jutting jaw and "What can I do you for?" energy is propelling him forward.

I met Tom once when Patricia and I were in junior high. She and Vicky had had a big fight because Tom was coming into town from Dallas, where he was living at that time, and wanted to take Patricia out to dinner.

"Barely pays child support and wants to buy you a steak," Patricia imitated her mother yelling at her. "He can pay for all those goddamn clothes you're always wanting and take you to McDonald's, the grandiose son of a bitch. A sirloin is not going to change what a piece of shit he has been and always will be, that goddamn mother f—no way in hell are you going out with him."

So, Patricia spent the night at my house, and the two of us went out to dinner with Tom, secure in the knowledge that my parents and Vicky never speak.

It was like having dinner with an imposter who was unable to hide the ruse. He seemed like someone my parents would be friends with what with his tall, agreeable, All-American looks; his ease in his business suit; his relaxed mastery of captains and waiters; but the picture wasn't complete. Little things would pop out like his bragging about a deal he made that even to my eighth-grader mind had obviously screwed the other party and the succession of ladies whose company he was enjoying, as Tom put it with a broad wink in his voice.

But the real peek behind the mask occurred at the end of the meal. He had paid the bill in cash with pointedly generous and conspicuously given tips all around and had returned to the table from the men's room. Patricia and I had just finished our bread pudding drowned in whiskey sauce, and Tom was clearly ready to leave. He stood by the table, looked at his watch, and jiggled his keys.

I reached down to pick up my bag, and when I looked back up, Tom was holding the glass ashtray that had been on the table out to Patricia.

"Here, sweetheart," he said, "stick this in your B cup."

"Daddy." Patricia looked quickly around to make sure that no one had heard, as her neck and chest got blotchy red. I wasn't sure exactly which part embarrassed her—the reference to her clearly developing breasts or her father's apparent ease with stealing. Or maybe both.

"What? You think that logo on there is for customers here to look at? That's for us to take home, for friends to come over and see. Makes them think of this place. Then next time they go out, this is where they'll come. That's advertising dollars at work, boy. It's not doing them any damn good them sitting in here." He looked at her as if his greatest fear had just been confirmed: she was like that damn mother of hers after all. He slipped the ashtray back onto the table in a move that was barely perceptible. I wondered why he didn't just pocket it himself, if he was so sure of what he was saying. Then I understood that he both was and wasn't, as if each side of his brain had no idea about the other.

"You have no understanding of how the world works, young lady. That's going to cause you a lot of trouble one day."

Patricia practically ran from the table to get to the parking lot, leaving me to walk out alone with Tom, as he smiled and nodded to all the waiters and captains and bus boys, like the end of some inappropriate and disastrous date.

Vicky's grip on the column is tighter. Her entire body is practically wrapped around it and for one fleeting moment, I imagine the whole tent coming crashing down, a wedding ruined by the mother of the bride's self-protection. Tom is towering over her. I have never seen them together before, so had no idea how much taller he is. His arms are gesturing and pointing through a story he is telling, and every jab he makes in the air seems to make Vicky tinier still. All these years after that dinner with Tom, I had always thought that his rampant uncouthness must have been the breaking point in that marriage for Vicky. My father and mother's condescension aside, Vicky always had élan. But standing here watching them across the room, I realize that it was an entirely different form of brutishness that made her get out.

If I had little interest in speaking to Tom before, I really don't now, so I decide to make my way over to Vicky later. I am pulling out my chair finally to sit down, and wishing that Neil were back already, when I hear a low voice in my ear. Its southern accent is dimly familiar, like some dreadful déjà vu that I know is really true. My stomach clenches as if it is holding on to a column of its own.

"Hey there, Fiona. Remember me?"

Chapter 16

I TURN AROUND and am looking into his face. It has been over two decades since I have seen it, but it is as if I am seeing him then and now all at once.

"What are you doing here?"

"Well, there's a helluva greeting," he says, smiling at me, as the mustache over his mouth stretches wide. I had forgotten that there are parts of this country where men still wear mustaches. "It's my cuz's wedding. Think I'd miss that? And her being famous and all. Shit. I made damn sure I got myself an invitation. Plus," he says, winking at me, "I figured you'd be here."

"Oh." I suddenly feel like I am in a cage with a wild animal and the people pressing around us are the iron bars trapping me in. I try to scan the crowd for Neil, for anyone, but everyone I see is a stranger.

"I've seen every one of your television programs. Got the TIVO set to find you." He tilts his head to one side and looks down at me through his lashes and I am transported back to before, as if darkness is all around us, and excitement and terror are leapfrogging through me.

"That beautiful face. You still look the same. And your red hair," he says, as he reaches out and caresses my hair near my face, "I've never forgotten that red hair."

I am suddenly numb, unresisting, and his voice is all I can hear.

"So nice and long. It was short when I knew you," he says as his fingertips and my hair stroke my head and neck into a deeper stupor. "And it's real, boy. Not that dyed shit. Course, the best way to check that—"

A charge shoots up inside me and I knock his hand away. I look around to see who, if anyone, has seen all this, and where in God's name is Neil? But people are engrossed in themselves or spotting stars.

"Hey, hey, hey," he says with a smile on his face, but not in his eyes. "No need to get unfriendly like. It's been a long time. Just thought we'd have us a little catch-up is all."

"Uh-huh," I say, nodding my head. My mind is suddenly trying to think of techniques for dealing with abductors, as if that will help. Warily agreeing seems the best thing to do. I glance around again for Neil. Get here already, for fuck's sake.

"Me, I'm out there in Galveston. Not livin' all high and mighty like y'all here. Just doin' a bit of this, summa that. Don't want to get tied down. Had myself a ball and chain for a while but got rid of that damn shackle."

I suddenly have an overpowering image of him on an orange bedspread–covered bed in the back room of a small, furnished apartment on a hot, still afternoon strangling a woman with his bare hands. I practically have to blink my eyes not to see it.

"Oh. Well. I'm glad you're happy."

"Happy?" he says, as if he's never said the word before. "Hell, yeah. I'm happy. What the fuck's not to be happy? Course," and he steps closer to me, making his cigarette smell and the starch of his shirt, that I can tell he ironed himself, which for some reason depresses me to no end, press against me like I know his body wants to, "I'll be real happy seein' you again. And not just on that TV screen."

I immediately have the horrible and illogical thought that we have made some plans that I have forgotten about but will be carried out anyway, as if my calendar is open before him, and he is grandly marking it with dates for us.

Neil materializes next to me. It is all I can do not to fall into him, literally into him, and let my body hide inside his until this person leaves and I can safely emerge.

"Sorry that took so long," he says, kissing my cheek and putting down the plates. "I'm Neil." And he extends his hand.

"Billy." As their hands meet, I feel a wave of disgust that their bodies are touching. I notice Billy's high school class ring embedded in the flesh of his pinkie, as he withdraws his hand. Neil is considerably taller than Billy and this comforts me immensely. I realize that Neil is waiting for me to say something.

"He's Patricia's first cousin on her Daddy's side."

Neil nods. "So, you grew up in Lake Charles, too?"

"Nah, all over. Pop would get an itch, and up we'd go."

"So you two—" Neil looks from him to me. I suddenly hear my mother's voice in my head, "If you have to tell a man a lie, and you will, stick as close to the truth as possible. That way, there's less you have to memorize without getting tripped up."

"He and his family came through town one summer."

"Yup, went to my uncle's fish fry, and there Fiona was."

"We haven't seen each other in all these years."

"Uh-huh," Neil says.

I can't look at either of them, so I stare across the room. If Neil sees my eyes, I know he'll see the truth, and I don't want to give Billy any encouragement to talk about the only thing the three of us have in common, me. Tom is still bearing down on Vicky, while Mike looks on awkwardly as if he doesn't know either of them. I suddenly wish Tom would come over and get Billy away from us. Rescued by Tom: Jesus, I am desperate.

"Hey, and congrats on that rug rat I see y'all got comin'." Billy reaches out his hand and slowly strokes my stomach, looking at Neil with a small smile while he does. It is all I can do not to scream. Neil's hand goes to the small of my back, as I back away from Billy's hand.

"Thanks," Neil says, then puts out his other hand. "Nice to meet you, but we need to eat." Then he turns me around to the chairs.

Even in the clamor of the crowd, I can hear a stunned silence from Billy as our chairs scrape against the temporary parquet floor.

"O-kay, I got it," Billy says to our backs. "Well, hey there, bye, Fiona. See ya." His voice handles my body with those last words, and I know he doesn't mean them casually. Okay, I'm being paranoid. He lives in Texas, for God's sake. I'm in L.A., with Neil, perfectly safe.

"Bye," I say, over my shoulder. I don't want to look at him, want to just say it without turning my head. But his face pulls my eyes toward his and I look anyway. It is like the horror movies that Louise wouldn't let me watch growing up because as she said, "Once you got those pictures in your head, child, ain't no gettin' 'em out." His eyes are ready for mine, and everything he knows is alive and there for me to see. I want to scratch it out forever.

Neil's hand on my arm gently pushes me to sit down. He pushes his own chair in, and it reminds me to do the same. I try to make out the sound of Billy's feet walking away. I just want him to get the fuck out of here. And for my thoughts of him to go back into the tiny and regulated part of my mind that I never allow myself to go into and for the real him just to disappear.

Neil takes a long, slow sip of his drink, then looks quickly around. I wish to God that I could have a bourbon on the rocks.

"Who the hell was that?" he says, switching our plates since his roast beef was in front of me.

"I told you."

"Yeah, Patricia's cousin, but, what?" Neil says, vigorously cutting his meat. "Was he in love with you or something? Seems like he still is. Or obsessed, at least."

"I met him once."

"What difference does that make?"

"Neil, he's not and wasn't ever in love with me. He told me he just went through a divorce, so he's a bit—off is all."

"Oh, that guy is definitely off, but not from a divorce. He probably keeps the body parts of small animals in his freezer to rearrange on rainy days."

I glance behind me just to reassure myself that he is gone, though I know Neil wouldn't have said a word if he weren't. The crowd is even thicker than before. It appears that all of the Laker Girls are crammed at the nearest bar. A new blast of magnolia scent hits the air, and I feel as if I am suffocating. I have the wild, improbable thought that Patricia had humidity piped in to make the space seem that much more authentic, but I know even she would draw the line there. Authenticity isn't worth bad hair.

I put my napkin up to my mouth and nose and take some deep breaths through it to block out that heavy and sweet floral scent. I suddenly get the sense that Billy has left the tent. This barely offers me the comfort that it should since I know that he left because his purpose in coming here has been fulfilled: seeing me. But he is gone now, I tell myself. And I am with Neil. So I can forget all about him again, forever. Even if I have to know that he watches me on TV. How fucking gross is that? So from now on, everytime I get a residual check, instead of its being a happy surprise, it will be a creepy reminder of him. Fuck. How did he get into my life again? It is so Patricia for her wedding to bring in something like this. And not to her either, but to me. Though I guess in a way it is to her too, but not as much as me. And why in God's name didn't she tell me he was coming?

I settle into my seat and try to focus on the food that Neil has brought me. But it is as if I am wearing Billy's body, and always have been, and no one, not even me, had been able to see it.

Until this evening.

Chapter 17

THE LIGHTS IN THE TENT SUDDENLY DIM, and two spot-lights start scanning the crowd like some wedding reception game show from hell. The drummer in the band begins a drum-roll, then an announcer, I swear the guy who does all the promos for CBS (Patricia's network), says, "Ladies and Gentlemen, please join me in giving a big welcome to the talented, the fabulous, the married: Patricia Woods and Zaaaaaaaane MacKenzie."

Ed McMahon couldn't have done it better. A cymbal crashes and the band starts up "Dream a Little Dream of Me" as the spotlights merge and land on the newly re-weds. Then the floor underneath them begins to rise until they are on a stage of their own facing the crowd. I half expect Patricia to start waving to us à la Evita.

A waiter appears out of nowhere, no small feat in this crush, and hands them glasses brimming with champagne, or rather, Dom, I guess. Zane raises his, and everyone in the tent follows suit. Neil and I had gotten up when their stage started to rise, so we lift our glasses up high into the air.

"This is one helluva night," Zane says into the cordless mi-crophone that he pulled out of his pocket. The crowd goes wild, whooping and clapping their agreement. "You guys should try this getting married thing sometime. But I guess a bunch of you already have, but hell, do it again!" The crowd laughs right on cue. They could hire themselves out to do laugh tracks, their spontaneity sounds so canned. "I know I intend to," Zane continues. Most of the crowd laughs while the rest try to look politely uncomprehending of what they just heard. Patricia smiles and giggles. It is clear that Zane has no idea what he just said, and I wonder how much he ever does.

"We want to thank some people here—"

"Here we go," Neil says into my ear. Neil has a theory that it is impossible for any social event in Hollywood to occur without, at some point, all involved acting as if they are at the Academy Awards, and usually as Oscar winners. AA meetings are filled with applause and acceptance speeches for years sober, and birthday parties have Academy Award quality montages of the celebrants' lives, as if they are getting the Irving Thalberg Lifetime Achievement Award.

The crowd has fallen into the usual hush of people either hoping that they will be one of the lucky who are mentioned and praised, or deciding whom Zane needs to thank for relationship harmony to ensue. There are circles in Hollywood that regularly bet on the fates of marriages of actresses who win Oscars when their husbands never have. And if the "lucky" actress forgets to thank her husband when she wins the golden statue, the odds of their union's ending before the year is out quadruple.

"And Patricia's family," Zane continues. "Coming all the way from New Orleans."

Neil looks at me. No one in Patricia's family lives in New Orleans or ever has. I imagine that in Zane's mind, south Louisiana is just one huge French Quarter filled with strippers and hurricanes from Pat O's covering the entire region.

"Her old man, Tom, there. Give it up for Tom." The crowd dutifully claps, while many look around mildly perplexed as for whom they are applauding. "Be sure to get him to tell you about the time he tangled with the SEC. You're my hero, man."

"And Vicky. Now if I ever doubted that southern women are the most beautiful in the world," Zane continues, "one look at Vicky sets me straight again." I can imagine Vicky on the other side of the tent beaming beneath a polite smile. Patricia's eyes get that squinty-but-still-open look they get when she is hurt and confused. She probably thought Zane hadn't even noticed her mother, or better yet, that her fame had finally catapulted her past her mother's looks, a peak she's been trying to surpass her entire life.

"But Patricia's brother, Mike. Dude!" And Zane throws his arm up into the air. Off to the side of the tent, I see an arm in an ill-fitting navy suit respond in kind.

"We had to of been separated at birth, my man. And you know, Patricia told me about how when they were growing up, Mike used to beat her up all the time, but now that I've met the righteous dude, I know there's no way that could've happened."

I suddenly lose my breath as if my stomach has just been punched the way Mike used to punch Patricia all those years ago. Patricia's smile has frozen on her face. Her color has drained and any giggle she had been manufacturing looks ready to come out in a strangled sob.

"What a fucking idiot this guy is," Neil says to me. He doesn't say it in my ear, and the people around us hear him easily. The crowd is silent, but Zane is smiling and talking on. It is like watching the audience for *The Producers* suddenly being shown *Schindler's List*. No one seems to know what they are watching, and I wonder whether even Zane does. This is definitely a man who needs a script.

"I need some air," I say to Neil, as I turn and push my way through the packed crowd. Another blast of magnolia scent has just blown down, and I feel as if I am being beaten to death by its cloying force.

"So, is that really true?" Neil says, once we finally break free from the antebellumesque reception and are sitting on a marble bench at the entrance of the hotel near the crème suited valets. They had rushed up to Neil when we approached, but he waved them off, so they are huddled around their stand, laughing and talking in Spanish, waiting for the next car owner to appear.

"What?" I know what he means but have the small, stupid hope that he is talking about something else.

"What that idiot said in there, about Mike's beating Patricia up. Did he really do that?"

I almost don't have the energy to answer. This entire evening has felt like a torture chamber wedding-style. I just want to go away and never have to talk to any of these people again. But I can feel Neil getting concerned about me, and I really don't have the energy to make him believe that I'm okay.

"Yes, he really did. He was angry and a bully and I think always jealous because Patricia's father had more money than his did, which isn't saying much. Not that Patricia or Vicky ever saw any of it. But Mike used to beat her up all the time.

She went through hell with him, which she clearly is going through now with that dick-wad she married. How she is even going to be able to look at him after what he just did I have no idea. I'd want to kill him. And I couldn't even imagine facing my friends, or—hello—all the industry people in there if I were her. What in God's name is she going to say to them?"

"It wasn't her fault. Zane's the one who should be embarrassed."

"Yeah, but he won't be. And most of the people in there will forgive him in two seconds because they want him to be in their next film, but she'll be left humiliated. It's always the victim who gets it worse. He told her secret. And not only that, doesn't even believe it. How can she ever trust him again?"

We sit in silence on the Mission-style terrace. A fountain is making soft music on water nearby. I imagine that Patricia and Zane are having their first dance and I wonder what kind of expression she is gazing into his eyes with. Or maybe she is spared from that moment of hell by his incessant scanning of the crowd. Thank God, he has never tried to do theater because breaking the fourth wall would be all he could do, though with the way careers go in this town, at some point it will be a notch he'll want on his belt, God help us.

I feel as if I have been beaten up. The idea of having to face Patricia after what just happened and having to be all happy and bright is more than I can bear. Not even to mention the surprise guest I had to see. If tragedies occur in threes, then I'm terrified to go back in. But maybe their getting married counts as the first one. Okay, I feel horrible thinking that way. And what do I know? Maybe Sarah is right and Patricia is happy. And maybe she had a lobotomy that I didn't know about. Okay, what that godforsaken husband of hers just did clearly affected her. I could see it affecting her. I just wonder whether she's going to do anything about it, though I don't even know what you would do about that. Flee? Instant wedding/instant divorce? She probably needs me more right now than she ever has. So, I just need to be there for her and see her through whatever this is. But I just hope it doesn't last too long because I don't know how much longer I can lie about the way I feel.

Then a truly terrible thought occurs to me. What if she doesn't think she needs me right now? What if she thinks all of this is fine, that Zane is still the crown prince, and what am I so upset about anyway?

And if that's the case, then maybe I am being pushed out. And maybe by me.

Neil stands up, takes my hand, and we make our way back to the wedding.

Chapter 18

MOMMA'S CAR WASN'T IN THE DRIVEWAY on the side of the house when Patricia and I rode up on our bikes from my pixie haircut. My stomach unclenched. I was safe for a little bit. As we went in the kitchen door, Patricia's dingy, soaked sneakers and my drenched sandals leaked out their own small rainfall onto the floor.

"Louise?" I yelled to let her know that we were home, and also that I was getting an old towel to clean up the water that I knew she knew we were tracking in.

"Fiona?" My mother answered me from the hall.

My stomach felt punched, and my knees started to buckle. I looked at Patricia and she looked at me. My hand automatically pulled down the back of my hair. I had a wild idea of running out the kitchen door, jumping on my bike, and pedaling as fast as I could, never to return. Maybe if I were all on my own, then the fairies and pixies would become real and could finally take care of me. My mother's footsteps were approaching. Maybe all I needed to do was leave home and join them, and then I'd be fine. My mother's purposeful steps were just on the other side of the kitchen door. I wished with everything

I had that I could go live with fairies, but I knew they weren't real. I looked at Patricia one last time. I felt like one of the three little pigs in the little straw house with the wolf so close, but with no brick home to escape to in sight.

"Let's see how—" my mother said, then she stopped as if she had run into a wall. Her features flattened as the rage came over her from within and pressed out through her skin.

"Time to go home, Patricia. Fiona is no longer allowed to play."

Patricia stared at my mother, her eyes wide and uncomprehending of what she was seeing or heard.

"You heard me, young lady. This minute." My mother banged her hand on the counter. "Louise," she yelled into the hall, "get Patricia's things from Fiona's room. It is time for her to leave."

I heard Louise sigh. I had a feeling I knew what it meant and the futility it conveyed terrified me even more. We all knew that Patricia was supposed to stay until six o'clock, when Momma would drive her home and Vicky would pretend that she would be there soon, only to call at 8:30 from a loud and dark restaurant to tell Mike and Patricia to heat up some Campbell's soup for their dinner, ignoring the candy and popcorn she knew they had already eaten.

"But I look like you, Momma, even the receptionist said so."

My mother wheeled around to glare at me, her eyes filled with a wrath that was ready to tear me limb to limb.

"Patricia," she said, still staring at me. "Get your bike and take it to my car." My mother turned her focus on my friend. "Now."

Patricia practically jumped at the last word, she was so used to my mother's perfunctory politeness. As Patricia turned to go, we gave each other a silent good-bye by brushing the tips of our fingers together.

"I'll deal with you when I get home," my mother said, her hand grabbing my arm. "In your room this minute." And she yanked me hard, hurling me out through the kitchen door.

I heard my mother's footsteps in the house when she returned from taking Patricia home. It was like hearing an army advance that I knew was going to attack, but having no idea how or when. And I was trapped. There was no point in securing the door. It was her door. It was her house. I was the unwanted one in it.

I dared not sit on my bed and mess up the coverlet. Beds are for sleeping or being sick, my mother always said. And sitting on the dressing table's stool would only remind me of what I had done. That left an antique chair in the corner that I hated because the cane bottom seat always scratched my legs. So I sat on the floor with my stuffed animals and doll. I told my doll she could cut her hair whenever she wanted to. My teddy bear said that he loved my short hair because he could see my ears for the first time, and he kissed them twenty times each. But even that didn't make me feel better.

I wanted to throw up. I hadn't eaten since breakfast and it was almost two o'clock. My stomach was empty, but it hurt. And I needed to pee. But I was afraid my mother would hear the toilet flushing and be reminded of me. I had listened to her moving through the house, eating her lunch in the dining room, laughing on the phone, going outside to get the mail, but never coming to me. And that was a relief and a terror all at once.

I tried not to make a sound. Not to exist, actually. To disappear as best I could and only reappear when her rage had passed. Somehow only to be alive when her deep and immense displeasure with me was done. But I wondered when, if ever, that would be.

Finally, I had to pee. I decided that I just wouldn't flush the toilet. But the minute the stream hit the water, I worried that my mother could hear it and would fly up to attack me. I held my breath. I didn't hear anything. Maybe when she finally did come into my room, she would see the pee in the toilet and kill me even more. I closed the lid when I was done, and closed the bathroom door, hoping she wouldn't notice either of them.

It was almost four. She had never made me wait that long. Maybe she was never going to come punish me. Maybe this was it. Maybe I would be stuck in this room until I died. I didn't know how long a person could last without food or water. Tommy Pensalotta at school had told me that roaches can live four days without food or water, but my goldfish had died after I skipped only one day to feed him, so maybe humans were somewhere in between. There was water in the bathroom faucet, but I couldn't use it because then she would hear me. Maybe she was calling other families for someone to take me, setting up an adoption this very minute.

The best times with Momma were when I could wear a dress and she'd pick out ribbons or barrettes to put in my hair. I'd stand in front of her as she sat at her dressing table, and she'd arrange the accessories in my hair as she talked about the long hair she had as a child and the long hair I had, too. And it was so warm and wonderful to be like her. But I had ruined that. Though wasn't I like her with my hair so short, just her as a grown-up? But I was wrong and bad for doing it. And she was going to kill me. Somehow, someway.

When my mother entered my room at 5:45 that afternoon, she did not look at me. She went straight to my closet, threw open the door, and pulled out a great big pile of clothes. Then she walked out of my room, went to the balcony railing, and threw the clothes over where I could hear them land in a suicidal jumble on the marble foyer floor. Back and forth she went, grabbing cotton dresses and colorful skirts, pastel pants and cheerful blouses, bright belts and flowered hats, pink bags and a rainbow of shoes, multi-hued tops and sweet little socks, be-ribboned and smocked nightgowns from my dresser drawers, methodically throwing them over the railing, where they piled up and up and up, like bodies any which way in a mass grave.

After dropping the last pile onto the heap, my mother reentered my room and finally looked at me. I saw the second person in her eyes that I would see sometimes, a whole other body inside my mother's that would examine me through her gray-blue eyes.

"For this entire summer," she said. "You will wear only boys' clothes." My mother's features were composed, her hands poised, her lips barely moving, but each of her words was a bullet into me. "Tomorrow, we will go to the boys' department at Maison Blanche to get you shirts and slacks. Since you have made the decision to look like a boy, then you can dress like one, too. And we'll just see how much you like it then."

Then she turned and walked out of my room.

Chapter 19

IT IS SAID that you can tell a lot about a woman by her clothes. Look into her closet, and who she is will unfold before you. Not so with me, because my closet is not just for me: I share it with thousands of characters whom I inhabit sometimes briefly (for an audition) or a bit longer (callbacks for producers or networks), but none of them is truly me.

Of course, when I do get the job that I dressed in costume for to audition for the role, the wardrobe mistress takes over from there. But even then, I arrive at my wardrobe fittings with a bunch of my own clothes to give her a more clear idea of the direction I think we need to go in, and also, more important, because nine times out of ten, she ends up wanting me to wear one of the items that I brought, usually a piece that I auditioned in, which I am then paid the union rental/cleaning rate to use.

So my closet has a good number of garments that if I were not an actress, I would never own: A (pretty, but come on) western-style shirt that I only hang on to for that possible, but improbable cowgirl audition, yee-haw. A lawyerish-type suit for that moment when I might cross over from "victim of the week" roles to defenders of such. And a one-piece bathing suit for those auditions when my body makes a difference in my getting a role—or at least when they are finally honest that it does.

There are times when I want to reclaim my closet: Just go through my clothes and throw out all those audition-only garments. Get rid of the suits, and the young mother khaki pants (which I won't wear even when I really am a mother), and the padded, push-up bras (okay, maybe not the padded, push-up bras), and only have clothes staring back at me that are really me and that I love.

But the problem with that is that I can't because of (1) my job and (2) even if I could, I don't think I would because I can't throw clothes out, ever. And probably for obvious reasons.

Other items, I can ditch with no problem. I have given all sorts of things to our housekeeper. Facial products and watches and colognes from industry event gift bags, a set of dishes that I never much liked from Neil's bachelor home, my old computer for her middle-school daughters to use. But never any clothes.

And, God knows, I want to. I even tried to once a few years ago. But the whole experience is a dreadful blur, like a month of withdrawal from alcohol, caffeine, and chocolate all rolled into one horrific hour that left me sweating and nauseous and feeling faint. It was enough to make me swear off that activity to the end of my days.

But I have been saved from still carting around clothes from my Lake Charles days because before I moved here to L.A., Patricia sent me out of my room, out of the house really, and went in with two or three big garbage bags—she never would tell me how many she actually filled—and threw out everything that she hadn't seen on me in the last year. She wanted to follow that fashion magazine dictum "If you haven't worn it in the past six months, get rid of it!" But that felt too scary to me, so we extended it to a year. Even so, what with all the years of clothes preceding that, there was still plenty to dump out.

And she did it for me again before I moved in with Neil.

"You're getting married," she said, "starting fresh. You don't need the clothes you wore as a student at UCLA."

"But they could come back in. You know how cyclical fashion is."

Patricia just gave me a look that she understood, but wasn't buying any of it. She knew as well as I did that I couldn't care less whether my clothes would "come back in." I was in sheer terror of throwing them out. So she did it for me, saving me from the embarrassment of Neil's seeing an obscene number of garment boxes coming off the moving truck that I would then unpack and put away as if I were actually going to wear them one day.

"And don't go looking for them at Out of the Closet 'cause they won't be there," Patricia said, referring to a chain of thrift stores around town that is especially popular because all of the proceeds go to AIDS research. "The charity place I'm taking them to you'll never find. It's time to let them go. Besides, it's bad feng shui to hang on."

Then she made me promise that I'd let her do it again in two years. I pushed for five, so we settled on three.

Today, however, I am not having any trouble imagining throwing out clothes, at least the maternity clothes that my friend Jodi (who is really more Patricia's friend, but still) has just lent me.

The other day my body suddenly seemed to cross the line from being able to wear my regular clothes, albeit flirty skirts with elastic waists pulled below the small but nonetheless there bulge, to not. And it happened to coincide with the mid-September summer-to-fall season change. Though maybe it doesn't seem as if that happens in L.A., a season change, but it does, four times actually.

And you hear that all the time out here. "There aren't any seasons!" the newcomer wails. Or "I just like to see the seasons change," a New Yorker will say, rather smugly, and usually in February when you know it is hell where he lives, but he has the impressionistic bouquet of fall in his eyes, and the rampant birth of spring in his voice, and you don't feel you can say, "It's colder than a witch's tit where you live right now; fuck the seasons."

But when you've lived here long enough, you become one of the ones who say that the seasons do change in L.A., you just have to know how to see them—or smell them, for that matter.

Winter in L.A. in the elite neighborhoods means steer manure. Everywhere you drive through Beverly Hills, Bel Air, Pacific Palisades, and Hancock Park, the air reeks of fertilizer from the giant bags of it that the gardeners are spreading over the ground. It is not an altogether pleasant smell, but I never mind it so much because I am always taken back to my first fall here, when I lived on campus at UCLA and experienced so many brand new things, not the least of which was a completely different form of heat, the dry kind, that I had never known before. It was one of those times when so much is new that it gives great and concrete support to the realization that not everything one's parents believe is true. Thank God.

So there's that for winter. And no matter where I am, or how warm the weather is, I can't wear soft, summery clothes past Labor Day. So the other day, when I moved my flirty, flowery skirts to the back of my closet and started to pull out garments that aren't wisps of cloth, it suddenly hit me that I wasn't going to be able to wear them this fall.

And it's not that I didn't know that this was going to happen. I did. It just was compounded because I was already feeling off kilter by the normal season change. I forget how to dress each time fall and spring come along. The nights get chilly or the days get really hot, and suddenly I am at a loss, as if I have never seen the clothes I own for that season before and have no idea how to wear them.

But no pregnancy wardrobe fairy is going to arrive and cast a spell over my closet, filling it with the perfect maternity clothes, so I needed to borrow them.

And I thought it was really sweet of Jodi when she called to say come over, get the clothes, she's had number two, and if number three happens, it will be a virgin birth. Her husband left her last year and she has resolutely sworn off men, which she keeps saying is easy to do in this town since she is nearing forty and they aren't looking at her anymore anyway, but I kind of wonder whether they would if she hadn't, but I'm not a close enough friend to say that to her, and I guess it's never occurred to Patricia to mention it. So I got in my car and headed to her house on the Westside.

I had to take Vermont all the way down to pick up the 10 freeway. It is not a pretty drive. Vermont Avenue is not filled with stretches of interesting and fetching stores like La Brea. Or magnificent and imposing mansions like Rossmore. Or even chaotic, but rewarding antique stores like Western. It is filled with a collision of true grit and tough breaks jumbled and jammed together in the form of businesses that I always wonder as I drive past, How are they still open? And in the middle of it all is L.A. City College ignoring its hard-up neighbors as it nurtures and supports fragile dreams. Vermont is so L.A. I love driving down it.

Jodi lives in Mar Vista, an area I am only acquainted with because it is just south of the Santa Monica airport where Barney's has its semiannual splurge of a sale, which I didn't go to last month for the first time. As I pulled off the 10 onto Centinela, I hoped that the clothes I was going to pick up would be at least almost as fabulous as the ones I missed at last month's sale. They were Jodi's maternity clothes, after all, and from what I've seen, she's got pretty good style.

"Look at you," she said, as she came to me for a hug when she opened her front door. "Just a little Madonna!"

Jodi lives in a house from the '50s that she just remodeled (after a top fast-food chain bought a jingle from her) into a Gehryesque box, which is great, but then she had it painted shades of avocado, bark, and almond. I suddenly worry about the clothes I am about to look at.

"*So* exciting!" she went on, as she pulled me into the house and shut the door. "Boy? Girl? Oh, of course, you're not telling. Well, either one will be absolutely perfect." Then she stepped closer to me, as if about to impart the one maternal secret that would make life with baby forever easy. "But pray for a boy because I don't care what people tell you, girls are hell."

I wondered whether her daughters had heard what she said, but realized that this probably wasn't the first or last time that they would. Then I thought how stupid to tell someone to pray for a girl when this far along, thank you, amnio, we would already know. So if it was a girl, and it is, then I would have no recourse but to feel bad. Which I don't, completely, at least. Okay, maybe some major fear that creeps up before I fall asleep, and that I don't tell Neil about because then he'll want to know why and that's a conversation I'm not ever having with him or anyone.

Even though Neil and I have been telling people what the gender is, I immediately decided not to tell Jodi after what she said, which is probably stupid because it's not as if Patricia doesn't know and can't tell her, though she is still in Fiji. You would have thought Patricia was getting the heir to the British throne when I told her the news. I've only seen her that happy when she got her TV show. Which was nice and fun, but I still don't understand how she only wanted a girl.

"Carolyn!" Jodi yelled. Each syllable was given a weight of its own. I thought that if the name had known it could ever sound like that, then it would have shortened itself to a nickname long, long ago.

A mouse of a girl with a floppy blue bow in her sandy hair appeared in the salad green hall.

"Time to get your sister. Go get in the car." Then Jodi turned to me as her daughter scampered out of the house. "I have to pick up Ashley; I'll be all of two minutes, but I got them ready for you; they're just in here."

She led me into her office, where there were even more varying shades of green. It was like being suffocated with chlorophyll. "Those two boxes." Jodi opened a walk-in closet and pointed in. "And I'll be right back. Oh, this is so much fun," she trilled, as she exited the room.

Two large boxes were shoved into the far back of the closet.

I had to move ancient stereo equipment, a desktop PC, and a file storage box filled with what sounded like old cassettes before I could wrestle them into the room. I wondered what it would have been like if she hadn't had them all ready for me.

There was a large mirror next to her desk, I guessed so she could imagine how the singers who would eventually record her jingles would look as they sang, but I wasn't going to try on clothes in a grass and lime green room. Though as I opened the boxes and started taking out the clothes, I realized that the room's greenish cast was the least of the problems.

Garment after garment was dark and matronly with high, high necks and huge flowing skirts. There was a forest green velvet dress that I swear was an exact duplicate of the one I wore in the Christmas pageant in third grade. And all the pants had waists that went up so high, you could practically pull your hair back with them. Were these the clothes I was supposed to wear and be happy in? Proudly flaunting my new pregnant body, as one of the pregnancy books that I had bought said, which was, of course, written by a man. Flaunt what? These things could be used to tent a house.

For a moment, I almost ran—left the clothes spilling out of the opened boxes, and the rest of the crap that I had had to pull out of the closet in the middle of the floor, and just taken off. But I heard Jodi's Volvo pull up, heard her marshaling her daughters in, and heard her voice, happy yet doom-sounding-to-me, saying, "How's it coming? Finding anything?"

I got ready to lie like a rug, as Sarah always says, when she's seen a friend's work on TV or in a film and has to pretend it was wonderful.

"Because what's the point in telling her she sucked?" Sarah said to me the first time I went to a film premiere with her, and both of us thought that a friend of hers had stunk. "She didn't ask me to critique her work, or teach her how to act, which I can't do anyway, so I may as well make her feel good about what she was able to do, even though it was hell to sit through."

And Jodi believed my lies. Though I don't know if that was the good news or the bad because the upshot was that I had to drive away with all the goddamn clothes. I tried to get by with taking just a few things, but Jodi insisted.

"No, really," she kept saying, as if my protests were only holdovers of my southern manners, and I was too polite to say that I wanted everything. That's one problem with being southern outside the South, I have found. People attribute politeness to you even when you really aren't being polite. Then when you finally have to insist and say, "No, really," they decide that you are just rude. Southerners can't be direct even when we want to.

As I got onto the 10 with the trunk of my car filled to the brim (the boxes wouldn't fit, making me think, "Thank God, I have an out," but Jodi just started yanking the clothes out of them and shoving them into my trunk; this woman could not be stopped), I wanted to call Patricia and say, "Why in God's name didn't you warn me? Jodi got pregnant and lost not only her mind, but worse, her sense of style. She needs serious help."

But Patricia is in Fiji, and when I finally am able to talk to her, the more pressing question I have is about the surprise wedding guest from hell, whose name I don't even want to think, much less say, but I will have to in some form because why the fuck didn't she tell me about that potential shock?

The pregnancy exhaustion has been gone for quite a few

weeks now, but the thought of that phone call makes me want to pull over to the side of the freeway and just go to sleep. Or maybe it's the traffic that I'm facing, which shouldn't even be happening in this direction at this time of day, but then the imported palm trees shouldn't have survived either, so there's L.A. logic for you.

As I get to a dead stop on the 10 just past the 405 interchange, it feels as if the back of my car is being massively weighed down. I am driving home with a closet's worth of clothes that I have no desire to wear, that, in fact, if I do wear, will make me want to go screaming into the hills. Where are the great maternity clothes that are supposed to be everywhere? Or are those just illusions like the outfits on models in magazines adjusted with clothespins to make them fit the way they never will on you? And these clothes are top-brand maternity, the good stuff, supposedly. But if I wear them, I'll look like some sexless, womanless, it thing walking down the street.

Though there they will be, taking over my closet, staring at me for months, until I am finally able to schlep all the way back out here, babe in tow, to get them out of my life. I can't believe I am bringing home a pile of clothes that all I want to do is throw away. I guess I should be happy that I finally want to dispose of clothes, but the irony that I can't is too depressing to be happy about any of it.

I am still stuck between the 405 interchange and the next exit off the 10, which is National, a no-man's-zone if ever there was one. I got off there once a long time ago, thinking I'd take a shortcut to Culver City, but I suddenly was trapped in this odd warehouse-filled, street-jumbled land that I thought I'd never be able to return from. Since then, I have avoided that exit at all costs. But there is no way I can stay on this freeway all the way to Vermont. And Robertson, the exit after National, feels like I will need to earn a purple heart just to be able to get there. Fuck. I suddenly can't be in this car another minute with all these clothes in my trunk. I immediately imagine them using their massive arms and legs to slither out around the backseat, creep up, and then throw themselves on me, attacking and suffocating me with their horribleness.

There doesn't seem to be any air left in the car. I roll down my window and stick my head out to try to breathe, but the stifling heat and exhaust deplete me. Okay, I really have to get away from those clothes and out of this fucking car. I look around to see whether some lane magically opened up. But spotting the Virgin of Guadalupe in the car next to me would be less of a miracle. I decide just to drive on the shoulder to the nearest exit—fuck the CHP—but I am stuck in the middle lane, and the guy in the yellow Humvee next to me does not look as if the milk of human kindness runs through his veins, big surprise. Okay, onto plan B, whatever that is. Okay, so, think.

I have a brief and happy fantasy of putting my car into park, getting out, opening the trunk, and calmly throwing every item of clothing over the railing of the freeway and onto the 405. For a moment, I think this is a perfect plan. Humanitarian, even, incorporating charity in my solution. Then I think of the CHP again and how they appear out of nowhere, and I really don't want to have to call Neil from the nearest police station to bail me out for endangering the lives of maternity clothes. There'd be no sympathy for me, especially when they see how expensive these clothes are. I can't even imagine spending that kind of money on this stuff. Jodi is fucking nuts.

I'll wage a clothing strike and wear sacks before I give in to wearing this crap. All that money on horrible clothes, like my mother paying for those—

Oh, God, not that.

The car behind me suddenly beeps to make me drive the three inches of space that have opened up in front of me. At the rate we are going, I will be home tomorrow night.

I wish Patricia weren't in Fiji. I could say two words to her and she'd know exactly what's happening with me and what this is about. Fuck. All right, so I have to tell someone because if I don't, they will find my abandoned car tomorrow morning with the clothes in the trunk torn into shreds and a note saying, "It was just too much."

I pull out my cell phone and autodial Sarah. Her home voicemail picks up, so I quickly hang up, and autodial her cell. Same thing. Fuck. Then I remember that she is shooting a big film in Vancouver this month. I so need to talk to her, to somebody. Need to and don't want to, but don't have a choice. I autodial the first number on my cell phone.

"Neil Perry's office."

"Hey, Janice," I say, trying to keep my voice light. "Is he in?"

"Fiona, are you okay?"

God, I hate that it is so obvious. "I'm fine, just stuck on the 10; you know how it is," I attempt a little laugh, but it comes out choked. "Can you get him, please?"

"One sec."

In two, Neil is on the phone. "Are you all right? Is the baby okay?" He sounds about to run out the door to find me.

"I'm fine, I just—do you have a minute? I need to talk."

Chapter 20

THE PILE OF CLOTHES ON MY BED to be put away was enormous. And drab, a heap of burgundy, brown, black, deep green, navy, gray, and tan. I had never noticed how dull boys' clothes were until I had to wear them.

The salesman had been perplexed. He didn't know us; the saleswoman in the girls' department did. Twice a year found my mother and me in that department, settled in for the afternoon in one of the large lattice-paneled dressing rooms with the rose vines painted in the corners, and a soft cloudy sky on the ceiling. My mother would lounge on the pink-and-white striped chaise while Hilda, the saleswoman, brought her a constant supply of Coca-Cola, the only time she allowed herself that high-calorie drink, "To keep my energy up," my mother would say, as if our task was a grueling ordeal and not the height of girlish delight that it was.

Hilda would carry armload after armload of clothes into the dressing room, outfits she had put together in advance, after my mother had called to say that we were coming in, with ancillary pieces of every kind. Pink pants and a paler pink shirt with ribbon trim. The floral or striped shirt to mix in. A deeper pink jacket for when it got cold, and we'd all nod as if that actually happened. The skirt to be worn to Sunday Mass. Light purple pants with pink piping on them. And a spectrum of socks, belts, and bags to "change the look." Then we'd start all over again with the next outfit. It was pure girl heaven.

Hilda saw us as we walked down the aisle in front of the girls' department. She immediately looked as if she had just walked into a surprise birthday party and, while thrilled at the prospect, was not totally prepared. Then her face registered confusion as we kept walking toward the boys' department. But she smiled and waved as if she had decided that we must be going to get a birthday gift for a nephew or cousin, especially since we had just been in her department a month ago buying a whole new summer wardrobe.

And that is what I had hoped my mother would tell them. As I sat silently in the car on the drive over, a drive that had always been filled with great excitement and joy, but now was nothing if not the journey to my death, I chanted over and over in my head the wish that my mother would say that the clothes were for some boy relative who was too ill to go to the store, so I would be trying them on for him, since we happened to be the same size.

"My daughter here needs a wardrobe for the summer," my mother said in a loud and clear voice to the older salesman with the rumpled face and dark gray suit in the boys' department who had inquired how could he be of help, ma'am? "Please show us to a dressing room and bring us what you think she'll need."

The salesman made a small and embarrassed laugh, then paused for a moment as if waiting for her to join in on the joke, too. Finally, when none was forthcoming, he said, "The girls' department is just across the way, ma'am. Surely the clothes there will be more suitable for a young lady to—" and he gestured to me as if my sheer presence completed the statement.

"As I said, please show us to a dressing room. I haven't got all day."

My face was as red as my short hair. I wanted to crawl inside myself and pull my body in after me so that none of it was left exposed. I studied the floor. I wanted to peek up at the salesman, to plead with my eyes for him to tell my mother that she couldn't do this, that it was against the law somehow. But I heard him sigh, just the way Louise did when my mother was about to punish me, and I knew my fate was sealed. As we walked through the racks and racks of boy pants and shorts, I wondered whether all grown-ups had that sigh and if so, why didn't they ever do more than that?

The wallpaper in the boys' dressing room was filled with balls: footballs, basketballs, tennis balls, baseballs. It made me remember how much I hated dodge ball and how I could always get out of playing it at recess because I was a girl. Patricia and I scoffed at the girls who played boys' games. But now that I'd be wearing their clothes, it'd be stupid for me not to play their games. And how were Patricia and I going to play with Paula and Jane, or do ballet in my neighbor's pavilion while I looked like a boy? And it wasn't as if I could go over to Patricia's apartment and switch into her clothes for the day because she was two inches shorter and one size bigger than me. Everyone was going to think that I was a boy. They'd see me with my short hair and boy's clothes riding my pink bike and think what? Not really a boy and not really a girl, just a sort of it thing going down the street. Maybe I'd just stay in my room all summer and hide. I couldn't wait for school to start. Never had I wanted the summer to end just as it was beginning.

"And don't forget the underwear," my mother said to the salesman after pants and shorts and shirts and belts and socks and shoes had been tried on then whisked away to the growing pile on the counter waiting to be purchased.

The salesman stopped dead still for a moment in his walk away from the dressing room. Then I saw his shoulders do a small shrug, and his step quickened as if he couldn't get out of there fast enough.

I nearly broke down and sobbed. The underpants I had on, the same pair from yesterday, as all my clothes were since my mother had gotten rid of every single other garment the afternoon before, were my favorite. They were green bikini underwear and I was always happy to see them freshly laundered in my drawer ready to be worn again.

One particularly hot day that spring while waiting in the girls' line outside the cafeteria to go in for lunch, I picked up the hem of my uniform's skirt and started fanning my face with it, creating a peep show flashing of my underwear. But only girls were around, so I figured, "Who cares?"

"Put your skirt down, Miss Green Bikini Underwear," my fourth-grade teacher, Mrs. Rizzouto, said. She was young and pretty and had just gotten married, and Patricia and I were constantly asking her to show us her wedding rings as if we'd never seen any before, but those had been on our mothers' hands, and Mrs. Rizzouto's was brand new.

The girls in front of me turned around and tittered, and my face turned red, then we all laughed together, but secretly I was pleased. I loved those underwear and didn't mind the other girls knowing I had them.

A sob was pushing up from my stomach and into my throat. I knew if my mother heard it in my voice then she'd be even madder still and do God knows what. I bent down to the floor as if to scratch my toe and gulped and swallowed and gulped, but could not get the sob back down. Where it came from was too full and other sobs were pushing up behind it, all lined up like beads on a necklace that were choking my throat. Finally, I took a deep breath and forced the sob down into my arms and hands. They felt cold and tingly with it trapped in there, and then numb, as if any hug I would ever get from then on would not be felt because of the cry that was stuck, unable to get out.

Chapter 21

"HEY." Patricia's tanned arms are encircling me as we stand at her front door. We break apart to go inside, and I look out over L.A. through the empty lot next to her house. It is a spectacularly clear and bright day. Every building and palm tree down below seems to be outlined by its own klieg light. There are days in L.A. when even the palm trees appear to have big careers.

"So was your trip just fabulous?"

"Oh my God," Patricia says, turning to go inside, "amazing." She pads barefoot across the floor, wearing a silk sarong from her Fiji honeymoon, as if the sands of the South Pacific are just outside her door.

"Zane taught me how to surf; that water is just unreal. And we were in this grass hut right above the water with a coral reef below us; it was insane. But mostly, we just made love all day."

"Oh, how great," I say, as I sit down on the couch. Then I want to clarify: great about the surfing and coral reef, but no comment about the made love part. Because what am I supposed to say? I'm so happy for you that you made love (okay, even that term is so scary Barry White) all day, if you really did, because who are we kidding: sex is like auditions, and all people lie about how much they are getting.

"It was perfect. And after the wedding, we needed a long break."

"Yeah." I automatically clear my throat. I didn't want to bring it up this quickly. I was hoping that we could talk about other stuff for a while, like my baby shower, which is the main reason we got together this afternoon to pick a date and plan it. And I want to talk about my baby shower. I just also need to get this other odious topic out of the way, or I'll never be able to talk about anything else, even though it's the last thing I want to talk about.

"Water?" Patricia is already heading to the kitchen. I wonder why she isn't getting the bottles from the mini fridge at the wet bar, then immediately realize that Zane probably has it stocked full with alcohol. Patricia has never been much of a drinker. I have seen her have all of two drinks, announce that she is "feeling it," and then switch to Diet Coke for the rest of the evening. But she can also smoke a few cigarettes, then forget about nicotine entirely, whereas if I even smell a cigarette, I want to start lighting up again. I wonder what she does while Zane gets blotto as he is famous for doing all the time, and if he did on their honeymoon.

Zane's stuff is everywhere. I can see Patricia's minimalist order trying to survive under his chaos, but it has been usurped. It reminds me of a home that a toddler lives in with parents who want to pretend that their life is the same even after the child has arrived.

Patricia comes back into the room with two chilled bottles of water. There are whole swaths of people in L.A. who live their lives as if they are constantly on a film set, particularly when they entertain. Water is served in plastic twelve-ounce bottles and handwritten signs are everywhere pointing to bathrooms or parking, as if the 2nd 2nd AD has been about. I always expect a hierarchy to be enforced at the food table, the way actors on a set get their meals served first while the crew waits in line.

"So, I found these darling baby shower invitations on the Web," Patricia says, handing me a bottle of water and settling in on the lounger chair. "Well, two, actually, so I was thinking you could choose. But they're both really cute. Who are you inviting anyway?"

Okay, why I thought I'd be able to hold this in, I have no idea. Especially with my best friend. And what is the point in sitting here, pretending that I can talk about baby shower invitations when all I want to know is—

"So, did you know he was coming to your wedding?"

"Who?"

"Billy." I look at Patricia, but she immediately looks at her water bottle, as if she has never before opened a twist-off cap.

I had thought on the drive over here as I rehearsed and prepared for this conversation, as if it were an audition that I felt particularly right for but was still nervous I wouldn't get the part, that I wouldn't say his name. Especially since I haven't ever talked to her or anyone about him, much less said his name. Even when I saw him at the wedding with Neil, I didn't say his name, so I don't particularly feel like starting to now, as if just saying it would endow him with a true and valid place in my life. Dreadful One or The Last Person We Ever Wanted to See were lines I had improvised on in the car, and I figured I'd use one of them, but when it finally came time to ask Patricia, I felt an uncontrollable need to slap his name in her face.

"Oh," Patricia says, as if at some point she had expected I might want to have this conversation, but in the nuptial bliss of her honeymoon had forgotten all about it until now. "No. Well, kinda. Look, Daddy called and asked me if I'd send Billy an invitation."

I can't believe that it doesn't seem to cost her anything to say his name, as if we've been talking about him every day all these years, and this conversation is just a continuation of those. And maybe it is, a voiced one, finally, after so many silent ones.

"He said Billy had just lost his job, or something happened to him, and it'd cheer him up to get one, is all." Patricia looks at me as if surely I can see how ridiculous all this is. "It was just an invitation from a star that he could show off to his friends."

I take a big drink of water to help me ignore that last comment. The fact that Patricia called herself that, and with a straight face, is just too much. It is all I can do not to go screaming off the edge of the cliff that her pool is barely hanging onto. Okay, yes, technically, Patricia is a star. Because of, God save me, *Sports Giant.* Though in a sense, that should basically cancel out her whole star status. But, okay, fine, reality TV is the big craze, so, yes, she's a star. But it is one thing to be one and quite another thing to refer to oneself as one. Katharine Hepburn could call herself a star, but Patricia?

"So, why should I even have mentioned it?" Patricia says. "I mean, who cares?"

"Uh, hello, actually, I care. And why wouldn't you tell me? You had to have known that I'd want to know."

"Tell you what? That I sent him an invitation? I didn't think about it. I mean, I never thought he'd actually come. And I slightly had more on my mind than Billy Knight's wedding invitation."

"But he came. You sent him an invitation and he came. Didn't you think I might want to be warned?"

"Fiona, it is not my job—"

Oh, here we go. About a year ago, after Patricia's fiancé dumped her and she discovered that he was a sex addict, Patricia went to a few Al-Anon meetings, and ever since then, she'll come out with one of their little sayings, usually mangled, when she wants to get out of something but make it seem as if she is being responsible in a higher-consciousness kind of way.

"—to tell you everything that I do," Patricia continues. "Like I said, I never thought he'd come."

"But he did."

"I know, you keep saying that. Not that I saw him."

"How nice for you. But I did. And I think the whole goddamn reason that he came was to see me."

Patricia just looks at me. I can hear her thinking, "Don't start. I've got *People* magazine and *TV Guide* affirming that there are millions more people in this country who want to see me than you." She takes a deep drink of water, then says, "Uh, I think he was there for me and my wedding."

"Yeah, well, I was the one stuck with the wonderful honor of his talking to me, so why the fuck was that?"

Deep in the back of the house, the phone rings. I know it is ringing in the bedroom, and I find it odd that the only phone with the ringer left on is the one that should be the most quiet of all. We both sit and listen to it as if it is Billy himself calling. I suddenly and irrationally have to convince myself that it is not. He probably doesn't have Patricia's phone number, but I wonder whether he has her address. I try to recall whether the RSVP cards for her wedding invitation were addressed to be sent here. I feel a panic in my stomach at the idea of his knowing where she lives, as if he could be right outside this very minute staking her house and waiting for me to show up.

"So what'd he say?" Patricia says in the quiet after the ringing stops.

It is what I have wanted to tell her for weeks, but my mind suddenly goes to sleep right where that memory is held. I can only feel the edges of it, like a dream that I have the sensations of, but no details.

"I don't know. That he's creepy. Neil finally came up and pried him away. But I had the feeling he might try to—" I look at Patricia, but she is examining the polish on her nails. I keep my eyes on hers to see whether she will look up at me, a sign that she wants to hear more, but she does not.

"Never mind. I don't want to talk about it anyway," I say.

"Then why'd you bring it up?"

We sit in the silence of her home. Despite Zane's clutter everywhere and Patricia's perfectly selected period pieces, I feel an emptiness here that is so full, that not another object could be crammed into this space. Then I wonder whether the emptiness is inside me.

"I have to go." The words shock me as they come out. Patricia's mouth opens in surprise, then she closes it quickly into a firm, grim line. If I had had any thought of changing my mind, her expression just dismissed that, so I follow through. I feel my body getting up from the couch, grabbing my bag, and walking across the suddenly very long room. I can tell that Patricia is stunned. She lets out a strangled bit of breath.

"Okay, well, thanks for stopping by," she says, walking behind me to the front door, as I open it wide.

Stopping by. As if I'm some actress she used to see at auditions, who happened to be on her set and went by Patricia's trailer to say hello. It feels like even more of a slap than her saying, "Then why'd you bring it up?"

"Yeah, well, bye."

"Bye."

I walk out into the white glare of the afternoon, where everything looks scorched by the light, and get into my car.

Chapter 22

THE WORST PART is that there is no one I can talk to about it. Though, okay, on a certain level, the worst part is what actually happened in the first place all those years ago to have had these things happen now for me to be so upset about. That definitely is the worst part in the grand scheme of things. But I have noticed that it is usually what I am feeling in the present moment that becomes the worst part, at least temporarily.

Not that this feels temporary because all I have needed to do since I saw Patricia last week is talk to someone about this. Sarah, preferably, and then after that probably Neil. But what would I say? I can't tell them the whole main reason I am upset and had to have that conversation with Patricia in the first place, which broke down so thoroughly as if it never could have gone well and maybe it couldn't have. Maybe that is why we have never talked about it to each other before, or to anyone, for that matter, until I said something and even then we didn't. Just said his name and that he was at her wedding. So if we can't even talk about what we need to talk about, how are we ever going to get past that we didn't talk about it?

Not even to mention my baby shower, which is suddenly feeling like some captive in the Iranian hostage crisis. I just hope I can free it faster than Carter did.

I am sitting in the reception room of Building 17 on the Warner Brothers lot, waiting to go in for an audition. The room is surprisingly empty, considering that it is usually packed with actors in all states of confidence and terror, waiting to deliver a few minutes' performance that they hope will get them hired on one of the many shows that are cast in this building. The walls are covered with huge, glossy pictures of the casts (the actors' faces are almost life size) of all the hit Warner Brothers TV shows going back a couple of decades or so. It is impossible not to stare at the pictures in the waiting room and in the halls as you are led to audition, and decide that (a) you are just like them, and therefore are going to get the job, or (b) that you may as well just hang it up now because, let's be honest, who are you kidding? I have no doubt that the pictures are intended to do exactly that. After all, if promoting their own shows in this setting isn't preaching to the choir, then what is?

I take my time signing my name onto the sign-in sheet, so I can scan the names above mine and see who has already been in. There is a small group of girls that I go up against for all the same parts, but I only see two of them on the list. Either the others haven't been in yet, or Rick Lowry, the casting director, doesn't see them as the pregnant type. I hope. I settle onto the plastic bench and pull out my sides—which is what we call the scenes from the script for the audition—to work on them until I am called in. This is the first audition I've had in five weeks (I've never gone that long without one before), since mid-August, when I went into my agent's office to tell him my news.

"How dare you get a life and be happy?" Brad said, sitting at his desk with a view of the Santa Monica Mountains and Boulevard showcased behind him in the floor-to-ceiling windows.

"Brad," I said, laughing, and thinking he would, too.

"Don't think you're going to get all goo-gooey with this baby and cut out on me. We've got a big pilot season coming up for you, and I want you out there."

I suddenly felt like that joke where the actor comes home to find his car stolen, his house burned down, and his family killed. A police officer tells him that his agent did it. The actor looks aghast, and says, "My agent?" Then he suddenly brightens up. "Came to my house?"

"No, I'm happy for you," Brad said. "Neil, too. Tell him I said so. No, I'll call him myself." He grabbed his phone, pushed a button, and said into the receiver, "Amanda, put Neil Perry on my call sheet." Then hung up.

"But look at you," he said, as he sat back in his chair. Brad has the well-serviced looks of someone who spends a lot of time with stars, so needs to stay on par. "You don't look pregnant. You look like you ate a Fatburger. Okay, so now I can send you up for all those pregnant roles"—as if TV and film are simply swarming with them. "And they don't want girls who really look pregnant; no one wants to see that, so you're perfect. You're going to look like someone stuffed a pillow under your shirt, I can tell."

"God, I hope so."

"January, huh?" I can see Brad's mind switching into quarterly fiscal year mode. "Okay, so you'll take a couple of weeks off, then you'll be good to go. Things don't really heat up for pilot season until early February, so we'll be fine."

"I hadn't really planned to go back that soon. I figured I'd take some time, you know, just to be with the baby."

Brad looks at me as if he is about to explain something embarrassingly elementary. "You're an actress. All you have is time. Hold the kid in your lap while you study your sides. Look, if I call you with an audition and you're not ready, just tell me." For a second, I almost believed him, then I remembered whom I was talking to. "But I'm not going to stop getting you out there. I can't let you break your momentum."

Driving home from seeing him, on one hand, I was relieved that Brad didn't want me to stop working. But on the other, I had planned to take a good two months off, Neil in agreement, just to be home with the baby, and not have to worry about appointments and what I looked like and early call times. Especially when I thought about a commercial audition I went to last February where an actress was in the waiting room with her six-week-old baby.

"Oh, she's daaarling," a cute and pert brunette actress sitting on the bench next to the new mother said, as she peeked into the carrier the baby was sleeping in.

The waiting room was packed. The commercial was a national for a new lightweight, sunscreen-added, antiaging moisturizer of a big skin care line sold only in drugstores. Usually those calls went straight to the modeling agencies, and I could tell that some of their girls were here (they looked at the most twenty-five, not the asked-for thirty). But for this one, they had wanted a more "accessible or unconventional beauty," as it was described in the breakdown—the job description that goes to the agencies. There were the blonde goddesses, the fabulous ethnic types, and every interpretation in between. Every girl and agency in town wanted this job.

"Thanks. Now if she'll just stay asleep in the room with me while I audition," the new mother said, "everything will be great."

"Well, if she doesn't," the pert actress said, "they'll just think she's cute. And they might even have a role for her for their baby skin care line. Hell, she could get a job and not you."

The new mother actress laughed with her, but not convincingly. "At this point, that might even be okay. With the way I've been feeling lately, it's all I can do just to get clothes on every morning." She unclipped, then reclipped the barrette holding back her overdue-for-highlights blond hair. "This is my first audition since I had her, and it's good, I guess, 'cause it forced me finally to put on something besides sweats, but—" She reached out to straighten the perfectly-tucked-in blanket on her baby. "This whole baby thing is really—kind of hard."

She said it in a small voice and I could suddenly imagine her in a nice, but modest home, somewhere in the Valley, all alone during the day with her baby, finally living a fantasy she had always had, but now shocked by it, as if she had signed on for a sitcom role she could shake off at the end of each day, but instead found herself playing *Mother Courage* twenty-four/seven.

"Oh, you'll be fine," the clearly childless pert actress said. "Once you finally lose all that pregnancy fat you're still carrying around, things will be much better."

The new mother looked found out, as if she had thought that by putting on audition-worthy clothes, she would be transformed into her old self and everything that she was before. "I know, that's what my husband keeps saying, but I just—"

"Marcie Redding?" The commercial casting director had

stepped into the jammed waiting area and was crossing out names on the sign-in clipboard.

"Oh God, that's me," the new mother said to the pert actress, as she stood up and tried to grab her diaper bag and baby carrier all at once.

"I'm here," she said, then she waved her arm with the diaper bag on it to the casting director, causing the bag to fall down her arm and hit the baby carrier, which made the baby let out a deafening cry.

"Well, nice to meet you," the pert actress said. "And good luck in there!"

"Oh, uh, thanks."

Then, as the casting director watched, the new mother stumbled over a statuesque Nordic girl's feet that were sprawled in her path, and that she couldn't possibly have seen thanks to the carrier that her screaming baby was in.

The pert actress sat back as if she owned the room. She couldn't have looked more comfortable and self-satisfied if she had just come. She may as well have just shoved the new mother to the ground and stomped all over her, since the effect was basically the same. Commercial auditions are notorious for actors' trying to psyche each other out. Unlike TV and film auditions, there usually aren't any sides to study, so everyone is trapped in a small room, staring at each other, and longing to get the job that will change, if not their life, than at least their bank account very nicely. I wondered why the pert actress had picked her. Then I realized that while the new mother actress had been on maternity leave, she must have lost her "fuck you."

When I first got out of UCLA, I met Rosie, my clothing designer friend. Her mother (whom she had called Danielle her whole life) was a huge movie star who won an Oscar for a film directed by her third husband, was politically outspoken, and began preserving her stunning looks long before anyone with an extra ten or fifty grand did.

"You have to have a 'fuck you,'" Rosie said to me one day at lunch at an open air restaurant-cum-florist shop on La Brea Avenue. "That's what Danielle taught me ever since I was born. A 'fuck you' in your back pocket that you can pull out when you need to, and, baby, you are going to need to."

The waitress brought over our salads without dressing, deposited them before us, and disappeared again. I had just come from a workout, was ravenous, and had to restrain myself from making about ten tomato, lettuce, and butter sandwiches with the whole grain rolls that Rosie was ignoring.

"I figured out early on that mine wasn't big enough," she said, "so I quit acting and became a clothing designer. You still have to have a 'fuck you' just to survive in this town, but not one nearly as huge as an actress does."

Sitting in the reception room at the Warner Brothers building, waiting to go in for this pregnant role audition, I think about the possibility of losing my "fuck you" after the baby arrives. Just being pregnant already feels as if it is changing everything, at least in my career, considering that this is the first audition I've had in weeks and that's never happened before. I kept telling myself on the drive over here that acting is like riding a bicycle: if you know how to do it, you never forget. But it wasn't the acting part that was unnerving me; it was the auditioning part because that's a game you have to do a lot, and regularly, to keep up. At least, with the pros.

I have just started studying my sides, when the tinted plate glass door of the waiting room opens and Angela Bowen walks in looking straight ahead. Okay, I should have known she'd be up for this role. She's been on every TV show that Rick has cast (I've done four of the seven), and he'd probably call her in to play an eighty-year-old man. Not that she is a chameleon; you basically get the same thing with her every time, icy patrician looks with a small smile as if she knows all of your secret dreams and has figured out how to get them before you can.

I will have to say hello to her, but I pretend to study my sides while she signs in. I know that she is scanning the names the way I did, but I also know that she didn't need to read mine because I know and she knows that I know that she already saw me out of the corner of her eye when she walked in. Like any great auditioner, Angela has perfected the "totally focused on why she is here, while sussing out the competition" survival skill.

But neither of us has any intention of acknowledging each other before Angela sits down because then there'd be that much more time when we'd actively have to pretend to be studying sides and not trying to figure out whether the other one looks more right for this role than we do.

And if that actually mattered, then I would clearly win, if this were a business with any logic in it. But this is television, so there's a problem. Do the leads on any TV show actually look like the kind of people they are meant to portray in the real world? So why would a real pregnant belly be any help now?

Angela gets all the way to her seat, choosing one at a right angle to mine so we don't have to look at each other head on, before she pretends to see me for the first time. And she's a good actress, but that's a hard one to make believable even if you're De Niro.

"Oh, Fiona, hi. Oh my God, look at you. Are you really—?"

As if I'm either suddenly fat all in one spot or raiding wardrobe departments for pregnancy pillows.

"Yeah," I smile. "Almost six months."

"Oh my God, that is so great." It is hard not to hear her thinking, "And now I don't have to worry about you for a nice, long while. Or maybe ever."

"Thanks, we're really happy about it," I say, emphasizing the "we."

"Wow. I was wondering why I haven't seen you around all this time."

Great, so there have been lots of auditions that I've missed. Or not, and she's lying. Auditions and sex, there you go. Okay, I'm not going to worry about it.

"But it's so much better to be a mother than do all these stupid jobs," she says. "I've just been *craaazy* busy working lately. All these new one-hour shows this season are just perfect for our type. It's like they wrote them for us."

Fuck. So, of course, there's been tons of work. It's the fall TV season, and Angela's right: every new goddamn show is using at least three guest star victim roles a week to keep the convoluted plots going, but by the time I have the baby and finish my maternity leave next spring, their shooting season will be wrapping up.

"Well, Brad's still been getting me out. I think he could get me auditions even if I was dead." Okay, I just name-dropped my agent. I knew that she would know who he is because all I have to do is just say his first name and everyone in town knows which agent I mean, the big one, but still. That must be some new level of base behavior I've just dropped to. But fuck it. There hasn't been a Geneva Convention about auditions.

"You're kidding. Wow. 'Cause this is the first thing I've seen in the breakdowns for a preggers role, but," Angela smiles, "I guess that's why he's so great at his job."

I start to say something about going up for roles that are only being shot from the neck up, but decide that even though my lie was completely lame, I have to commit to it, like a bad improv that finally really will end.

"Well," Angela says. "it's just been *craaazy* busy for me. And actually, I was going to see if I can go in first, do you mind, ahead of you? 'Cause I have to get all the way down to Sony for a producers' session, and you know how traffic at this hour to Culver City will be hell." Then she smiles, as if I have been waiting my entire day to do this favor for her.

It is so Angela to have asked that. I have seen her do this a million times to other actresses in waiting rooms, but never to me. And I always thought that she wouldn't pull this on me, because I thought she knew that I was on to her game. But here she is, smiling at me, as if I just got off the bus yesterday and haven't watched her working this for over five years. What's happened to me?

Though I am the only one here, so it's not like she could pick anyone else. And, of course, I am pregnant, and therefore an easy target because where else do I have to go? It's unlikely that Rick would believe that I also have a producer session somewhere. The odds of that for a pregnant actress are way too low. Okay, will it be better or worse to go in right after Rick has seen his favorite actress? Not that he doesn't like me. He has cast me a bunch and always brings me in, but Angela has always been his golden girl. Though I really don't have any choice but to let her go in first, because if I don't, I'll be the pushy pregnant actress who has nothing else to do, except go

to Old Navy to look at bad maternity clothes that I'm supposed to love because they're cheap. And at least if I let her go
first, I can use the time to pull myself back together before I
go in. Fuck you, I think, as I tell Angela that of course, that's
fine; go ahead.

We both settle in either to really study our sides or to pretend that we are. Rick's assistant comes bustling in, but before
she can read my name off the sheet, Angela jumps up, like
Nadia Comaneci about to deliver a ten, and explains about her
(purported) producer's session and that's she's going in first.

As Angela walks to the door to follow the assistant down
the hall, she stops for a second, turns her head, and smiling,
says, "Good luck!"

Has that phrase ever been uttered sincerely by an actor before? I smile and nod in response.

Once they are down the hall, I pick up my sides again to really, truly, this time study them. I'll be damned if I let her
screw up this audition for me. God, it is so annoying that of all
people, she had to walk in. Okay, stop. I have about ten minutes, at the most, before I'm up, so I just need to stay concen-
trated on this audition for the next, say twenty, and then after
that, I can vent about her.

And worry about my career. Or what's left of it. Okay, stop.
I'm pregnant; that's all. It's not like I lost my legs. Plenty of
people keep working after a baby comes along. But I've already
lost tons of work. Though a baby is much more important
than a guest star role, not that I have the baby now. And I
won't even have this role, if I don't settle down and try to focus
again.

I read through the sides, then start to read through them
again, but put them down, and close my eyes. I try to concen-

trate on my preparation, but I realize that I need to do something even more pressing. After quieting my thoughts by doing a short relaxation exercise of letting out a long, silent exhale while rolling my neck and doing a lower back stretch in my chair, I make a silent vow to myself that no matter how long I go without an audition or a job after the baby is born, I won't ever lose my "fuck you."

Feeling refreshed and renewed (Angela, who?), I pick up my sides, when suddenly I wonder whether I've already started to.

Chapter 23

"HEY, FIONA, IT'S PATRICIA."

Okay, first, just that is annoying: Like she needs to tell me who it is; like we haven't spoken in so long that I won't remember her voice. Not that we have talked very recently. It's been almost two weeks since we had that not-mentioning-it fight at her house, but still. After twenty-nine years of friendship (this month) I think I slightly know what she sounds like on my voice mail.

"So, I just found out that I'm leaving tomorrow for Iceland, I mean, Greenland. I mean—Zane?" I can hear the phone being pulled away from her mouth. "Which one is it that has more snow?"

"Greenland."

"Right. Okay," Patricia says back into the phone. "I'm going to Greenland; I just found out. We're doing this big Iditarod competition for the show, and a bunch of other snow sports, too, because, well, you know, winter and all, but mostly, because no one else has ever gone there."

"Except Leif Eriksson," Zane pitches in from the background.

"Who? Oh, right," Patricia says, laughing. "That's why I'd heard about it before. Okay, but anyway, so I just wanted to let you know that I won't be here for a while, and obviously cell phones won't work at the North Pole—"

I wonder whether that is true, but I sure as hell am not going to call hers to find out.

"But the minute I get back, we'll plan your shower. They haven't told us when that is, but I figure some time in the next, I don't know, month or so. And your due date's, what, early January, so we'll be fine. So anyway, okay, well, talk to you then. Bye." And the message clicks off.

I depress the 1 key and listen to it again. I don't know whether it is shock or masochism that makes me do that, but I can't resist. Her message is almost breathtaking in its complete lack of thought about me. Even when she does acknowledge me, she doesn't acknowledge my reality, so in a sense, it is kind of worse that she even mentioned the baby shower because now she doesn't have the defense of completely forgetting about it because of being crazed before a trip.

And, come on, who are we kidding, she just found out today that she is leaving tomorrow? One of the be-all judges of the show? They've probably been throwing cheesy fur coats at her all week to get her wardrobe ready. If she does an all-white *Dr. Zhivago* thing, I will have to throw up.

She could have just grabbed her date book, suggested a couple of dates in December for the shower, and told me to call her back with the one I want, so at least it is set before she takes off for the fucking North Pole. Unbelievable: the anti-Christmas elf if there ever was one. I hope she gets eaten by the Abominable Snowman. Though I don't think he's up there. Well, whatever is up there, I hope it eats her.

And at least if she had suggested a date, I could be telling people while she is in Greenland contributing to the melting of the Arctic Cap with all the fucking production equipment they'll have up there, so people will know about the shower more than two weeks in advance. Not that anyone here cares about the "mail out invitations one month prior" rule, but I do. And the shower is in December, for God's sake, when everyone is swamped. I could kill her. It is so like Patricia to do this. Greenland. She probably suggested it. Or would have, if she had remembered that it exists. Like me and my shower, completely invisible to her.

"Can I help you with something?" a young and pleasant salesgirl asks.

I realize that I have been glaring at the rack of clothes in front of me as if they are the message from Patricia. S'il Vous Plaît is one of the great clothing store finds in L.A. that only exist thanks to large sections of town where there is still inexpensive real estate, i.e., the Valley. It is on a corner of Moorpark, in a strip of stores that includes a dusty Judaica shop, a forlorn-looking pet store, and a check-cashing-cum-telegram place. Sarah stumbled upon it years ago after a meeting at Universal, and we meet here periodically for a cheap, but fabulous apparel fix. And as she said when we made our plans for today, with most of the clothes here being knits, why go anywhere else for maternity?

"Oh, no," I say to the salesgirl. "I'm just—well, looking for clothes, obviously, but I'm meeting a friend, so I'll just yell when I want to try something."

I turn back to the rack of T-shirts. There is a long sleeved, V-neck black one for $14.99 that is halfway between sheer and opaque, perfect for layering or by itself at night. I grab one for each of us. Sarah definitely embodies the highest level of female friendship: she shares her clothing store secrets with me.

The bell on the front door jingles, so I look up, ready to show Sarah the great T-shirt that I found for us, when I see her. Samantha Kelly is a writer/producer I read for years ago when she had a pilot at NBC. I didn't get cast, it didn't get picked up, and she bounced around in staff writing jobs for a while until two years ago, when she broke out with a hit series that she produces and writes for Showtime. Not HBO, but still. She is very easy to remember with her long Brigitte Bardot–styled hair, dark red lips, and propensity for wearing dresses from the fifties, all the more to flatter her "Come to Momma" figure.

I am shocked to see her here. Barney's, okay, but S'il Vous Plaît? Though maybe she found this place during her pre-working years and stayed loyal. She immediately walks over to the rack of dresses on the other side of the shop, so I figure I don't have to initiate a reconnect. And God knows, she has read tons of actresses over the years, and my one producer session with her was much too long ago for her to remember me.

Besides, I don't feel up for an industry meet-and-greet. Not that I don't look okay for it. One thing about meeting Sarah someplace is that she always looks so incredible that I feel like I need at least to try to stay on par. Though who am I kidding? Just going anywhere at all in L.A. requires a certain level of getting ready.

One morning last year, when there was nothing to eat in the house, I threw on some clothes, ignored the actresses' imperative to swipe on some bit of makeup (and being a red-head, that means light brown mascara since our eyelashes are invisible), and just ran out of the house to Trader Joe's. I was waiting in line with my o.j. and energy bars, when I saw a casting director who had hired me months before.

Now, on one hand, the fact that she had hired me should have been enough. She likes me, likes my work, and gave me a job, how great to see her. But it was not. That job was the season before so on a certain level, it may as well not have even happened at all. There is a fabulous meter that appears next to everyone's head in Los Angeles, and the needle is constantly going up or down, declaring to all around what your status is, and it changes by the minute. Schlumpy sweats and no makeup at the grocery store did not bode well for a high rating.

I glanced at the casting director out of the corner of my eye, and just as I was looking away, I saw her see me. But I couldn't tell whether she saw that I had seen her, too. So then I had to figure out which would be worse: the danger that she knew that I had seen her (if in fact she did) and was intentionally avoiding her, or saying hello and letting her see me full face without mascara to hide my albino eyelashes?

And it's not like she was wearing any makeup. But as a casting director, she gets to look tired and beleaguered in a powerful-over-actors-but-no-one-else sort of way while she juggles the demands of finding Ambulance Driver #2 and the movie star who has suddenly decided that TV cannot live without him, while he ignores the fact that the film world certainly can. So she doesn't have to wear makeup. But she is the hunter and I am the prey, and no one ever wanted an antelope with no discernable lashes.

But anyway, I wish Sarah were already here. So I'll just look at clothes that I might be buying if I weren't pregnant and see if some of them will work even though I am. Not that I'm minding that pregnancy is totally changing my body, unlike that studio executive's wife who infamously hired another woman to carry her child, so she wouldn't have to deal with pregnancy messing up her perfect, private-trainer sculpted body. But this whole getting dressed thing for it requires a new set of wardrobe skills.

I glance up at the door to see if Sarah is there, even though I haven't heard the bell. She is always on time, but I am early, so I turn to look at some thin knit sweaters when Samantha walks over to me. Her eyes are on my face and hair, then she says, "Didn't you read for me once before?"

I am thrilled. Even though I didn't get the job, after all these years she still remembers my work.

"Yeah, I'm Fiona Marshall."

"Right. I thought so."

"It was for *Family Matters*."

"Oh, that!" she says, as if anything she wrote before her current hit show was a collective bad dream we all had.

She doesn't bother to give me her name, knowing full well that one of my jobs as an actor is to remember every producer I've ever tried to work for. And especially one who was just featured in the "My Favorite Weekend" column of the Calendar section of the *LA Times*. Not surprisingly, or very originally, hers included hitting the Rose Bowl flea market for wardrobe finds. Though I guess she was keeping S'il Vous Plaît to herself.

There is a pause. On one hand, the natural and, in any other world, polite thing would be for me to congratulate her on her hit show. But on the other, I am an actor, so there is always that unspoken "I need a job" under every conversation because every actor always does, so I have to refrain from mentioning her show.

"Such a great little store, isn't it?" Samantha says. "One of those places you just don't want anyone else to know about."

"Exactly," I say, silently thanking Sarah for being the kind of friend she is. "And some of this stuff will probably work even with my belly." I give my protruding stomach a slight rub, as if trying to include a shy friend in the conversation.

Samantha looks down at it, then looks up at me, as if she has no idea who I am or why she is talking to me.

"Huh. Well, bye." And she turns and heads out the door.

I stand there for a moment with my hand still on my stomach, then I quickly drop it as if I was doing something indecent. Okay, what was that? Did I completely mess up by saying that I'm pregnant? But how could she not tell? Though maybe she just had some tragedy about that. But, no, because the *LA Times* piece said that she takes her husband and three kids to the Santa Monica farmers' market every Sunday. But Jesus God, you would have thought I had just picked my nose.

And I didn't expect her to ask about my career. There is an unspoken rule in Hollywood that when two people of unequal success interact, the greater of the two not only does not have to, but invariably will not, ask about the lesser's career because help could be asked for and, God forbid, that simply can't happen.

But surely my pregnancy would have been a good neutral topic. Hell, it even takes me out of the running, so I can't ask her for work. Not that I would have. Brad can do that. But we could have had nice, neutral mom/almost-mom talk.

The front doorbell rings, and Sarah comes striding in. She gives me a big hug, then pulls back and looks at me.

"What?" she says.

"Nothing. Well, Samantha Kelly just walked out of here."

"I thought that was her pulling out of the parking lot, but I figured, no way."

"Yeah, it was."

"So?"

As we move through the racks, I tell Sarah about the conversation.

"She was probably just having a bad day. Thought she could pop in here without seeing anyone, and—"

"But she initiated it with me. I wasn't even going to speak to her, and she came right over; that's what was so weird."

"Well, whatever it is, it's her stuff. It always is with people. That's one thing you can count on."

"Her stuff that will keep her from ever wanting to hire me."

"But she remembered you."

"Yeah, but it was probably just my hair. They always remember my hair."

"You can't worry about it. I promise you: she's forgotten already."

"I know; you're right. I know."

"Here," Sarah says, holding a low-riding knit skirt in three colors. "Try these."

On the car ride home, it hits me that being a pregnant actress is basically the same as being an over-forty actress. I am invisible, no longer in the game. Being pregnant is practically a preview of life after forty. Or life after I look forty, since forty is only five years away, but I still go up for roles of thirty-year-olds, thanks to my mother's genes, and the fact that on my twenty-fifth birthday, Rosie instructed me to start lying about my age. Unless being a mother will make me age faster—there's a terrifying thought. All that lack of sleep. "God's plastic surgery" is what Rosie once said that Danielle called sleep. Before any big film, Danielle would disappear into bed for weeks, and Rosie and her sister would have to whisper and walk around on tiptoe the entire time.

But God knows, that is not how I want to live. And not how I want my child to live. Though maybe, after I have my daughter, things will just go right back to normal with auditions and jobs. I hope.

But who am I kidding? I am already experiencing how much things have changed. I may as well have already been sent to the over-forty, few-to-no-jobs land, like elephants trudging to their special place to die so they won't be constant reminders of the terrible fate that lies in store for them all. Or for all the females, at least.

My entire old self has become invisible, and I wonder whether I'll ever see it again.

Chapter 24

LOOKING INTO THE MIRROR was not what it used to be. First, there were the clothes. They just never felt right. The shorts were baggy on my body, not like the little dark purple cotton velvet shorts with the coordinating lavender top that my mother had gotten me the summer before and that I lived in so much, she finally relented and bought me a second set, so I could wear the outfit all the time, and still be clean. The boys' shorts were loose and longer on me, and the fabrics were stiffer than the soft cottons and linens and knits that my girl clothes were made of. All the boys' shirts had high necks. I felt choked. Just putting them on, I'd have a moment of my head being caught and the fear of not being able to get back in or out. I wanted my tank tops and V-neck shirts and button front blouses back. I wanted the way I looked back.

The first time I wore the boys' clothes, my mother and I had just gotten home from buying them. Momma made me march straight upstairs to my room to change. Louise had lined up the shopping bags in front of my closet the way she always had when there were pretty things in them. After those shopping trips, Momma would be in my room with me, deciding which outfit I would wear first, and while I put it on, she would pick out barrettes for my long hair and put them in for me. Then I would sit on my bedroom floor waiting for Daddy to come home, playing quietly with my dolls so as not to muss up my new clothes before he saw them. When I heard him come home, I would wait until he had fixed his drink and sat on the couch with his paper and finished his drink, before I would go down and show him what we had bought.

But this time Momma didn't come upstairs with me to pick out an outfit. She told me just to stay in my room until I was called down to dinner, so I figured I wasn't going to show the clothes to Daddy. I guessed he didn't want to see them. I didn't want to see them. I wanted everything back the way it was before I cut my hair and ruined everything.

As I began unwrapping the bright blue tissue, there was none of the joy or excitement I always had when I took new clothes out of the bags. My girl clothes had always had pale pink tissue. I hated this blue and I didn't want to wear any of the clothes that it held. I wanted to stay in the last outfit of my girl clothes that I still had on and crawl into bed, and not leave until the summer and this horrible punishment were over.

But I pulled out the clothes and put them away. When I finished, I looked into the closet. It was so dark in there—gloomy. And I was going to have to wear these things day after day, week after week, all summer long. I picked out a pair of tan pants and a dark green shirt to put on. At least dark green was a color that Momma said was pretty on us because of our hair, though I had never worn it in the summer before. As I took off my girl clothes for the last time, I suddenly wanted to hide them. Put them under my mattress and be able to look at them every day as a reminder of what I once had and would again.

But Momma had told me to put them by my bedroom door for Louise to throw away the next day. After I placed them there, I felt as if I had left my dolls out in the rain and was doing nothing to save them.

I went back into my room and made myself go to the dressing table mirror to see how I looked. The second I saw myself, I wanted to throw up. I ran to the toilet, but nothing came up. I sank down to the floor, the pants' stiff fabric cutting against my legs.

Finally, I heard my mother calling me down to dinner. I got up from the bathroom floor and looked in the mirror. I was a boy—or could have been. I couldn't believe I had done this to myself. Why had I told that stupid woman to cut my hair? And why had she listened to me? The tears that had started in the store's dressing room were threatening to come up again. Momma always knew when I was about to cry because my chest would get flush, but at least with the high neck shirt on she wouldn't be able to tell. I would just have to figure out some way to speak without the sobs bursting through my mouth.

I left my room and walked down the hall and down each step of the long staircase. I always liked to walk down it with one foot on the carpet part and one foot right next to the banister on the hardwood part, liked hearing the difference in the sound that each step made. I would try to make the foot on the carpet loud and the foot on the wood part soft, so that they would be even somehow, but today, I didn't even try. I was too busy hoping that I wouldn't start to cry when I looked at Daddy and said hello. He had never stopped one of Momma's punishments before, but maybe this time he would. He had always told me he was so happy that he hadn't had a son and here was Momma trying to turn me into one. Surely he wouldn't put up with this. Please, I hoped.

My parents were already seated at the dinner table when I walked in through the open double doors. Momma looked up quickly, and I saw that barely-there smile she would have sometimes during her bridge games when I would peek into the living room and later she would tell me that she had won. I looked at my father. He had his head down, spreading his napkin open on his lap. I was about to say, "Hi, Daddy," when he glanced up at me, then immediately looked down at his plate. He had never not said hello to me. I may as well have not even been there. I wasn't his son, but I wasn't his daughter anymore either. I slid into my chair and forced myself to eat while my parents talked to each other, but not to me. The food just sat on top of the hard twists in my stomach like my mother's cold hand.

For a few days, my father didn't look at me. Then when he finally did, he never mentioned the clothes. As if they weren't there. As if what I looked like wasn't there. I wondered if I would ever be seen by him again.

The first two weeks of having to wear boys' clothes, I stayed home. Louise didn't need me to explain to her why I didn't want to go to Drew Park to play Ping-Pong or swing or practice flips off the jungle gym. I think she was surprised that I went outside with Patricia. But we either stayed in my backyard or in paradise or in the neighbor's pavilion, so I wasn't worried that people would see me.

"It's not so bad," Patricia said, when she first saw me in the boys' clothes.

"I look like a boy."

"No, you don't."

"If you saw me walking down the street, would you think I was a girl or boy?"

Patricia bit her lip and looked at me, considering, and then didn't say a thing. I ran to the bathroom and cried.

The next day, Patricia brought me a pair of her favorite bikini underwear, the pink ones with the little red ladybugs all over them.

"None of my other stuff would fit you. Not that your mom would let you wear something anyway, but I figured these could be secret. Just so you have something as a girl."

I took them in my hands. Their shiny nylon over my skin was like entering a room I had been shut out from.

"Don't worry, Fi. This'll be over soon. And no one can tell. Really, I promise."

I hid them in the space under my dresser drawer, next to my mother's fairy book, where I could take them out every so often and look at them, reminders of what I'd have again.

The next day, Patricia got shipped off to her grandmother's. Every summer, Mike's father would pick Mike up to go stay with him and his new wife and child for a few weeks, and Vicky would send Patricia to her mother's in Breaux Bridge while Mike was gone. Patricia always begged Vicky to let her stay home, or at least not to have to be gone the whole time, but Vicky always forced her to go, saying that it wasn't safe for Patricia to be at home without her older brother. Little did she know.

At first, I figured I could handle three weeks of staying inside the house. I read some books. I watched TV. And I spent hours in my room in make-believe. I'd find ways to make the boys' clothes look like a girl's. I'd twist the front bottom part of a T-shirt up, put it up through the neckline, and then pull it down, making the shirt into a kind of genie midriff. I'd roll up the shorts so they weren't so long, and I'd put on some lily-of-the-valley cologne that Momma had forgotten I had and pretend that my room was all sorts of fancy places, and I was the most fabulously dressed girl there. But after about a week, I got bored.

It was like being sick. The minute I woke up, I knew there was nothing to look forward to. All of the days until Patricia came back were lasting longer because of these empty hours in them. I didn't want my other friends to see me like this, but finally, I couldn't take the boredom anymore. I had to get outside. I figured I'd just ride my bike for a little while, early in the morning, and get back home before anyone was out and saw me.

I hadn't ridden my bike since I went to the beauty parlor for the haircut that started all this mess. I wished that I looked the way I looked the last time I rode it with my hair down my back, and my favorite pink shorts and pale pink shirt on. Just being on my bike again felt weird, the same, but different. I couldn't feel the wind pushing through my long hair, just a slight ruffling around my face. And the long shorts moved up and down on my thighs with each pump of the pedals.

But it was a relief to be outside. Even the heat was like an old friend after all the air conditioning. It was still early in the day, so the streets were quiet; the sidewalks in front of the houses were empty. I even felt kind of safe.

Before I knew it, I was at Drew Park. There were some mothers and small children at the sandbox. I wondered whether they could tell that I was a girl in boys' clothes, or whether they thought I was a boy, and which one was worse, but then I realized that they weren't even looking at me. No one else was there. I had never been at the park this early before. The light through the giant live oak trees dappled the ground. I propped my bike against one of them and walked across the park, the ground dusty and filled with roots and leftover acorns from last fall. I passed a hole in one of the trees where Patricia and I used to leave notes for the fairies. The little scraps of paper were always gone when we came back the next day, which only furthered our hope that we'd get an answer soon, but then we realized that the custodian had been taking them, thinking they were trash.

I went over to the swings and sat down, pumping my legs hard to get up high, then swooshing through the air. I could feel my too short hair in the wind again, but I closed my eyes, and pumped my legs, and let myself not be there. Not be there, and not be what I was wearing; just legs and sun and wind and outside and motion and free and air.

When I opened my eyes again, the park was still empty, except for the mothers and their children who had moved to a picnic table and were eating snacks. I put my legs down, letting the swing jerk to a stop, then got off to leave the park before anyone else came. But as I was walking to my bike, I saw the jungle gym.

I tried to figure out how long I had already been at the park. But even if I knew, I still didn't know when other kids were going to come. It could be an hour before anyone else showed up, and then I would have left for nothing. A few quick flips on the bars wasn't going to hurt anything. I would do those, and then go home. And if I saw someone coming, I'd just run to my bike and leave.

I went to the jungle gym. I jumped up, grabbed a top bar, then swung my legs up and through my arms, and flipped to the ground. I did a few more of those and then stopped. The palms of my hands were bright pink, and the skin felt squishy and soft. I rubbed them together, and could smell the rusty metallic smell of the bars. I looked around. The mothers were putting their children into strollers, throwing napkins away, saying good-byes. No one else was at the park. The day was getting loud. Frogs in the long puddles that ran alongside the parking lot were making their song and the cicadas' sounds were underneath them. The heat held everything together, compressing it tight, then pushing it against you, so that the sound was part of it, and you weren't sure which was louder or which was hotter, the sound or the heat. I looked at my bike, looked at the deserted park, then climbed up the jungle gym to the top bar and was hanging from my knees about to flip to the ground when I saw them.

Two girls from my grade at school were walking near my bike straight toward me. They weren't in my class, so I barely knew them, but I knew enough about them to wish that they weren't there. Or at least didn't see me, though I didn't know how that was going to happen since I was hanging in clear sight. I thought about flipping down and running behind one of the oak tress, but they were coming right toward me. I had forgotten that they came here.

"Please go to the clubhouse, please go to the clubhouse," I repeated in my mind, as the blood continued to rush into my head and I felt myself start to feel weak. I had to drop down. Where was Patricia when I needed her?

I pulled my torso up, grabbed onto the bar with my hands, let my legs come off the bar, and then jumped down. I landed in a squat. I looked up and saw the taller of the two, Teri, look-ing over at me, shading her eyes with one hand. She was standing like one of my grandmother's friends. Her other hand was on her hip and I imagined an old lady's bag dangling from her elbow. Then I saw her say something to the smaller girl, Ann-Marie, and they both started walking over to me. A mile away on a dark rainy night, and they would have known it was me. My hair was a beacon for all to see, even very short.

"What happened to you? Get into a fight with a lawn mower?" Teri said, marching up to me.

"What kind of haircut is that?" Ann-Marie started to laugh.

I was still crouched on the ground. I figured they couldn't see my clothes that way, so I'd stay like this until they went away. All the past year, in fourth grade, I'd been teased about my hair, so now there were two reasons I'd have to hear about it, but at least they couldn't see my clothes.

"Flame Head got a haircut!"

"Flame Head, shorn head, your daddy's a creep and your momma's dead!" Teri's voice sang out against the summer day sounds in the park.

"Shut up," I said.

"Flame Head, shorn head, your daddy's a creep and your momma's dead!"

"Shut up."

They were both singing it now, and Teri had started kicking dirt at me. It sprayed over my shoes and against my legs and side and some of it went into my nose.

I couldn't just stay down there. They weren't going away. They were on each side of me and their taunting song was getting louder each time. Staying down was making it worse, but I didn't want them to see my clothes.

"Flame Head, shorn head, your daddy's a creep and your momma's dead!"

Then Ann-Marie kicked me. Her foot came at my legs hard and fast, and I remembered her on the dodge ball field, always winning points for her team. I jumped up and ran straight at her with my arms out in front of me, but Teri grabbed me from behind, as Ann-Marie danced backward away from my reach. I twisted and pulled to get free of Teri's grasp. Her hands were clenched on my shirt, pulling it and me back.

"What's that shirt you're wearing?" Ann-Marie stopped chanting and skipping to look at me. "My brother has that shirt."

"Those are boy clothes!" Teri yelled.

"You're wearing boy clothes!" Ann-Marie's voice was even louder still.

"I am not."

"You're a boy!"

"Flame Head, girl dead! Flame head, girl dead!" Teri's voice rang out over the park.

"Shut up!" I broke free from her hands and turned around to push her away, but she grabbed both of my hands with one of hers, and twisted me around, so I was backward with them, then pushed me to the ground.

"You're a boy! Fiona's a boy! I'm telling everyone; Flame Head's a boy!"

I was on the ground with Teri on top of me, and Ann-Marie jumping around singing their chant.

Suddenly, I saw Mrs. Ritts, who ran the clubhouse summer programs for kids, standing over us. My hair was wet with sweat; dirt caked my legs, arms, and face; and my shirt was stretched out of shape.

"What in the world—Teri Guidry, get off of her right now, you girls—"

Then she stopped when she saw me. I didn't know if it was the dirt on me, or my hair, or clothes, or all of it at once, but she breathed in quickly, then let it out again.

"Fiona, get up. Ann-Marie, Teri, in the clubhouse, this minute. I'm calling your mommas."

As the two girls turned to walk away, Ann-Marie stuck her tongue out at me, and Teri mouthed, "Flame Head is a boy!"

"Are you all right? Do you want first aid?" Mrs. Ritts was always asking kids whether they wanted first aid, like it was lemonade or something.

"I'm okay. Thank you, ma'am."

"Can you make it home? Should I call your momma to come pick you up?"

"No, I'm fine. I've got my bike here; I'll just ride it home."

"Just terrible. The likes of which I've never seen." She was looking at me but wasn't seeing me, and I couldn't tell if she was talking about the other girls or my haircut and clothes or both.

"Yes'm."

"You get along now."

"Yes'm."

I walked slowly to my bike. My legs were hurting from the kicks and I could taste dirt in the back of my throat. I wanted to be home. Wanted to take off my clothes, wash off the dirt, put on one of my frilly pink nightgowns that I didn't own anymore, climb into bed, and eat cookies that Louise would bring me.

By the time I reached my bike, the tears were coming down. I wiped the back of my arm across my face without thinking, and I saw the streak of dirt on my skin and knew there was a matching one on my cheek.

And now everyone was going to know because they were going to tell them. But when I go back to school in the fall, I'll be dressed like a girl again, and maybe no one will believe them. Please, no one believe them.

I kept repeating that to myself over and over as I pedaled home. I just needed school to hurry up and start (I had never wanted that before) so I could dress like a girl again. And then I'd be exactly like I used to be. I hoped.

Chapter 25

MICHAEL LEVINE, INC, on Maple Street in downtown Los Angeles is over 60,000 square feet of textile heaven. Situated in two huge buildings on a block crammed full of tiny storefronts with fabrics spilling out of bins under signs reading "Todo 99 cents," it is the god of the garment district. Though usually only interior designers or denizens of the neighborhood shop here. The rest of L.A. (or those redecorating, at least) spend their money at Diamond Foam and Fabrics on La Brea while munching on Red Vines and La Brea Bakery baguette samples at the checkout counter as they are rung up. But when compared with Michael Levine's selection and wholesale prices, free candy and bread don't mean much.

I am here to find fabric for the baby's room. Though I guess I should start thinking of her by her name, since Neil and I finally did pick one last week, but it feels like tempting fate somehow, like the Victorians who didn't speak the baby's name until it was christened for fear of evil fairies casting a spell on it while it was unprotected by God. Not that I think that is going to happen. And it's not like I believe in fairies anymore or anything. But show me an actor, and a Catholic one at that, who is not superstitious, and I'll show you a movie star who doesn't behave like a narcissist. It just doesn't exist.

I was all set on the name we picked, happy about it even, until a few days ago when I was surfing the Web, and ran across this stupid online book, *How to Name a Baby*. I shouldn't have even read the goddamn thing because basically it was just one big fear screed all about people mispronouncing names, and kids at school teasing about names, and people not doing well in life because of their names. I kept trying to tell myself that it was clearly written by a person named Bill or Bob (not surprisingly, the author's name was nowhere to be found) who was finally getting revenge for having a boring moniker, but it didn't help.

When Neil and I found out the baby was a girl, we had no idea what to call her. We had already picked a boy's name. Not Neil. I have no interest in calling my son the same name as the person I share my bed with, thank you, Oedipus, and Neil isn't into that whole junior thing, thank God. But for a daughter, we had nothing. I didn't want to go the family route, though I did want Celtic, so I ended up looking on a Web site for baby names, which seemed the least personal thing to do, but I realized that maybe in the end, that is better somehow. The name can become personal because of who our daughter is.

After the amnio, when I told Patricia that we were having a girl, and she dropped the phone to scream and jump for joy, when she came back on, she asked me what name we had chosen, but at that point, I didn't know. Neil and I promised each other last week that we wouldn't tell anyone what we picked, but now I don't know whether I'll be able to. That stupid book made me realize that I need to try it out on someone. How can I not get a second opinion on my baby's name? It is so male to think that I could do that. And to be able to do that.

And as much as I am still annoyed with Patricia, if I am going to tell anyone the name, I want it to be her, considering that she knows the name of every important person that was ever in my life, so has information that no one else does. And Jesus, we named our dolls together. It's not like Neil will ever know, and I'm not going to tell anyone else but her because, one, that way I'm sort of pretty much keeping my promise and, two, people have no manners about names when the baby isn't born yet. Patricia told me horror stories of what Jodi went through, and that was with her kids' conventional names of Carolyn and Ashley.

And especially since the name we chose can hardly be called conventional, I really need to get another opinion on it, and soon, because I don't want Neil getting too attached to it if I need to tell him that I think we should change it. Because maybe it would be a terrible mistake as a name. I don't want to ruin my daughter's life with it, and how will I know if I don't run it by Patricia?

So when she called yesterday to say she was back and tell me about her trip, and let's pick a date for the shower, I suggested that she meet me here to find fabric for the nursery. I could tell that she wasn't going to mention our conversation about Dreadful One, but the fact that she brought up the shower so immediately made me feel a lot better and I really needed to get her opinion about the name already, though I wanted to tell her in person so I could see her face, so next thing I knew, we were arranging to get together today. And she didn't even go on forever about her trip. So maybe it does make sense just to move on about that wedding guest thing. There's nothing we can do about it now. It's over. The wedding and he and what happened. I just want to think about my baby.

I look over tables stacked high with bolts of fabric toward the store's entrance. Patricia still isn't there. She should have been here in the last few minutes if she was going to be on time for her being late. At least with her minimalist house, I don't have to worry about her wanting to spend an hour looking for fabric for throw pillows.

I walk to the far wall where the baby room textiles are. Bolts of fabric are hanging horizontally five high in U-shaped sections. I am looking through ginghams and toiles and chintzes, when I suddenly realize that Patricia is coming up behind me. She has been wearing Chanel Number 19 since we were fourteen. Her father gave her some birthday money that year, so we rode our bikes to Maison Blanche and spent over an hour picking out a cologne, our noses practically scorched on the inside from smelling every one. For months afterward, Patricia would spray the cologne into the air in front of her, then walk through it so the scent would land softly on her clothes, creating a "cloud of fragrance," as the magazine that she got the tip from called it. Then one day Vicky walked in while she was doing that and explained that all that did was stain her clothes, so Patricia started putting it on her pulse points like everyone else.

"Hey." Patricia moves in front of me to give me a hug. Her huge handbag presses against my body like one of her appendages. "Oh my God, look at you. Your belly's getting so big! But you just look like you swallowed a basketball. Is she moving?"

"Tons."

"If she does while I'm here, you have to tell me." Patricia turns toward the fabrics I was just considering. "Okay, not gingham, but you weren't going to do that anyway, were you? Although as an accent with a toile it could be fun."

"That's what I was thinking."

"Have you picked the color?"

"I thought I'd see what's here. But not pink."

"Sea green could be fun."

"Or pale purple."

"I still like your idea of the chocolate brown accent. Speaking of—" She pulls out two half-dipped chocolate chip cookies from Mani's Bakery. "I know we're not supposed to have food in here, but you're pregnant and I was over there, so."

"There should never be any rules about chocolate."

"Exactly. Though I feel like Sr. Rosary is going to take them away from us any minute. Oh, before I forget," Patricia says, as she rummages in her giant handbag, "get out your date book."

I almost tell her that I have left every Sunday in December wide open for a possible shower date, but I pull it out anyway.

"How's the nineteenth?"

"That would be perfect." I write it in my book, as if I could possibly forget.

"And if you get your list to me in the next day or so, I can get the invites out by Friday, so they'll still arrive a month in advance."

"That'd be great. Thanks."

"It'll be fun."

We move along the aisle and walk into the next section of fabrics. Patricia pulls down a pale orange floral print.

"This could be fun."

"But if she's a redhead, that'd be way too much."

"I guess you're right. But it's funny, I've only been thinking of her as that."

"She could have Neil's dark hair. And for her sake, I hope she does."

"I love your hair."

"Yeah, well, the teasing wasn't exactly pleasant." I finish the cookie and fold the napkin up and put it in my bag.

"Okay. So we finally picked a name." I feel like I am announcing the actual birth.

"Oh my God, what is it?" Patricia says, stopping and turning toward me.

"But I told Neil I wouldn't tell anyone."

"I'm not gonna tell anyone already. C'mon, I'm dying to know."

"Okay," I move closer to her, as if some underground network of baby naming spies are nearby. "We both wanted Celtic, but not a family name, so I went on the Web and found this one. But you have to promise to tell me if you don't like it."

"I will, I will, what?"

"*Aislynn*."

There is a pause. Patricia looks absolutely blank. I have never seen her so devoid of reaction. It is as if she has amnesia of facial expressions.

"It means a 'vision' or 'inspiration.'"

"Uh-huh."

"Okay, you hate it."

"No, I don't, I was just—Aislynn Perry. I was trying to figure out how it sounds and what nicknames kids at school would do."

"That's what that stupid online book I read said I should worry about, but I can't think of any; can you?"

"Nooo." Patricia bends down to look at a fabric of turquoise and yellow alphabets. I can't decide which is more disturbing on it, the colors or the fonts.

"And besides," she says, "you can't worry about that anyway." It sounds as if she is talking about something inevitable, like L.A.'s next earthquake.

"But I do. That's why I wanted to tell you. And you don't even like it; do you?"

"No, I've just never heard it before."

"That's part of the point. I want it to be new for her, without all that baggage other names have." Then I immediately wonder whose baggage I am referring to.

Patricia stands up. "What matters is that you like it." For a second, I wonder if it's my mother I'm hearing.

"That is so not reassuring."

"Fi, I like it. Really, I do."

"I don't believe you."

"I'd tell you."

"You kinda did. I thought you'd like it."

"C'mon, we pick out each other's headshots together. I think I will slightly tell you if your daughter's name isn't good."

"Well, there weren't any others that we liked. Not that she should be named by elimination, but—anyway, we like it." Then I realize that I suddenly like the name much more, as if Patricia's aversion to it gave it a resoluteness before my daughter even wears it.

"It's going to be beautiful on her," Patricia says, putting her hand on my arm, then she glances at a bolt hanging next to me. "Did you see this chintz?" she says, pulling out a length of the fabric. "This could be great. I have to be on the Westside in an hour, so we should get in gear."

Chapter 26

NOW THAT I KNOW that I like my daughter's name, thanks inadvertently to Patricia, I realize that I am nervous that I won't like her. I mean, I know that I'll love her. Of course, I'll love her. But what if I find her impossibly annoying? Or worse, what if she doesn't like me?

And, yes, okay, the teenage years will be whatever particular circle of hell they will be, but I'm talking about sooner, like in a few years. Because even though she'll have a personality as an infant, it's not like that of an older child. Though actually, what could show personality more than communicating about one's three most basic needs: food, comfort, and sleep?

It is odd and a bit disconcerting to have a whole life, and not in the scientific when-does-the-soul-enter-the-body definition of life, but the friends-school-heartbreak-jobs-illness-career meaning of life, growing inside my body and to have no idea who this person will be. And yet she will be part of mine. Completely.

No wonder some people, like Sarah, believe that we choose our own parents. It must give them an illusion of control since we can't choose our kids. But if that's true, then why did I choose Ed and Margot? He was benign enough, but she—though I can't really separate him from her since I wouldn't be here without both of them.

But I don't want to think about her right now. I want to think about my baby and this first birthing class I am driving to. Though it is unnerving that all roads seem to lead back to Margot. I still can't believe she's not coming for the birth.

Neil says I should be grateful because now there won't be any way for her to create any drama. Exactly, I said, because she already has. What could be more dramatic than not coming to your only daughter's first birth? The entire thing will be all about her not being here. No, it won't, Neil said. It'll be about the birth of our child. I hope so, I told him. Then he hugged me and I pretended to feel better because of what he said.

Though thinking about it later, I did start to feel better because I realized he was right. The birth really won't be able to be about anything other than our daughter because no matter what, birth, like death, trumps all. Even Margot, I hope.

While I was getting dressed this morning, knowing that we have our first birthing class tonight, I kept telling myself that it should be the easiest occasion to dress for. It's not an audition with a bunch of actresses who aren't pregnant and for a role where they don't even want someone who really is pregnant. It's not a big Hollywood party where only box office counts. It's a birthing class with other pregnant women and an instructor who is a mom, a friendly group if there ever was one.

But this afternoon, I suddenly got seized with panic. Okay, maybe that's too strong a word. Intense nerves, I'll call it. I found myself staring into my closet, trying to figure out what outfit I could change into that would look like what the other women will be wearing. And that was absurd because we're all going to be in maternity clothes. But then I realized that I was thinking of them as if they already were mothers, even though I know this is a class for first-timers.

And despite the fact that I am pregnant and—knock wood that all continues to go well—am going to be a mother, I am having a hard time believing that I actually will be a mother because I have never been one before. Sarah has a cat that she adopted from the pound right after the cat had kittens, and I remember a few years ago looking at her cat one day and realizing that she had more fully fulfilled her job of being female than I had.

But I was still in my late twenties, so it wasn't a big deal, and with the cat, I could handle it. For one thing her offspring weren't around constantly to remind me of the fact, and for another, I never had to be in a social situation with her, in a roomful of others the same as she was, futilely trying to look like her, as if my non-cat-ness could ever not show. So, the cat was easy, but these other mothers that I'll suddenly have to be with once my baby is born—it's as if there is a higher level of femaleness to which they ascend and automatically receive the perfect wardrobe as their membership badge. And I can't help but feeling that mine's going to get lost in the mail.

But I'm not going to worry about that right now. I'll just only hang out with all my nonmother friends. It's not like I need any new ones anyway. And I'm still only pregnant, so maybe I should just worry about how I'm going to get this baby out of me instead of whom I'll hang out with once I do.

Neil is sitting in his car, parked in front of the instructor's home, e-mailing on his BlackBerry, when I drive up. Deborah, the birth instructor whom Rosie's sister used and loved, lives in a house in the flats of Beverly Hills, a neighborhood distinguished by charming Spanish stucco houses from the 1920s that are being squeezed out by enormous, brand-new, built ten feet from the property line, grotesque mausoleums. I mean, mansions. Deborah, thank God, lives in one of the older, authentic homes.

When she opens her front door, we hear a shriek as three young children go barreling up the stairs, screaming and hitting each other the entire way. A fourth child immediately careens straight into Deborah, then, hooting loudly, takes off after its bigger siblings. Deborah just pushes her wire-rimmed glasses up her nose and smiles at us, as if having four children is its own form of lobotomy.

In the living room, three couples are arranged on two deep, low sofas. I wonder how the women are going to get up from them and whether Deborah thought about that when she bought them. Two of the women look ready to pop, and the third appears about five weeks away, like me. They are all dressed in maternity-style, but great looking, workout clothes. It is a small relief. Neil takes a straight back chair from the side of the room, moves it next to one of the sofas for me, then sits down on the floor beside it. I notice one of the women looking pointedly at her husband, but he refuses to meet her eyes.

After going around the room and saying our names, jobs (God forbid a networking opportunity be missed), due date, and hospital, Deborah jumps in.

"Okay, so. The method of childbirth that I teach is all about achieving a nonmedicated birth experience. And, as all of us know, the only way to get good at something is to—" She looks around at us, her smile an eager encouragement for us to join in.

"Practice, practice, practice," she finally says, pushing her glasses up her nose.

"And I thought that was how you got to Carnegie Hall," Neil whispers to me.

"Neil," I say quietly.

"So, that's what we're going to do here," Deborah says, "practice giving birth."

I start to ask how we are meant to practice something that is physically impossible to simulate, especially since we have no idea what it will be like, when suddenly one of the children who careened up the stairs when we first came in, runs into the room, stops just inside the doorway, next to and a bit behind her mother, and stares each of us down. She appears to be about six years old with soft, blond curls and is holding a pink hula hoop in front of her as if daring us to take it from her.

"Two of the most important tools in achieving a nonmedicated birth are squatting and relaxation. Squatting makes a huge difference in the birth process. It opens the outlet of the pelvis by 10 to 15 percent. It also is the only exercise that gives elasticity to the perineum." Then she beams, as if she has just told us that our deliveries will be pain-free.

I give Neil a "The peri-what?" look, but he is just as stumped as I am. Then I wonder why it is that at the age of thirty-five, I am still discovering parts of my genitalia that I had no idea even existed.

The child, while still looking straight at us, lets the hula hoop fall to the floor, where it bounces up and down, rattling loudly, until it finally comes to a rest. Deborah ignores this unsolicited percussion accompaniment and continues on.

"And that makes a huge difference in avoiding an epi-siotomy." Deborah nods her head, her blondish brown curls shaking as she does.

The child, still looking at us, suddenly takes off her shirt and throws it wildly behind her. I look at Deborah to see whether she has noticed what just happened, but she is fully engrossed her in topic.

"But most women haven't squatted since they were five years old because someone probably told them that they could see their underpants."

Clearly not a concern this child would have. She is standing in the doorway, topless, with a rather purposeful expression on her face, as if she is part of the lesson somehow. The other couples in the room are now looking at the child, causing Deborah finally to glance over her shoulder.

"Oh, hi, Delilah," she says. Then turning back to face us, she pushes her glasses up her nose, and does a quick little clap of her hands. "Okay, so. Why don't we all try a little squatting right now?"

I wait for her to tell her daughter either to get dressed or to go back upstairs, but Deborah is looking at the eight of us, waiting for us to get into the prescribed position. I wonder whether this is some odd protracted bathtime ritual they have, this shedding of the clothes all over the house. But in front of strangers? And men to boot?

The child, as if filled with the enthusiasm that we should be having for the squatting, picks up the hula hoop and begins swinging it expertly around her half-naked body. It is impossible for Deborah not to know what her child is doing. The hula hoop is making its trademark rattling sound. Not to mention the whirl of activity in her peripheral vision. But she just starts talking about the correct foot width for a good squat.

I look at the other couples to see whether they are looking at the child, but the women are focused on trying to disentangle themselves from the couch, while the men try to hide their obvious thoughts of "Why do I have to do this? I thought this was just for her."

Neil is waiting for me, so I get out of my chair, and onto the floor. As I take hold of Neil's hands and squat down in front of him, I hear the hula hoop fall to the ground. Well, thank God. Maybe Deborah whispered something to her after all. I glance over to see whether the child has already left, but she is still there, practically showcased in the doorway, where she has begun a dance that can only be described as schoolyard stripper. I half expect a pole to descend any minute now. The child doesn't have hips, her torso is smooth and flat, yet she is moving her body as if Mata Hari could learn something from her.

Deborah glances at her daughter, pushes her glasses up her nose, and then goes back to extolling the virtues of nonmedicated birth. I suddenly wonder whether having gone through four nonmedicated births, Deborah is enjoying a completely medicated life because it is all I can do not to yell, "Can you please tell your daughter to stop dancing and put her goddamn shirt back on? What is your fucking problem? There are men in this room. Does the name Roman Polanski mean nothing to you?"

I want to jump up, throw my coat over the girl, and carry her from the room. I glance at the other couples to see which direction the men are facing, but they are focused on their wives, complaining with them about the physical discomfort.

I suddenly wonder whether I am either really sick or losing my mind.

"Well, that was an experience," Neil says, once Deborah's front door is safely shut behind us and we are walking to my car.

"Yeah." I wait to see what part he is referring to.

"Her whole diatribe at the end about breastfeeding as long as the child wants. And not baby, but child. You know she's talking about three-year-olds."

I don't know whether I'm relieved or worried that he wasn't talking about that child. Then I decide relieved because maybe I was just imagining things. Imagining that there was something to feel weird about a child doing a completely and fully sexualized dance in front of adult strangers while her mother looked on and did nothing. Okay, there is no way I can ever go into that house again. I immediately wish we were having a son. Not that they don't have their own share of dangers, but at least they aren't—

I suddenly realize that Neil is looking at me with concern, so I scramble to get back to what was last said.

"I know, and I don't feel like hearing all that crap for four more weeks."

"Rosie recommended this woman, right? Just like those feng shui women. Doesn't that tell you something?"

"Well, the feng shui actually worked."

"Fiona, that is not why we got—"

"C'mon, we've been using that second bathroom again for months."

"Because you called your psychic, who said that God is in charge of the health of our child, and you decided that psychics trump feng shui, so, presto, we got our bathroom back."

"Exactly. See?"

Neil just looks at me.

"Okay, so maybe I get a little extreme about this stuff, but I know people who are a lot more."

"I'm not married to other people."

"I'll find another birthing class."

"Or not. And we can do it the old-fashioned way. With medication."

We stop at my car, and watch one of the other couples from the class drive off. I start to wave, then don't. Their car stops at the end of the street, turns, and disappears. The low sounds of Wilshire Boulevard come to us on the cold, dark air.

"Look, I just really want to see whether I can do this." I turn to face Neil. "I mean, if we aren't able to have a natural birth, fine, but at least let's give it a shot, right?"

"Fiona," Neil says, putting his arms around me. "You're going to be a different mother to this child than your mother was to you. You don't have to put yourself through hell just to prove it."

"What are you even talking about? Is that what you think this is?"

"I just think you need to relax." Neil draws me in toward him. "I'll support you however you want to do this. It's your birth."

"No, it's not. It's our daughter's."

But as he holds me in his arms, with my face buried in his neck, I suddenly wonder whether it is mine, too.

Chapter 27

"HOW ARE THE CLASSES GOING?"

"Great. I found a teacher I really like, Nancy Weissmann; I don't know if you know her. Though I've been doing all that relaxation stuff for years thanks to acting classes. But the techniques are great. I just hope I can do them when I need to."

"You're gonna be fine."

As Dr. Walker squirts the ultrasound gel on my tummy, then smoothes it across, I wonder what it would be like to have just even that bit of conversation with my mother. When I told her on the phone the other day that Neil and I were taking classes to prepare for a natural birth, having to bring up the subject on my own and completely out of the blue, her response was "That's how I had you, and I didn't take any classes."

She then launched into a monologue about her upcoming bridge tournament. I imagined interrupting her to say that there is no way in holy hell that she had me in a natural birth. Vaginal, yes, but natural, no. Because who are we kidding? My father had his cocktail, and my mother had her epidural. It is so my mother to think that natural means vaginal.

Then I noticed that she had changed the subject to how well my father's new bank building was coming along and it looked as if it would be right on schedule, which is a miracle, you know, particularly down there. But I knew that what that really meant was that the building and I still have the same due dates, so don't think they'll be here for my natural birth.

Dr. Walker presses the ultrasound wand on my belly. "There she is."

My baby appears on the screen. She turns her head and moves her arms, like Isadora Duncan in a cramped dance.

"Hi, baby," Dr. Walker says. She is wearing her engagement and wedding rings, as she normally does, on a gold chain around her neck. All these months that I have been seeing her, the chain was a plain gold serpentine, something she might have found at the bottom of her drawer, left over from the '80s when people were wearing those things. But today it is a gorgeous golden woven rope that I have a feeling I would find in the Tiffany catalog if I looked. I commented on it when I first walked in, and she sheepishly grinned, saying, "My anniversary."

"Any questions about anything?" Dr. Walker says. "Everything okay?"

"Yeah, except recently, I've gotten this funny little pain right here." I point to a quarter-size circle just to the left of my belly button. "It feels sore sometimes, but only right there. Like it was burned somehow from the inside."

"It's from your umbilical cord. The baby's stretching out your skin and pressing against it, so you're finally feeling it. I had it for all three of mine, same place each time. It's kind of nice though. It's where you were connected to your mother."

No wonder it hurts.

Driving home from the appointment, I decide to stop at Mani's Bakery on Fairfax for a chocolate chip dipped cookie since it is on the way. And since I could eat one every day. And they're completely natural, so I pretend that that makes it not really a cookie somehow.

I am sitting on one of the metal chairs outside the bakery, eating my cookie, and enjoying the low-wattage warmth of the December sun. The cars on Fairfax are reeling past, their occupants like actors in a silent film that is only a moment long. As I put the napkin on my empty plate, and get up to leave, I realize that using the term *natural* for a nonmedicated birth is, frankly, elitist. It's a birth, for God's sake. Any way the baby needs to come out is natural. All that matters is that it's healthy.

And that the mother is there for it.

I get in my car, put my head down on the steering wheel, and start to sob.

Chapter 28

PATRICIA'S HOUSE IS VERY STILL TODAY, despite the pending party. Whenever I walk into it, I feel as if I have dropped back thirty years and the seventies' sitcom star is still living here. She had her own hit show, which was a spin-off of another hugely successful TV show, then never got another job once her series ended.

I imagine her during her glory years, with no idea how numbered they are, arriving home at the end of a day at the studio, and throwing her script down in the round conversation pit, as if it were Brecht and only she can interpret it correctly. She kicks off her shoes onto the shag rug, and complains to someone—a friend, an assistant—what a goddamn rotten day it was. But she enjoys the complaining, is happy about the goddamn rotten day, wants it to be, so that it will all continue to be so important. The complaining is one of her perks, one of the joys of her career. How hard it is to be funny and paid obscenely for it. They just don't understand.

When Patricia first moved in here, I told her to burn some sage to get rid of any lingering energy from that failed career. I always forgot to ask her whether she did.

Pink candles of all sizes and shapes are burning in the fire-place, even though it is not yet two in the afternoon. One of Patricia's dining room chairs has been moved to the living room and is completely wrapped with pink ribbons a la Christo. Every tabletop is filled with perfect pink roses in banana leaf wrapped vases that are similar to the ones at Patricia's wedding reception, clearly the same florist's handiwork.

"It's just beautiful," I say to her, as we hug hello. "Thank you."

Patricia doesn't say anything, just squeezes a little harder. I immediately can tell what her face looks like, so I pull back to look at her, and it is exactly as I thought. Her eyes look worn down, like pennies handled too much, and her mouth is in a sad, firm line.

"What?"

"He left. Last night."

"Like, for Vegas or something, what?"

"No, like left as in moved out. Last night."

"Are you kidding me?" I suddenly understand why the house feels so still. And why its uncluttered look has returned, not because of things being put away for my shower, but because all of Zane's stuff is gone. "Where?"

"I don't know and I don't want to know." Patricia walks over to the conversation pit, steps down into it, and sits down. I follow her in.

"What happened?"

"Nicki fucking Coleman happened."

"No. Oh, no."

"Oh, yes. Apparently, it started while I was in Greenland. But who knows? She was at our wedding party. It probably started then. Or before. The fucking dog, I don't put it past him."

"Jesus."

"Exactly. At first, it was all about this film they're going to do together, but then there were little things, like he suddenly started wearing cologne. I mean, what man wears cologne? So that was weird. And then—well, he never wanted to—you know—I mean, even on the honeymoon, he wouldn't really touch me. So, it became kind of clear that there was something going on, and then last night, he admitted it."

"That's horrendous."

"And she is such a slut. That fucking billboard of her all over town with her tits hanging out for her big, serious film. I mean, please. Academy Award, here she comes. Maybe for best implants, but that's an even tougher category than acting in this town. I didn't sleep a wink all night. I was so angry, that finally at four in the morning, I cut up his side of the bed."

"You cut—what do you mean?"

"I took a knife and slashed the mattress on his side of the bed," Patricia says, as if that is the prescribed and normal behavior after a spouse has moved out.

"Oh."

"I felt better, but then it made sleeping kind of hard. Feathers kept floating up from the gashes everytime I moved. It was really annoying. I wanted to call him and tell him to buy me another fucking mattress and come get this one for them. But I don't want to see him or talk to him. Ever again."

"Yeah, I wouldn't either. So, what are you gonna—"

"You know, get the divorce attorney. I called Pamela."

How perfectly Hollywood to call one's publicist before a best friend or therapist. But, Jesus, her husband of seven months just walked out. She can do whatever she wants.

"She had a few names for me, so I'll use one of them, but

what she really cares about at this point is that we don't let it get out. At least not yet. So, you can't tell anyone." Patricia looks at me as if she is about to pull out the knife from last night, and make me do a blood oath.

"I won't."

"Pamela has a whole plan, and I'm just letting her handle it. I mean, Brett and Sheila were shacked up in Malibu for months before the tabloids finally figured out that he'd left TV Queen Rebecca, so we should have some time."

"Well, that's good."

"Yeah."

I glance up and see that a pink piñata in the shape of a giant teddy bear is hanging above the center of the pit. Pink sticks festooned with ribbons are lying on the floor. It takes me a second to understand that it is for my shower. The image of a bunch of women thwacking the hell out of a teddy bear is not the sort of gentle and love-filled maternal atmosphere that showers usually are. I wonder whether Patricia got the idea for it before or after she found out about Zane.

"But, Jesus Christ, this is the last thing I need with my career," Patricia says. "I could just kill him. Everything was going so great, and then he has to turn around and just—"

She shakes her head, staring off into midspace, then her eyes land on the sticks. I have an almost uncontrollable urge to jump up and hide them. Maybe she got that piñata just for her.

"I mean, Christ, Fi," Patricia says, looking at me as if we are back in ninth grade, and she doesn't understand why the algebra test she didn't study for was so hard. "Why can't I ever get a goddamn break?"

I stare back at her at a complete loss of words—or, rather, a complete loss of words that I can say to her. As I try to think of some response, we hear a car pull up on the gravel half-circle driveway outside the front door. It is probably Sarah, thank God, the first guest, always on time.

"Ugghh, I just really can't face guests right now," Patricia says, then vigorously rubs her eyes. For someone who is so fanatical about the way she looks, I can never understand why she hasn't figured out that that just ruins that delicate skin. It is almost painful to watch.

"Can you get the door? I need to go touch up my face."

She gives me an absentminded hug, as if I am the one who needs consoling, and with the way this baby shower is starting, maybe I am; pulls herself up from the pit; and leaves the room. Fucking Zane. I don't know whether to be happy that she is finally rid of him, or pissed off that he picked this weekend to do it. I hear Sarah's footsteps coming up the walk. I have never wanted to talk to her so much and had to be so mute.

I get myself up from the low step to let Sarah in. As I pass the hall closet, I notice part of a jacket sticking out, so I automatically open the door to push it back in. It is clearly one that Zane forgot; his old sports sponsor's logo is emblazoned across the front. As I take the sleeve in my hand, a sharp and sweet scent rushes at me from the jacket, pushing me back to another party from a long time ago.

Chapter 29

IT WAS AUGUST and the heat never let up, not even at night. After the sun finally went down, it would just change to a colorless form that stifled not from its glare, but from its impenetrableness.

So there were moments when I actually appreciated my short hair. Alone moments. Moments I was barely aware of until they had passed. But most of the time, I was counting the days for school to start, so that Momma and I would finally go shopping in the girls' department again.

I stayed inside as much as possible that summer, not daring to go back to Drew Park, or even to ride my bike on the streets. After Patricia returned from being stowed at her grandmother's, she and I spent the days playing at my house. She didn't care about going to the park and was just as glad to be away from her apartment because of Mike.

There were only two weeks left before school and all I wanted to do was wear pink again, to be a girl again, that the world recognized as one again.

Whenever I went out, people mistook me for a boy. Just on that Friday night, I had gone to Piccadilly's Cafeteria with my parents for dinner. Louise was on vacation and my mother wasn't cooking. "Not in this heat," she'd said, as if she ever did. But even with having to go out in public, I was thrilled. I loved the long line of perfectly prepared and presented food that gleamed and glistened behind the sparkling glass windows: the bright cubes of Jell-O in green, orange, and red; the regal roast beef sitting under the hot lamp with the carving knife poised above; the small round dishes of corn and lima beans and black-eyed peas and rice and gravy; and the cheerfully fattening desserts that even my mother ate.

And on that night, everything had gone fine. The women in their hair nets and gloves that were lined up behind the food and holding their spoons at the ready in the air said the same thing to me as they always had, "Serve you?" and didn't give me a second glance. And during dinner, I even had one of those wonderful moments, which had never happened before in public, of forgetting that I looked like a boy.

My father was in line at the cash register to pay for our meal. My mother had gone to the ladies' room, and I was at the table finishing my strawberry sundae. I scooped up the last bite, looked around to see whether my parents were watching, then picked up the glass boat bowl, and licked the inside clean. I made sure to wipe all around my mouth with the napkin before I slid off the booth.

My father had just handed his money to the cashier when I got to the register. It had one of those little silver shoots that the change came down in, landing in a bowl at the bottom like Santa down the chimney. I loved picking up the coins from the bowl, its gentle sloped sides helping them fall into my hand, and Daddy always let me keep them.

My father's quarters, dimes, and pennies clanged their way

to a stop. I reached into the bowl and was just fingering their raised surfaces, when the cashier's wrinkled and spotted hand shot out and grabbed mine.

"Sir, this little boy here is a-tryin' to steal your money," she said.

I jerked back my hand, empty of change, and looked up at my father, waiting for him to correct the old woman. He glanced down at me, then looked up into the distance, silently shaking his head. Then he picked up the change, put it into my hand, and patting me on my back said, "Let's go. Your mother can meet us in the car."

"Oh, sir," the cashier said in a wavering voice. "I'm so sorry, sir. I had no right way of knowin' he was your son."

My father pressed on my back to move me along, so I pushed open the heavy glass door into the thick bleak night. Then my father walked past me and crossed the parking lot ahead of me. I didn't try to catch up. I wanted to run off. Hide behind the building or among the tall grasses and weeds on the side of the lot until I could wear girl clothes again and my hair was long, and everyone, including my father, could see who I really was.

In the late afternoon that Sunday, Vicky picked Patricia and me up at my house to take us to Patricia's uncle Dave's for a fish fry. He was Patricia's father's brother, and not only was Vicky not really invited, she had no interest in seeing any of them either. It was practically all we could do whenever we went out there to get Vicky to pull into the driveway when she dropped us off and picked us up instead of waiting down the street.

At first, I didn't think I would go. But, "It's just gonna be my stupid cousins," Patricia said. "And, besides, what would you do here?"

I realized that staying home would be worse. Since the incident at Piccadilly's, I hadn't wanted my father to see me. I had stayed in my room as much as possible and was counting down for the next two weeks to end (surely Momma would take me shopping on the Saturday before school started, since that was when the punishment was supposed to be over) with as little contact with him as possible. Everytime I thought of my father staring off into space and shaking his head, like I was just too awful to claim as his daughter, I wanted to die. Being a girl again would change everything. So I changed into a pair of tan shorts and a light blue T-shirt with stripes across my chest and headed off with Patricia.

Uncle Dave and his family lived on the outskirts of town in an area that was almost rural. The mailboxes lined one side of the road; they weren't up at each house. And there was a farm next to Uncle Dave's with a bunch of goats, hens, cattle, and a mean pony that Patricia and I tried to ride one year and almost got bitten.

Uncle Dave's house sat far back from the street in what looked as if it could have been a field, if it had been cleared of some trees. There were some patches of dead grass in the large front yard that looked as if they would hurt bare feet. Patricia and I walked down the long gravel driveway, past two pickup trucks, a station wagon, and a long, shiny motorboat on a trailer, through the carport, and into the kitchen door.

Patricia's Aunt Frances and Aunt Geri were at the stove, putting breaded catfish filets into the deep fryer while two other women sat on high stools at the counter, alternately rolling hush puppies while tapping their cigarette butts in an ashtray. Bowls of coleslaw and potato salad were on the table, a watermelon was sweating in the sink, and a huge cooler with a beach towel shoved underneath it and filled with Jax beer was on the floor next to the kitchen table. Bottles of Coke and 7-Up and Jim Beam were on top of the fridge. Uncle Dave and Aunt Frances's four children, their three nieces and nephews, and some neighborhood kids could be heard in the deep back-yard playing a raggedy game of softball. Patricia's two uncles and their buddies were in the den off the kitchen, drinking beer and sprawled on the couch behind bowls of potato chips and dip, yelling to each other about a fishing show on TV. In my rush to get out of my house, I had forgotten how boring it was here.

"C'mon," Patricia said, as she went out the sliding door behind the kitchen table. She was always ready for a game of softball. I dragged myself behind her.

The Thunderbird pulled up in the driveway just as we were all sitting down to eat. The men were eating in the den, the women had commandeered the kitchen table, and the kids had been put out at a picnic table on the cement patio outside.

"Well, look-it who's showed up," Patricia's uncle Dave said, coming into the kitchen and going out to the carport. I peered in through the open sliding door. A moment later, Uncle Dave walked back in followed by a short, very tanned man; a woman with high, whipped-up hair; a boy of about ten; and him.

His blond feathered hair was longer than mine, and the snug T-shirt he wore had "Keep On Truckin'" in a balloony script across his solid chest. His tanned skin looked warm, like a towel you're grateful for after a swim. He walked to the cooler, grabbed a beer, opened it with something on his key-chain, took a long pull that drained nearly half of it, put it on the counter, then turned around and picked up one of the young cousins who had gone in, and threw him, squealing, into the air.

Aunt Frances busied herself with filling up more plates, as the rest of Patricia's cousins jumped down from the picnic table and went flocking into the kitchen. Aunt Geri yelled for everyone to go sit back down, for Christ's sake. Jesus, you'd think no one had ever walked in late before, and she whacked two of her kids' bottoms to get them to go outside. The kids started whooping as they ran around the kitchen table a few times before finally beelining it back to the picnic table. Uncle Dave was pouring his brother a drink of a little Coca-Cola and a lot of Jim Beam, when through the ruckus, I heard Billy's voice as if his eyes on me were carrying the words just so I could hear,

"Who's the foxy little redhead outside?"

I looked at him and smiled.

Chapter 30

IN THE PAST WEEK OR SO, whenever my telephone rings, I automatically think it is my baby calling to tell me that she will be here soon. And considering that I am only one week away from my due date, God willing, she will be.

Everything is pretty much ready. The nursery has been painted, furniture arranged, and the curtains, pillows, and bumper pad in the lavender fairy toile with the chocolate brown gingham accent have been sewn and put in place. Diapers, bottles, and blankets are at the ready. The birth announcement has been selected and will be printed once Neil calls in the information. So I'm just in a waiting game, trying to do all those things that everyone says I won't be able to do once she is here.

And for me, that doesn't normally include watching TV, as hypocritical as that may seem, especially during the day, but Patricia's publicist booked her on *Jessica* and I promised that I'd watch.

Word of Zane's decampment had somehow gotten out, and not because of me, though I did end up telling Sarah because when she saw me at the shower, she could tell that something was wrong, so I whispered it in her ear, then told her the rest later, but I know that she didn't tell anyone because she promised she wouldn't and what would she gain if she had? And besides, she's had her own tangles with the media and has no interest in inflicting them on anyone else.

Patricia is convinced that Zane's publicist let it leak to the press because she never liked that Patricia was with him and was always angling to get Zane seen at parties and stuff with other stars the whole time that Patricia was dating him before they married in Vegas. Once the publicist even accidentally-on-purpose booked Patricia on the wrong flight, so Zane showed up in a city with the costar of his film and not his girlfriend. That spawned a whole bunch of pictures and "Are they together?" headlines in the press, but Patricia just ignored it and rode it out. This time, however, it looks as if Zane's publicist had finally won.

"It's just a little spin control," Patricia said to me on the phone the other day, when she called to say she'd be on the talk show. "Jessica's making it a whole show about how to move on, so, you know, it'll be very upbeat. And this way, people can see that I'm doing great, and I can say it was amicable and all that other bullshit, so no one will think I was dumped. But we're including mental anguish in the divorce suit against him for putting me through this, that mother fuckin' dick. Thank God, I have such a great lawyer."

I almost started to say, "But you love going on these talk shows," then was glad that I didn't because obviously the press she does for *Sports Giant* could be considered fun, but this sounded like the worse kind of acting job, lying while having to pretend to be your real self.

"You're going to do great," I said. "Everyone already loves

you, and people always take the woman's side. Not that you need to worry about sides—"

"No, I know what you mean, and thanks. It'll be fine. Jessica loves me. It'll be fun to see her again and I'm doing *Allure* right after this, so Pamela is going great guns for me. And, as she keeps saying, this could end up being the best thing that could've happened to my career. And to me."

"I certainly think so," I thought, as I hung up the phone. But probably for different reasons.

I settle into the couch and click on the TV with the remote control. A breakfast cereal commercial that I was up for is playing when I get to the right channel. It figures they hired Kelly for it. She is making a tidy little living being the ubiquitous pretty American Mom, though she has never had a child and doesn't look like she possibly could have had the child giants that they paired her with. I reach for my cup of herbal tea, as the music for *Jessica* starts up. Even if you didn't know that it is the top-rated talk show in the country, you could tell just from the opening. The mostly female audience is going nuts. The stage set looks as if it costs as much as a five-bedroom home. And the male announcer sounds as if he is introducing God.

Jessica appears on the screen. At some point in her early past, she must have been a brunette, but thanks to the ministrations of makeup artists and hairdressers, all traces of her roots have been erased, and I wonder whether they have been from her memory, too. I suddenly imagine only pictures of her blond years existing, all previous ones destroyed, like the Soviet Union cutting out the faces in photographs of those who fell from favor.

Patricia is sitting on the couch, looking the way she used to before a big volleyball game: ready, a little scared, but excited for the thrill. After some extremely chummy chitchat—you would have thought they'd seen each other last week for lunch, but that is why Jessica is number one in her field—Jessica gets Patricia to tell her what happened. For a moment, I can almost see Patricia in Pamela's office rehearsing for this interview the way we used to study for our science exams. Patricia describes the months of dating bliss, the fairy-princess wedding party she had always wanted, then the mutual realization that they just weren't right for each other, after all. And the decision they'd made together just to be friends and move on. But she's stronger for it now, more clear, only wishes him well.

Jessica nods her head, as she has been doing through the whole interview with a look of absolute care and concern. "That's a lot to go through together," she says.

"Yeah," Patricia says, "but now it's time to move on." I can almost hear her publicist reminding Patricia to work in the theme of the show, to let it seem to have originated with her.

"Uh-huh," Jessica says, as a huge picture of Zane and Nicki Coleman descends silently on the back wall of the set. Then Jessica asks Patricia to turn around. Patricia looks out at the audience with a small nervous laugh, as if hoping one of them will clue her in, then she looks behind her. And stays there frozen. When she finally faces forward again, she is smiling, but her eyes are doing that squinty thing where I know she is holding back tears.

"It's okay," Jessica says, putting her hand on top of Patricia's. "It happens to a lot of us. That's why we're here." Then after the slightest, but most effective pause. "It was a shock, wasn't it?

It is hard to tell whether Jessica meant the breakup or the

picture, but like any good prosecutor, she leaves it open to the witness to interpret, and Patricia stumbles straight in.

Tears come to her eyes as she tells Jessica what it was like: the shock, the betrayal, the worry that it was all her fault. "I hear ya, honey," Jessica says at soothing intervals, "I hear ya."

When Patricia is done telling her tale of woe, Jessica wraps an arm around her, and Patricia gives her the same appreciative and adoring smile that she used to give the coach of the high school volleyball team that she was captain of. Then Jessica half turns her body toward the audience and looking out at them, says, "Anyone out there relate?" She could be leading an army to charge.

The audience goes wild, clapping and shouting their identification, a seething mass of sisterhood, ready for blood. Patricia looks at them as if they have just given her an Academy Award.

"I want to hear some of those stories of yours," Jessica says to the women, who look ready to confide all. "But first, we're gonna take a short break. And remember," she says, looking straight into the camera for her signature line and smile, "keep breathing."

Without even thinking, I immediately click off the TV and look around. Then I realize that no one can see me and even if they did, all I am doing is watching a friend on a talk show—but a friend getting ambushed and used on a talk show. I wonder whether Patricia wants to run off the set right now. And what Pamela, who is surely standing in the wings, is thinking about what just happened. Was that on her publicity agenda? How can Patricia even continue to go through with this? If I were her, I'd want to slap that ratings-craving Jessica across the face and walk away. I don't even want to turn the TV back on. I feel as if I've been listening to stuff that I have no right to hear, and Patricia didn't even say anything I didn't know before. Jesus, it was so slimy the way Jessica got it out of her. Maybe I am really grateful that I'm not a star and no one cares about whom I've slept with.

I could just not watch it anymore and when I talk to Patricia, act as if I had seen the whole thing. It's not like she'll need a blow-by-blow from me. Mostly, she'll just want to hear good things. And after what she's just been through, she should, the poor thing. Jesus, I can't even imagine what's going through her head now. Say as little as possible to this conniving woman and get the fuck out of here, is what it should be telling her.

I decide to go fix another cup of tea and just catch the end. I don't need to listen to a bunch of women that I don't know and will never see again bare their souls on national TV. And they're not even getting paid. At least, when I have stripped, physically and/or emotionally, for a role, I've gotten good money for it. Then I suddenly wonder which is worse.

After I fix my tea, I take it and a chocolate chip cookie from Mani's back to the couch and turn on the TV. The camera is on a woman in the audience who is crying. Her shoulders are hunched forward as they move up and down, and loud, liquidy breathing can be heard, as Jessica, with her arm around the woman, keeps saying, "It's good that you shared." The entire set is silent. Everyone is entranced by this woman and her grief. It is as if Patricia is not even there. Then out of the stillness, a voice is heard.

"I know just how you feel."

Immediately, the camera on Patricia picks up the shot and her face fills the screen. Then the screen splits, and another camera shows the audience with all eyes on Patricia, waiting for her to say more. The crying woman has stopped and is looking at Patricia as if she just found out that they are sisters. Jessica has started moving silently away from the woman, down the stairs, and onto the stage, as if she doesn't want to distract Patricia into not divulging more, but can barely contain herself from running to get next to her.

"When I was ten," Patricia says, and the screen immediately fills up again with a close-up of her, "my best friend and I were both molested by the same guy, and since then, it's been real hard for me to trust men."

My breath is kicked out in a gasp that is as loud as the audience's. It looks as if a neutron bomb went off on the set. I can almost see the air rise up in one collective shock, mushroom out at the top, then rain down in a torrent of exclamations. Even Jessica herself looks momentarily nonplussed, but recovering quickly, practically leaps to the couch, puts her hand over Patricia's, and, while trying to appear as if her entire career doesn't depend upon moments like these, says, "Tell us about it."

My mind feels pinned to a slot, as if my body can move, but my mind is stuck in a little, dark slot where Patricia said the words that we swore we never would. But my eyes must be attached to my mind, too, because I am unable to move them off the TV, off Patricia's face that is filling the screen, and off the scene she is describing of what happened to her, but also to me. To me. The things we swore we never would tell.

"I've tried to hide this my whole life," Patricia says, after she has told everyone what happened, or her version, at least. "But I want to live in the truth now. Every day, I carry around so much pain and vulnerableness from this, and I just want to be the powerful me." The women respond with a resounding cheer.

"You are powerful, honey," Jessica says to her. "Isn't she?" Then she holds up Patricia's hand in a victory wave, as the camera pans the audience, which is on its feet, clapping and stomping its lifelong affection.

The diet soda commercial is almost over before I realize that I'm no longer watching *Jessica*. I look at the remote control, irrationally hoping for some kind of erase button as if life is TIVO and this whole episode can be deleted. I click off the TV.

She told. She actually, finally told.

I look around for a moment, my mind blank but on hyperalert, then I realize that I am waiting to be attacked. As if the walls of my home will be beaten down and crowds of men, all looking like Billy, will come in, and it will be the end of me.

It is the end of me.

When I was ten, my best friend and I were both molested by the same guy.

Molested. To put that word on it. As if that can describe what he did to her. Or to me, for that matter. I got a haircut. I was punished. I was molested. Do any of those words even begin to explain what that experience really was?

And *ten. Best friend.* How many people know that Patricia and I were friends back then? Only practically every person in our lives, thanks to her big, fat mouth, always going around at parties and stuff, yapping, "Fiona and I have been best friends since first grade." Jesus, I could just absolutely kill her. What the fuck was she—okay, but calm down. There's no way that anyone in L.A. watches that show. Even though it has the highest ratings of all daytime TV. But, I mean, surely they're all at—okay, if there is any city where the majority of people don't work nine-to-five jobs and can be home watching TV, it is L.A. Fuck.

But maybe they don't watch it anyway, and the only thing the press is going to care about is Patricia's story. It's not like they'll be looking for me. So I just have to hope and pray that no one we know heard that "best friend" part and it can be just all about her. Not even to mention people in Louisiana seeing it because what the fuck do they have to do all day long? Jesus fucking God. Just out it came. I wonder if she even thought about it first. And the worst part is that it is so Patricia that she did that. What the fuck have I been thinking having that secret with her? Like I had a choice about it, like Billy asked me first. And I love how she very conveniently left out the fact that he was her cousin. God forbid she let it be known that it was basically incest for her and that she comes from goddamn scum.

I stare into space, shaking my head. The silence in the house suddenly feels ominous, as if it is meant to be broken, but badly. Then I hear the sound that I realize I have been dreading. My phone begins to ring.

Chapter 31

THE SOMNOLENT SOUND of the crickets and frogs pressed upon the tree house almost as much as the August heat. I had noticed the tree house a few summers before when Patricia and I had gone into the neighboring field to pick wild blackberries. It was high up in a clump of trees, far back from Uncle Dave's property. It looked as if it had been there for years. The wood had weathered to a soft gray, and two of the slats that were nailed into the tree for steps had broken in half, so were hanging crazily down like a broken zipper.

I had forgotten it was there.

"Best place to see the stars," Billy said to Patricia and me. "And there's supposed to be a meteorite tonight. Y'all ever seen a meteorite before?"

I didn't even know what one was, so I figured I hadn't seen one. It sounded like one of those things that Daddy would talk about at the dinner table with my mother that I never understood, like amortize. But since Billy was talking about it, and it was gonna be in the sky, I figured it wouldn't be boring.

Patricia looked at me.

"I wanna go," I said. "Let's go see."

"What if the tree house breaks while we're in it?" Patricia said.

Billy laughed. "Can't. I helped build the damn thing. Eight years ago when I was about y'all's age. Me n' Rodney from next door and his daddy, we all used the lumber they had left from that big kennel out there they built. Ain't no way old man Cooper gonna let them dogs have nothin' but the best. Hell, his own house won't stand up as good."

I looked at Patricia.

"Okay, but Momma's coming for us in an hour or so."

But even as Patricia said it, we both knew we'd be sitting there in that kitchen, waiting for Vicky finally to remember where we were and to haul ass out there, pull up on the road, and beep her horn for us to come, so she wouldn't have to see her ex-husband's family and remember what she'd married into.

"Okay, then," Billy said. "Let's just get us some refreshments, and out we go."

He turned and went into the kitchen through the sliding door. His jeans fit tight and smooth on his legs until they flared out over a pair of worn, dark brown, pointy toed cowboy boots. Roach-stompers, I had heard Patricia's Uncle Dave call them, because they could kill the bugs even in the corner of a room.

I watched Billy put ice into three tall red plastic cups and pour Coca-Cola into all of them. Then he looked around the empty kitchen, and through the open doorway into the den where all the grown-ups had migrated. The kids were scattered about the house or in the backyard catching fireflies. As Billy turned back, he saw me watching him. He smiled, then quickly opened the cabinet above the refrigerator, clinked through some bottles, grabbed a small one filled with a dark brown liquid, and slipped it into his back pocket before picking up the three plastic cups, which he pressed together like a triangle in his warm, strong hands.

"Okay, then," he said, as he stepped through the open sliding glass door. "Let's do it."

The tree house had a roof. On the whole walk over, through the thick-grassed and shimmering field, I kept remembering it as an open platform, like a ship moored and caught in the trees whose deck we would lie on to look at the heavens above. I imagined lying in between Patricia and Billy, the flare of his jeans just touching my calf, and watching the meteorite, giant in the sky, flashing and sparkling and bursting its starlight upon us.

"You go up first," Billy said to Patricia as we stood at the bottom of the oak tree, its massive canopy so wide, tall, and long that it almost reached the ground in some places. "So's I can steady these steps for you."

Patricia kneeled on the ground, retied her shoes, then scrambled up the wooden slats, and swung herself up into the opening.

"Your turn." Billy smiled at me. He smelled sharp and sweet, like cut grass with honey thrown in. I realized it was cologne. My daddy never wore any, and I wondered whether Billy kept his bottles lined up on a dresser the way my momma did.

With his hand, he straightened the lower slat that was hanging diagonally down, and as I put my foot on it, he held the back of my ankle with his other hand and kept it there until I pushed off to climb the next step.

When I got to the top and was inside, Billy whistled up into the darkness, and I looked down to see him holding up one of the plastic cups. He pulled himself up a few slats and handed the cups to me one by one, then was suddenly in the tree house with us, his boyness seizing the space.

"Je-sus," he said, looking around. "Haven't sat up here in a coon's age."

The tree house floor was smooth and wide. Walls on all four sides went halfway up to the roof, then stopped, like a porch that had been torn from a house and plopped down in the branches. Billy leaned over to a wooden box that was built into one of the corners of the room. He lifted the clasp, pushed some things around, then pulled out a fat candle and some kitchen matches, and let the lid shut close. He struck a match on the bottom of his boot, lit the candle, and set it down in the center of the box.

"There, now."

Then he reached into his back pocket and pulled out the bottle. In the small light, I could see the word *Rum* written on the label, and I thought of a ditty from one of my fairy books that the pixies would sing while they worked, "A-rum-a-tee, a-rum-a-tee-tum, a-rum-a-rum-a-rum-a-tee-tum."

Patricia was giggling. It was hard to see the stars what with the tree house roof, and the oak branches so thick and close with leaves. But there was one good-sized patch of sky, so we were lying on our backs, looking out through the opening, trying to glimpse a meteorite. The rum in our Cokes was good, better even than the way Billy said it would be. It was a hot candy, fire sweet, but gentle like a really warm bath for the inside. I felt smooth and floaty, as if the night sky had moved into my head. Billy tipped the bottle into our cups again. As we drank, Patricia started another round of giggling.

Then suddenly Billy jumped up, moved to the side of the tree house, and pointing out with his hand, said, "Look-it, there's one. A surefire meteorite. I'll be goddamned."

Patricia and I scrambled up to see, knocking into each other as we did, which caused Patricia to fold over in giggles again. When I reached the side of the tree house, Billy put his hand low on my back, and with his other arm reaching out into the dark, tried to direct my eyes to see. It took me a second to get my vision to adjust.

The night was its own explosion. I couldn't see all those stars from my house in Lake Charles because of the street lights and the big buildings lit up just around the bend on the lake. But here they were, and I suddenly knew that they had been there the whole time waiting for me to find them: to see them, and for them to see me. Clearly—like Billy.

Billy's hand was warm and wide on me. It could have been the back of a chair. I leaned into it a bit and it stayed solid, not moving. I wanted to sit into it.

"You know whatcha supposed to do when you see a meteorite, don't cha?" he said, his head tilted to the side, and looked down at me through his lashes.

I stared straight ahead, into the sky, into the stars that were winking and smiling their blessing at me.

"You kiss somebody. So's to make a wish. And it'll come true. 'Cause of that kiss."

I could feel him still looking at me as I looked at the stars, then the stars seemed to slip and I felt them shower down upon me, and move into me as his lips closed on mine and then his tongue entered my mouth.

My stomach grabbed at me, and if it had been my legs, I would have run. But my legs were soft, as if at any moment they were going to tumble down the way the stars just had. My stomach tried to make my body go, but it wouldn't move, and I didn't know which part to listen to.

"Whatchy'all doin'?" Patricia suddenly yelled.

Billy broke away and, removing his hand from my back, turned to his cousin and squatted down next to her.

"Just makin' a little meteorite wish with a kiss. Ain't you never done that before? That's the kind'll come true."

Patricia looked at him, and then at me. My mouth was still bursting with the firestorm inside. Stars had replaced my eyes, so the edges of everything seemed to twinkle and blur in the low light.

"Here's all," Billy said, then he sat down and put his mouth on hers. Patricia sat very still, like in a game of swinging statues that she was determined to win. But then I saw her mouth open, saw her lean in, then the light got too bright, and I turned my eyes back to the night to let more stars in.

I had been counting, but couldn't remember what number I was on. Probably because I wasn't really using numbers, but some kind of special star system to determine how many were still up there and how many had come into my head. There were blanks in the sky from where the stars had been. I wondered whether anything would ever fill them again.

Then I heard Patricia. It wasn't a word, was hardly a sound, it was more a movement and a breath and a thought all at once. I turned around and saw that Billy was still kissing her, but her shirt was up, and the tanned flatness of her chest was the same color as his hand, which was moving slowly and circularly on it.

She jumped up and back all at once. She wiped her mouth

with one hand, while tugging down her shirt with the other, and looked at Billy the way she had looked that afternoon I walked in on her and Mike.

Then she looked at me. She could have been Vicky. Her eyes were a silent lecture. I suddenly wanted to stay up past my bedtime, eat only dessert, and tear something apart just to know that I could.

Patricia could tell that I wasn't going to leave with her. She went to the opening, turned around, and as she lowered herself onto the top slat, gave me one last glance, then disappeared down into the dark.

I looked at Billy, then turned back to the stars. And waited to see what would happen.

Chapter 32

"WHO TOLD YOU?"

"Janice. One of her friends who also used to be an assistant, so is still part of that gossip tree, saw the show and had to tell Janice before it got on the Internet."

"Did she say something about me?"

"Who? Janice or the friend?"

"Either of them. Do people know?"

"She told Janice it happened to Patricia and her best friend. That's what's so creepy, Janice kept saying. But I can't remember whether Janice knows you grew up with Patricia or not."

"Jesus God." I close my eyes and lean my head back on the couch. I haven't moved from here all afternoon. I let the phone go to voice mail, didn't even look at the caller ID. Didn't turn on the lights when the sun set around five, just waited in the darkness for Neil to come home, and wondered who would be the one to tell him.

"Do you want to tell me about it?" Neil says, finally sitting down and putting his hand on mine.

"Not really."

"Fiona."

"What?"

"I thought we told each other everything."

"There isn't enough time or memory to tell each other everything."

Neil just looks at me.

"And I did anyway, tell you everything. Just not about—this."

"It's the biggest one to skip."

"I skipped it with everyone. Why should I tell? It happened. A long time ago. I barely remember it and—" I immediately can tell he doesn't believe that part. "I don't see what it has to do with anything now."

"Are you kidding me? Miss Emotional-Memory, Method-Trained Actress doesn't see what this has to do with anything? Has this made you totally nuts?"

I grab the throw from the back of the couch and wrap it tightly around me. "I'm not going to talk about it. I never have, and it wouldn't make any difference if I did now."

Neil just looks at me, shaking his head. I pull the throw up to the top of my nose and tuck my head in, focusing on my knees. The baby starts jabbing me in the ribs, and for a horrible second, I think that she wants me to tell, but I remember her wordless state and wish that I could be like that, too. Then the thought of someone like Billy getting to her makes me almost grab Neil and tell him everything all at once, including for him to get a fucking gun and stay with our daughter at all times.

"Wait just a minute," Neil suddenly says. "It was him, wasn't it? That guy at Patricia's wedding party, her cousin. That's why you were so weird about him, and he was so obsessed with you."

"He wasn't obsessed."

"Yeah, and Jeffrey Dahmer wasn't into boys."

"Neil."

"You need to talk about this. I saw how you were with him. You were totally freaked out. Whatever he did, and what a sick fuck, you need to tell me."

"I'm not telling anyone, I told you. No one needs to know."

"Except Patricia."

"Because it happened with her, sort of."

"Fiona, I'm your husband. When are you going to start trusting me more than her?"

I look at him for a second then have to look away.

"I do, I just— Look, I've never told anyone for twenty-five years, so I don't see how telling you now is going to change anything."

Neil is silent for a moment, then his eyes are sad on mine.

"Just our marriage," he says.

Then he gets up and leaves the room.

Fuck.

"I could fucking kill her. None of this would even be happening if it weren't for her big goddamn mouth."

"No," Sarah says. "None of this would be happening if you had been honest with your husband from the beginning."

"Honest? Patricia and I promised to keep it a secret. But I guess I'm the only one who knows what that means."

"That's a separate issue you're going to have to deal with with her."

"If she ever fucking calls me because I sure as hell am not

calling her. And I bet she's too chicken to. She knows what she's done."

"Okay, but right now, we're talking about you and Neil."

A car with a bad muffler drives down the street.

"Where are you? Did you go out?" Sarah suddenly sounds concerned, as if I might be pulling into a bar.

"No, I'm sitting on my front steps. I didn't want Neil to hear me. Not that he would because he went to sleep. At least, the light is off in our bedroom. Not that he told me good-night. We haven't said anything to each other since our blowup."

"You need to tell him."

"Why?"

"Because he's your husband and this is your marriage we're talking about. And not telling him is giving this thing much more power than it deserves."

"All it has had is power, especially since I found out we're having a girl."

A couple in their early twenties comes out of the house across the street and starts walking to their car. Despite the chilled December air, she is without a coat, and is wrapping herself around her boyfriend for warmth.

"I just want it to go away," I say. "And it had, that's the worst part. Everything was going fine. And then suddenly it's been like the whole goddamn thing has just been exploding in my face. Like it won't fit inside me anymore—and has decided to come out."

"That's the best thing. You're ready for it to, or this wouldn't be happening."

"Was I ready to be—whatever—by Billy when it happened?"

"You know what I meant."

"I know, I'm sorry, I just—"

The boyfriend starts up the ignition on the car. It is from the 1950s, and I watch as the girl slides across the seat to sit close to him.

"Feel like I'm being ripped apart."

Chapter 33

EVEN WITH THE ATROCIOUS PAIN, at no point have I thought that I can't do this. In between the minute-long contractions, during the two minutes of Thank God, pain-freeness, I don't want drugs and I don't think that I can't do this.

But I do want it over with.

Neil is holding my hand. We have barely spoken to each other in the past three days, and when we did, it was freighted with an embarrassed anger, and I couldn't tell whether it had started with him or me. But it didn't matter because it had grown between us, bigger than my tummy, like an awful child begat long ago.

I had been hoping that everything would magically clear up, especially before the birth. Neil would realize that the past didn't matter, that our life together is in the future, and things could just go back to the way they were before.

But before what? Because suddenly it was as if that memory had always been alive, living with us, and had never not been part of our life, the way everyone says once the baby is born, it'll be hard to remember what things were like before.

Another contraction comes up and my stomach grips down hard. At least, I think it is my stomach, my stomach that has become my entire body, and is trying to open me up while clenching me so tight that I feel as if I'm going to explode and compress all at once.

Then it stops, and I turn to the side of the bed that Neil isn't on and throw up. The nurse jumps up from her chair to clean it up and brings over a bed pan. Neil hands me a bottle of water.

We had talked about having Bach playing, "The Goldberg Variations," so when we got here to the labor/delivery/recovery room at Cedars-Sinai, he put the CD on, but the sound was too bright, like lights going off in my head, so I asked him to turn it off. I also wanted to ask the nurse to turn off the cologne she was wearing. I couldn't believe that she was wearing some; considering she's in obstetrics; then I figured that I couldn't ask her that because how would she remove it? But its sharp and sweet smell is making me want to tear my skin off.

I look at Neil and he squeezes my hand. I am naked, on my hands and knees, and as I lean forward on the birthing ball, he starts rubbing my lower back. But his eyes are halfway distant, as if the front part of him is with me, but the rest is not. I wish I had the energy and privacy to say something to him. Then I realize that he only wants to hear one thing, the one thing I won't tell him.

My body seizes up again and I try to breathe into the pain, the pain that is everywhere all at once, forcing me down, and I try to relax into it, the way I learned in class, but it is like trying to relax in an electrical storm. I am being knocked out and am floundering from the flashes of light and the sensations on my skin. The pain has taken me over.

I get a reprieve, throw up, sip some more water, and back it comes again. But this time, I am being torn wide open. I want to push this pain off me, out of my body and off my skin. I raise my head up to look at the ceiling, and the lights start to blur, edges of them raining down on me and into my mind, and the nurse's cologne moves across the room to enter me, and the pain is clenching me tight yet ripping open my belly and groin, and they are everything all at once, my whole being is belly and groin, and suddenly underneath this birth, an older agony that has never been delivered comes roaring up.

"I can't do this."

For the last hour and a half, on every push, my mind has been filled with one loud, tremendous, and all-encompassing thought, "I can't do this." Finally, I said it.

Neil immediately looks alarmed. Dr. Walker stares up at me from where she is perched on her stool at the foot of the bed. I am holding onto the top of a birthing bar; my legs are wrapped around its sides, so that I am sitting up; and it is very clear to me that I can't do this.

"Yes, you can, Fiona. You don't have a choice." Dr. Walker's voice is sharp, not the honeyed smile she has always had. "And you're almost there. Now, push and keep pushing while I count, and don't stop until I tell you to. One, two, three, four," she says, as I bear down hard. Then I feel those old sensations rising up again, and my body clenches and stops.

"No, don't stop, keep—okay," Dr. Walker says. "Just relax."

I let out my breath.

"You did so well with the labor without even an epidural," she says. "I thought the pushing was going to be easy for you."

Neil takes my hand. I can't look at him.

"You can do it," he says.

"No, I can't," my head tells me inside.

"You've gotten this far." He rubs my hand.

"Fine, but I can't go any further and I won't," my head continues. "Because if I do, I'll die."

Then a contraction comes up again, and Dr. Walker starts her counting, and I can't believe she thinks I can make it to ten because just trying to push for as long as four or five makes me feel as if I am suffocating and being pressed down and turned out and don't they know that this shouldn't be happening?

"Okay," Dr. Walker says, after not even five counts.

I know I can stop, so I close my eyes.

"Just relax, Fiona." She sounds disappointed.

I want to tell her not to have any goddamn mother fucking feelings about my birth, but I am too humiliated. All I can hear in my head is "I can't do this," over and over again. And the worst part is that I agree with it because I am too afraid of what will come out if I am able to do this.

Neil tries to take my hand again, his wedding ring pressing against me, but I pull mine away.

Another contraction rises up, and I hold my breath, pushing down hard, but this time, I don't even make it to four counts before I stop.

"Okay," Dr. Walker says. I can hear her sliding her rings up and down the chain that they are on. "But if this doesn't get any better, we're gonna have to use the vacuum."

The vacuum? No one ever talked about a vacuum. How fucking scary and draconian a punishment is that? Like she thinks I can't even push my own daughter out. Like she thinks I'm not female enough. Like she can just decide all on her own what it will be like, and I have to go along because she's in control, but I'm the one who has to live with it, has to walk around an unwomaned female, and meanwhile, fuck her, I'm more female just like this, unbirthed and stuck, than all of her fucking ideas about what it should look like for me to be a girl.

Then suddenly, I feel an urge that I didn't before and a push comes up, all on its own, though part of me, and not of them, but of my baby, and something else that was always there, but just covered up.

"Look!" Dr. Walker says. "Your daughter!"

I look into the mirror that Dr. Walker had set up at the end of the bed, and there she is. The top of her head is visible and it glistens like fairy-painted dew.

"Wow," Neil says.

I reach down and touch the soft head. Then another push comes, and it is as if the past came swooshing out ahead of her, and my daughter is being carried aloft on a future that will take her places that I have never been.

And suddenly I understand that she isn't me. Was inside me, is part of what makes up me, but she is not me. She has her own separate life, with her own separate birth that isn't about what I need to get rid of.

Then in one push, my daughter's head comes out, and on two more, she is free.

I look into Neil's eyes and see our baby in them as he looks at her. Dr. Walker puts her to my breast, covers her with a warmed blanket, and helps me to help my daughter latch on. I put my hand out to Neil's and he takes it, holding it tight, but I know that I still have another delivery to go through with him.

Chapter 34

THE DAWN LIGHT through the east-facing window into my room at Cedars-Sinai could be packaged and sold to aging film stars. It comes in all once, soft and golden-pink, as if reflecting off newborn skin. I have been awake all night, ever since we came out of the labor/delivery/recovery room at one a.m. Thank God, Cedars only has private rooms. I had no idea how quiet a hospital could get until there was nothing to listen to at four a.m., except my own head.

Neil is asleep on the daybed on the side of the room. Aislynn is sleeping on my chest, so I ease her gently down onto the bed and push pillows all around. I swing my legs out over the side of the bed and try to stand up for the second time since giving birth. I waver for a moment, but by holding on to the railing, I am able to stay upright. I take the few steps over to the daybed, sit down, and put my hand on my husband.

"Neil?"

He opens a drowsy eye.

"I'm ready to talk."

Chapter 35

BILLY'S TONGUE WAS IN ME. I didn't know how long it had been. The tree house had started spinning right after Patricia left, then my knees buckled and I was on the floor, and my body so squishy and the floor so hard made me feel even more off balance. Then Billy came over and kneeling next to me, lifted my torso and rested it on the top of his legs. He tilted his head, looked down at me through his lashes, and took my hand in his. His heavy high school class ring pressed against my skin. It was cool and bright with its newness. His finger looked as if it was still getting used to wearing it. I touched it with my other hand, which made him smile, and then he began kissing me.

It was like running into the street, and playing sick to get out of school, and lying to Louise, and all those things all at once, except more, because I had a feeling that this was permanent somehow. Like a pixie haircut, but for the inside, but opposite, since this was making me a girl again. And even more of one than before. I wanted to know what I'd be like when it was done.

Billy moved my shirt up with his hand. It made me think of

Dr. Taylor, with his wide pink face and white hair fringe. I almost expected the cold stethoscope, but Billy's hand was warm, and its circular motions somehow made the tree house stop spinning around and made the stars in me sparkle brightly.

So this was all it was gonna be, like Dr. Taylor, but to make me feel nice. And I was feeling nice, nice and sleepy, and like if I kept lying there, then when I woke up, the awful spell would be off, and I'd be a girl again. Like I was once upon a time, but now would be ever after.

Billy took my hand, put it on his jeans, and covered it with his. My fingers and arm immediately stiffened, but his jeans felt like the ones I had had to wear all summer long, and I had a flash of happiness when I remembered that soon I'd be done with them. There was a bump in Billy's jeans and as I realized what it was, he wrapped his other arm around me, unbuttoned my shorts, and slid his hand in.

My stomach froze up and my legs turned to ice. I tried to kick myself up, but Billy's arm clenched closer around, re-straining me down. His cologne went into my nose, suffocat-ing me with its grip, and his mouth was mashed so hard against mine that it pushed my head all the way back. Then his fingers got themselves in me and as they moved in and out, his palm and thumb pressed down, keeping me from moving.

I tried to open my eyes, thinking that would somehow help me get free, but his blond hair was on my forehead and against my cheek, like the long hair I wanted so desperately, so I shut them again and tried to make a sound through my tongue-filled mouth, as my legs kicked around.

His fingers were moving faster; it was like being torn apart; there was no room for what he was doing, no space inside, but each jab spread me open wider, each withdrawal stretched me out, until it felt as if my whole body was going to come apart, when suddenly my stomach bolted and threw everything up.

Billy made a giant leap backward to standing upright, causing me to slip to the floor, then as he cursed and spit out the vomit that had gone into his mouth, I jumped up, dashed to the opening, and half-stepping/half-falling, slid to the ground, then tore across the field under the bright starry night, my legs of ice coming back to life as I raced away from the tree house and the lights of the kitchen came into sight.

Chapter 36

"HOW'D YOU FIND OUT?"

"I got the group e-mail from Neil this morning," Patricia says, "though I guess you took me off the phone tree."

"He must have. I haven't called anyone."

"You shouldn't."

"I don't think so either."

She stares at me from her chair. The remains of my dinner are still on the high table wheeled next to my hospital bed. Aislynn is asleep on me. When Patricia entered the room two minutes ago, it was in a burst of exclamations over my beautiful baby girl. I wondered whether she could even see my daughter past her barrage of ready compliments. They were practically a shield for her to hide behind, but not big enough.

"So," she says.

I look down at my daughter and smooth the blanket around her neck.

"I know what you must be thinking," Patricia says.

"About what?" I still don't look at her.

"About—oh, come on, Fiona, about what happened."

"A lot's happened. Like just last night, I gave birth. Is that what you want to talk about?"

"No, I mean, yes, I mean, look—" Patricia is silent for a moment, then smooths down her coiffed hair. "Do I have to spell it out for you?"

"I guess so." I am being horrible, but I don't care.

"Okay, *Jessica*, all right? Is that clear enough?" Her eyes have a challenge in them like in high school when she'd tell me about the fights she'd have with Vicky.

I look back down at my baby.

"It came out. I didn't plan for it to; it just did. But it's not like anyone knew it was you."

"No, no one knew. Except half of all Lake Charles, and practically every goddamn person here that we both know thanks to you and your big fucking mouth constantly having to yap about how we grew up together and have always been best friends. Did you think that no one watches that stupid piece of shit of a show? My goddamn phone's been ringing off the hook, and not about my baby girl."

Patricia stares at me. Her mouth is tucked in, in that tight little frown, and she looks cowed and defiant all at once.

"I mean, what the fuck were you thinking? Did we promise to keep it a secret or what?"

"I guess I realized that some secrets shouldn't be kept."

"How very convenient for you, but that wasn't for you to decide. Part of it was mine. Frankly, most of it. Go ahead, spill your own goddamn secret, but why the fuck did you have to drag me into it?"

Patricia looks down into her lap.

"And acting as if the same thing happened to both of us, as if yours was some big horrible thing. 'I've been carrying around all this pain and vulnerableness from this.' Oh, please. Don't make me throw up. The only thing painful about it for you was that he was your first cousin—not that you happened to include that little detail."

"Fiona, it was not okay what he did to me."

"No, it wasn't, but it really wasn't okay what he did to me after you left."

"You could have come, too."

Her eyes pin mine.

"That's what you're feeling so shitty about. It's not that I told; it's that you could've left." She looks at Aislynn, and then back at me. "Why didn't you?"

Her words shoot straight into my stomach, tearing it apart inside.

"You know what, Patricia? Fuck you."

Patricia pulls her mouth farther in and down, then gets up.

"Okay, I'm gonna go."

"Okay."

She hesitates at the foot of my bed. Aislynn is still asleep, as if she exists in a separate realm from the one we are talking in. Thank God.

"She's beautiful. I'm happy for you."

"Thanks," I say, looking away.

A second later, I hear my hospital room door click shut.

Chapter 37

I AM TWO WEEKS IN AND SO FAR, I am loving being on baby time. Before Aislynn was born, people kept asking whether we were going to get a baby nurse, one of the de rigueur accoutrements of having a baby in Hollywood, to stay with us in the beginning "to get us over the hump," as they said, but all I could wonder was what hump were they talking about? Though, really, I knew that they meant the "up in the middle of the night" and the "sleeping only two to three hours at a stretch" hump. But what I didn't understand was why they thought having a stranger in my house twenty-four/seven to take care of the baby while I pretended to be on some just-totally-relaxed time was going to be helpful since, one, the nurse would have to leave eventually, and, two, then I wouldn't be in sync with my baby and would have to scramble to get onto her rhythm.

Because isn't the whole point right now just to be with and take care of my daughter? As far as I can tell, the very particular physical state that I am in from just having birthed a baby is mostly there to remind me and everyone else to leave me alone, so that I will do nothing except be with my baby. And all this time that I've been feeding her, and holding her, and learning her little cues of what she needs is like the best improv I have ever been in. The concentration is complete. The objective is pure. And I am playing off the most direct partner I've ever had. Now if only other people would leave us alone, it'd be great.

Like Patricia, for one. Not that she is here, or has called, or has come over since I saw her at the hospital less than twenty-four hours after I gave birth, but she is in my head, present all the time, her eyes and mouth asking me that same question over and over, "Why didn't you?" and I just want her to leave me alone so I can forget all about that again.

Not that other people are making it easy to forget. I've gotten e-mails and phone calls from people I haven't heard from in ages, and after the requisite transparent and insincere chit-chat at the beginning, they inevitably ask the big question, "Weren't you best friends with Patricia way back then?" In a weird way, the timing is almost good that Aislynn arrived right after it happened because I have this ready-made excuse not to answer the phone and just delete all those e-mails.

Except I couldn't delete my mother's visit. Not that she called after Patricia was on the talk show, even though I am sure that at least one of her friends told her about it. Or if not one of them, then definitely this woman that my mother only and always sees at Clarkson's, the neighborhood grocery store, who wears her hair in one long braid and is obsessed with Patricia's career, which drives my mother up the goddamn wall because if there is one thing she can't stand more than the spotlight not being on her, it is the spotlight being on her daughter's best friend, and indirectly Vicky.

So I'm pretty positively certain that she knows. But as Neil said, right after I give birth to my first child is not exactly the time to mention something like that, to which I replied, yes, but she had three days before I delivered to call about it, and besides any mother who shows up two weeks after her grandchild's birth clearly is not very concerned about making the baby a priority.

So even though my mother must know that I was the one it also happened to, I doubt we'll ever talk about it. And that is fine. I barely wanted to tell Neil, much less have a conversation with my mother about it. Though I did feel better after I told him. And I was kind of shocked because it wasn't so terrible and scary after all. He just held me, and didn't ask yucky questions, and told me how brave I am.

Not that I feel brave, especially with my mother coming. And alone, without my father for her to compete for all his attention and win. But maybe she figured with a baby in the room, she might finally lose.

"Crisis at the bank," my mother said, when she told me about her solo travel plans. "And besides, at times like these, men just get in the way." As if suddenly she was some girly girl who was looking forward to female bonding over the baby.

But I'm just going to focus on my daughter while she's here and get through these few days, and then she'll be gone and some other celebrity will do or say something astonishing, but not really surprising, and everyone will forget all about what Patricia said, and I will, too.

I hope.

I switch Aislynn to my other breast, as Neil comes into the living room with a glass of water for me. I haven't been nursing in Aislynn's room very much, supposedly because it is easier to be in other parts of the house, but really because the fabric reminds me of Patricia.

"How're you doing?"

"You know. One hand great," I say, motioning to Aislynn, "on the other— What time is she coming?"

"She didn't say. I told her you were sleeping, and she said she'd take a cab over from her hotel sometime tomorrow."

"God forbid I have warning."

My mother sweeps into my living room as if she is making her entrance at a movie premiere. She has been sweeping into rooms this way my entire life, and I suddenly wonder whether that had something to do with my becoming an actress. Hollywood isn't the only place where people act like stars.

For the past twenty years, she has worn her hair in a chin-length bob, the style she let the pixie cut grow out into. With her recent face-lift, in a well-lit (i.e., dim) room, she could almost pass for the age she was when she first got that haircut. As it is, the diffused morning light through my front windows knocks off a good ten years.

"Darling," she says, with her arms opened wide.

I almost turn around to see who she is talking to. Her greeting seems much too effusive to be just for me.

But I step forward into her arms and receive her air kisses and hug. Then she steps back to appraise me.

"Well, other than needing a little lipstick and hair combing, you're holding up." She nods, as if relieved. As if my doing so were for her. "You look just the way I did. I barely gained the weight I was supposed to with you and no one could even tell two weeks after I delivered that I'd ever been pregnant."

I wonder whether she thinks that is supposed to make me feel good. God forbid, I affect my mother's life, much less body, while I'm in her womb.

"Well, let's see her. Is she asleep?"

No, she's wide awake, in her room upstairs, staring at the ceiling for hours on end, all on her own. She's two weeks old, for God's sake; of course she's asleep, if I'm not holding her.

"She's right here." I point to the Moses's basket on the floor next to the couch. Aislynn is lying inside, surrounded by rolled up blankets so she'll fit snugly in. It is still hard to believe that two weeks ago, she was inside me. As I stand with my mother, looking down at my daughter, it is even harder to believe that I was ever inside her.

"Well, she's beautiful, as I knew she would be. She got those good Connor genes; I can already tell. I hope Neil doesn't mind that his daughter doesn't look like him. Men are so funny about that. I could never understand why."

"Yeah, well, he trusts I haven't screwed around on him."

An annoyed alarm rears up behind my mother's face. "And what in God's name is that supposed to mean?"

I suddenly realize that she thinks I am somehow referring to Patricia's announcement on the talk show, as if a sexual encounter I had years ago qualifies as screwing around on my husband now.

For a moment, it is all I can do not to yell, "I've fucked a lot of men, Mother. Starting with, kind of, Patricia's cousin when I was ten, if being raped with a hand job can be considered fucking. What were you thinking, that I was a total nonsexual being? Or is that why you made me dress like a boy for an entire summer, so I would be. You must've hated when that was over."

My mother is staring at me, on guard for what I'm going to say next.

"That, uh—you know, the whole point of the baby looking like the father is to assure paternity."

"Oh." Her anger begins to empty out from the middle of her face. "Of course. Well."

I look down at Aislynn again. I have to stop myself from picking up the Moses's basket with her in it and running from the room.

"I thought I'd make some tea; want some?" I say, as I turn to go to the kitchen. I look back at my daughter. It would be too odd to take her into the kitchen with me, and she is sleeping soundly. I am being completely irrational.

"If you have Earl Grey."

I have no desire for tea, and the only Earl Grey I have is decaf, a sacrilege as far as my mother would be concerned, but I choose to let her stay in the dark about that part.

While the water is set to boil, I fill the teapot with hot tap water to warm it up, pull out a tray, put a cloth on it, take down two teacups and spoons, fill the milk pitcher, and put tea biscuits on a plate. I know how my mother likes her tea served. In an effort to calm down, I try to concentrate on each small task. But in my head, I am still screaming at her.

I turn to get the tea cozy from a drawer and catch a glimpse of myself in the mirror that is set into the cabinet door above the sink, one of those funky design features of Hollywood houses from the twenties that were built, surely, to cater to actors.

This morning, after I showered, I started to blow-dry my hair. Then Neil came into the bathroom and asked me what I was doing, and I had to tell him, trying to look good for my mother: casting directors have nothing on her in terms of judgment. "Fiona," he said, "you just had her first grandchild. She should be kissing the ground you walk on."

That will never happen, I thought, but he's right. I shouldn't have to knock myself out for her, so I put the blow-dryer down.

Then Aislynn needed to nurse, and while I sat with her, I tried to imagine myself in front of my mother with messed up hair, and frankly, the idea of it made my stomach sick, so I figured I'd finish blow-drying it when I was done nursing, but some-how that never happened, what with the burping and the walk-ing, and suddenly my mother was ringing the doorbell, so I just pulled it back into a haphazard chignon.

Some strands of hair are falling around my face, and for a second, in the kitchen mirror, it almost looks as if it were cut short, pixie cut short. I suddenly feel exhilarated and sickened all at once.

The kettle starts to whistle, so I turn off the stove, pour out the warmed water from the teapot, put the loose tea leaves in, and fill the teapot with the boiling water, as Patricia's voice comes into my head asking the same question it has been for the last two weeks.

"Why didn't you?"

Chapter 38

WHEN I GOT HOME that August night from Uncle Dave's house, my mother was still awake. My father had gone to sleep early as he always did. He used to brag that not only could he sleep through a hurricane, he had once as a child. My mother would just smile and say nothing.

I let myself in through the kitchen door that was never locked unless we went out of town and headed to my parents' room. My mother was sitting up in their bed, reading a fashion magazine that was propped open on her raised knees. The bedclothes were bunched at her feet. I stood in the doorway and leaned against the jamb. My legs still didn't feel solid, and the lamplight was blinding my eyes, making pointed, piercing starbursts around everything.

"Did you have a good time?" my mother said, glancing up at me, then looking back at her magazine.

I knew what I was supposed to say, knew what she expected to hear, and what would make all this go away. But for one split second, I wanted her to know. Wanted her to look at me and be able to tell and say it for me, to explain it for me. I felt so marked. How could she see me and not know what happened?

"Hmm?" she said, flipping a page.

"Uh-huh. It was just Patricia's cousins."

"That's good. Well, come here, and give me a kiss." My mother's arm reached out over my slumbering father toward me. She rarely hugged me, but the kiss she got every night was mandatory.

I hesitated for a moment. I figured my breath probably still smelled like the rum, and the floor suddenly seemed to be filled with dips and valleys. But my mother snapped her fingers a couple of times, so I pushed myself off the doorway, and walked carefully, trying to look steady, around to her side of the bed. As I passed the footboard, I glanced toward her and saw that her short summer nightgown was up on her thighs, leaving her unclothed private parts fully exposed.

It was like looking at an animal I'd never seen before and hadn't even known existed. An entirely new and strange creature that in a few years, I suddenly understood, was going to be me—whether I wanted it to or not.

She held her cheek out for me to kiss.

"G'night," I said, after my lips had brushed her skin.

"Sweet dreams." My mother lifted her magazine.

When I passed the end of the bed again, I made sure to look straight ahead, but my legs filled with ice, and I could feel Billy's hand in me, and I had to keep my mouth shut tight, so I wouldn't throw up. Once outside her door, I ran to my bathroom and made it just in time.

As I heaved into my toilet, I decided to tell Patricia everything, but only after each of us swore, on our Red Birds honor, to keep it a secret for the rest of our lives.

Chapter 39

"IS YOUR BED ALL RIGHT?" I say, as my mother sips her after dinner tea. We are sitting at the dining room table filled with the detritus of our meal. Neil is at a screening, and Aislynn is at my breast.

"It's fine. No, it's fine. And it's only for one more night. It's just you'd think with all that luxury, they could do something about the noise."

"You can hear through the walls at the Beverly Hills Hotel?"

"Yes. Well, I can, at least. Up and down through the halls, I just get this sense of people walking around. But never mind; I'll stay at the Beverly Wilshire next time."

"Well, I'm sorry you haven't been comfortable." I unlatch Aislynn's mouth, resettle her on the nursing pillow so that she is at my other breast, and get her nursing again.

"It's fine."

"Maybe it's the ghosts of all those dead film stars wanting to be near you."

"Then they should act like good southern ghosts and be entertaining."

"Exactly. I told you I'm out here with the heathens."

My mother refills her teacup. The dark dining room windows reflect our images, as if projected onto a screen.

"Speaking of, did I tell you I saw Vicky last week?"

For a moment, I try to think of a film star with that first name, then wonder how my mother could have seen one last week, even if there was one, since she was still in Lake Charles. Then I suddenly realize that she means Patricia's mother. Heathen, that's a new one in my mother's catalog of descriptions for her.

"No, where?"

"At a luncheon for the Auxiliary Guild of the hospital. Your father is spearheading the capital campaign for the new neonatal ward."

"Oh." I wonder whether she'll visit those babies sooner than she visited her own granddaughter.

"She was in another one of her outfits." My mother shakes her head before taking a sip of her tea.

Why my mother has always taken such offense to Vicky, I will never know. It's not as if my mother is style-challenged. Okay, so she's never been as flashy as Vicky, but she also has never entered a room unnoticed, or unappreciated, for that matter.

"But, of course, if someone devotes all her time and energy to the way she looks, instead of things that matter, that's the way she ends up."

Things that matter like tennis and bridge?

"It's why Patricia turned out the way she did. I always knew she was false. It's why she sold out to that reality show instead of sticking to her dream," my mother says, her eyes focusing on mine, "the way you have."

She looks at me as if to make sure that I heard this award of a compliment she has given me, as if it is a statue that I will put on my mantle and can look at if I ever forget that she said it. "Better late than never" must be her motto, but it isn't mine.

Aislynn's head drops back from my breast. Her mouth is partially open and her eyes are half-closed in the lush, dreamy fullness of postnursing. I put a burp cloth on my shoulder, lift her up, and begin patting her back.

"But," my mother continues, "if you have a mother who cares more about her store and all those men Vicky ran around with and never notices a thing about you, then that's what happens."

A white-hot flash leaps up from my stomach, and I have to slow down my hand on Aislynn's back.

"Vicky had to support herself and Patricia and Mike," I say, as a gentle burp moves out of Aislynn's mouth, "with little to no help from either of their fathers. While you had my father working and Louise at your beck and call."

I start rubbing Aislynn's back in small, careful circles to help her fall asleep, but also to try to help me calm down.

"Well, really, Fiona, I know that," my mother says, "better than you did. It was very clear to me what was happening in that apartment."

I feel Aislynn's tiny body surrender itself to sleep against my shoulder. I lower her to my lap and cradle her in my arms.

"What was happening?" There is no way she knows about Patricia's being beaten up regularly, so what the fuck is she talking about?

"Let's just say she wasn't the most on top of it of mothers." My mother dabs at the corners of her mouth with her napkin. She has eaten her entire meal and drunk her cup of tea with no effect on her lipstick, as if it did not dare not to hold up its end of her perfection. This makes me want to scream. "And really, Fiona, you were a child. How could you know anything?"

"And you did?"

My mother looks at me as if I am both a mother to fear and a daughter to punish. "And just what is that supposed to mean?"

"How much did you know when I came home that night from Patricia's uncle's fish fry?"

"Fish fry? What, in God's name, are you talking about?"

"That night, that summer when I was ten, when Vicky got me home so late after being out at Patricia's uncle's house. For Christ's sake, didn't you wonder what was happening all that time? Did you even notice what state I was in when I got home?"

My mother looks at me as if I am describing the plot of a TV show I guest-starred in that she had no desire to watch.

"I was drunk, Mother. Drunk. Patricia's eighteen-year-old cousin got me and her drunk and then—"

"You may not speak to your mother in that tone of voice."

"—did what he wanted to to us. Or tried to. Patricia ran away, and then I, thank God, threw up and got the hell out of there before he completely raped me, but not before he molested me and totally fucked me up, so that is what I'm talking about, Mother—"

"I will not listen to this."

"—the molestation that Patricia blabbed about on that talk show. I was the best friend that it also happened to. Though why in God's name I have to tell you that, I will never know. Maybe because you didn't want to notice then, and you don't want to notice now. But it's true and you have to. Did you just think that I stopped being a girl with all those fucking boys' clothes you made me wear that you figured no one would even look at me? And I was so goddamn deprived that by the time that sick fuck Billy saw me and started touching me, I was grateful, practically. So I let him, Mother. And that's the worst part, I let him at first, because I was just so goddamn happy that he saw me as a girl, that someone finally saw me as a girl. And it was the worse mistake I ever made in my life."

My mother is staring at me with her hand over her open mouth. I can imagine her mother saying to her, "Cover your mouth." God forbid that there be any sign that she actually has orifices.

"I had no idea."

I can barely hear her words. They could be coming from years and years ago.

"How could you not know? Especially now?"

"No, I mean—" My mother covers her eyes with her hand. I have a feeling that if she was wearing a scarf, the whole thing would be over her head. "I didn't think, when I made you—with the clothes—I just—"

"I gotta tell you, sometimes I don't know which was sicker, what Billy did or what you did."

The silence that follows my words is so heavy that it feels as if something has broken. Then I realize that maybe something has. My mother lowers her hand and looks at me across the table. I have an odd sense that she is seeing me for the first time. Then she looks at Aislynn, and for a moment, it seems that my mother doesn't know where she is. Or at least, she is not here with me in the present. Then she quietly gets up from her chair, goes into the living room, picks up her bag, and walks out the front door, shutting it carefully behind her.

I stare at the closed door for a moment, waiting for it to re-open with my mother in the doorway, then I understand that she is not coming back in. I consider running after her. She doesn't have a car; she is miles from her hotel. But I remember her cell phone, and my neighborhood is safe and populated after dark. Besides, other than offering to call her a cab or drive her, I don't know what I'd say, or what she'd say, and maybe she doesn't either.

As I turn my head back from looking after her, I catch a glimpse of myself in the mirrorlike windows holding Aislynn, and for a second, I see my mother holding me as a baby. I blink my eyes, grab my napkin from the table, put it up to my face, and begin to cry.

Chapter 40

I HAVE JUST GOTTEN OFF THE BUS at the corner of La Cienega and Beverly and am walking west toward Jerry's Deli. It is a bright and shining afternoon, the light almost too powerful even for L.A. but I head straight into it, into the force of that brightest of stars.

A glint catches my eye, and I look to my left and see the giant, grayish white hulk of Cedars-Sinai. I immediately try to figure out which room I was in with Aislynn when suddenly it hits me. Aislynn.

Where is she?

Oh, fuck. On the bus. I have left my baby on the bus, the L.A. bus that right this minute is heading downtown toward Skid Row, and my car isn't even here for me to chase it down, and it's not as if I can call them; I mean, I can, but if ever there was a dysfunctional entity, then L.A.'s Rapid Transit System would have to be it, so maybe the police is better, but is she still alive even? Maybe she flew off the seat when the bus came to the next stop, landed on the floor, hit her head, and died immediately. Or worse, is still alive and has already been taken by someone who will keep her and—

Neil is shaking me awake.

I stare at him for a moment, wondering how he got to the sidewalk that quickly, then I realize that I'm at home, in our room, not outside, so I immediately start searching for Aislynn, but she is nestled safely beside me in the cosleeper on my side of the bed. I touch her chest, feel her breathing, and let out a huge sigh.

"Oh, thank God."

"Bad one, huh?"

"Uh. Horrendous. I had left her on a bus. And I've never even ridden a bus. It was horrible, beyond horrible, like no fear I've ever had. It was like being sucked down into a giant hole of complete helplessness, while she was going to be—and I was responsible and grieving all at once. And all her pureness was just destroyed. She was destroyed, because of me."

"She's right here with us. She's fine."

"Thank God." I look at her again, then lie down close to Neil and put out my hand to rest gently on my daughter's leg.

"Because I don't think I am."

Neil and Aislynn have been sleeping soundly for over an hour, ever since I woke up from that dream, but I haven't. And I should be, because any minute now, she could wake up for a feeding, and I need my sleep, but I can't stop thinking.

On one hand, just to dream about Aislynn, even though it was horrible, was pretty amazing. During the pregnancy, I had generic girl (and sometimes boy) baby dreams, but since the birth, I've been wondering how long it would take for her to become so much a regular part of my life that she would show up in my dreams, as a whole separate entity. Not that I don't know the theory that everyone in our dreams is supposed to be us. And, okay, it doesn't take Freud, or Jung more specifically, to interpret what I just dreamed. But now for the rest of my life, God willing, there is this whole new person that is so much a part of my life that I will dream about her regularly.

I wonder how long it took for my mother to dream about me. And if she let herself remember them. And what they would have been like if she had let herself know what happened to me that night.

But, I suddenly realize, maybe that's why she didn't.

Aislynn begins to stir, making her little need-to-nurse sounds. I pick her up, put a pillow on my lap with my other hand, push aside the neck of my nightgown, and help her settle in. The bedroom is dim from the small nightlight. I suddenly imagine Aislynn at ten years old, with her deep red hair, walking in to tell me goodnight, fresh and smiling. I close my eyes and am holding that image of her when suddenly I realize that for me to be able to see who my daughter will be, I need to stop seeing who I was then.

Chapter 41

"IT'S GOING TO BE FINE," Neil says, as he takes off Aislynn's diaper, wipes her, and puts on some ointment.

"Fine?" I am pacing behind him, so I can peer around to make sure he is getting the diaper on okay. "She's probably not going to come. Did you even hear what I told you I said to her?"

"Fiona, your mother is not going to get on that plane this afternoon without seeing you and her granddaughter one last time."

He starts to dress Aislynn in the yellow onesie that she was wearing, but I take it from him, throw it into the dirty clothes bin, open her dresser drawer, and start rooting around.

"She's going to act as if everything's fine," Neil says, as he watches me consider and reject an endless pile of pink clothing. "But she's not going to run."

"When did you become such an expert on her? This is my mother we're talking about." I pull out a delicate lavender onesie with matching pants and socks that my mother sent two days after Aislynn was born, once her status as a redhead was confirmed, and hand them to Neil.

"I know, but just—" He stands there holding the clothes, as if he isn't sure which situation is harder to navigate, the one with my mother or getting our daughter dressed. I take the clothes from him and start putting them on her squirmy, tiny body.

"Focus on Aislynn with her. It's why she came."

"She came to make sure that I wasn't going to blab to everyone about what happened, the way Patricia did. That's why she came. And the minute I did blab to her, she flipped out, and ran. I flipped out, too, but I'm not running."

"Yes, you are."

The doorbell rings downstairs. My mother has always had such perfect timing, she should have been an actress.

"You've been running from this your whole life. But it's out. It's done. And you're a mother now. Move on."

"You move on," I say, picking up Aislynn, "and anyway, maybe I have."

Neil looks at me, kisses me on the cheek, and then goes down to let my mother in. I wait a moment, then walk quietly to the top of the stairs. I can hear my mother in the living room, making fake and bright exclamations about the day that Neil responds to. I suddenly can't decide which one of them I want to be with less, him or her.

"Oh, she's wearing my outfit! That lavender is sooooo darling on her," my mother says, when I finally walk into the living room carrying Aislynn ten minutes after she arrived.

I almost say, "Well, she didn't put it on herself," but Neil catches my eye, so I quickly change it to how much we love the clothes and thank her for sending them.

My mother smiles, sits down, and asks Neil whether it is difficult for him not being at Sundance now. Not that he doesn't have the best reason in the world for not going, but how are things at the studio; she'd read that last year was their best year?

Neil carries the conversation with my mother during our Sunday morning brunch. I am so grateful to him for doing this that I have to keep reminding myself to be pissed off for what he said. I sit at our dining room table and eat the pecan waffles that he made, and hold Aislynn, and practically use her as a screen to hide behind. As I listen to my mother talk about my father's work, I wonder whether she ever needed to use me as a screen when I was a baby, and if so, against whom.

Aislynn is asleep in her Moses's basket, and Neil is upstairs in our office talking to a producer about a scene that is shooting tomorrow. I insisted on doing the dishes, knowing that my mother would sit on the couch, and it would buy me a little time. And I told her I'd make some tea, so I'd have another excuse to be in there alone.

The kettle starts to whistle, just as Aislynn begins to cry. I immediately turn off the stove, move the kettle to another burner, and hurry into the living room.

Aislynn's face is wrapped tightly around her clenched eyes and mewling mouth. I pick her up, sit on the couch, grab the nursing pillow, and put her to my breast, trying to remember which one I left off on last time. As she begins to nurse, her face softens into its pale fullness.

"Where's the tea?" my mother says, looking up from the magazine she has pulled from her voluminous, this-season bag. I wonder whether she went to Dallas to buy it.

"It's—" I almost blink for a second, confused. "It's in the kitchen. Or the hot water is. I didn't have time to make it. But

I can after I finish—or—" I try to imagine my mother in my kitchen, making herself at home, carrying in tea for us.

"Waiting never hurt anyone."

"Thanks. I'll make it when I'm done."

"No, I meant Aislynn." My mother turns a page and begins examining a lipstick ad.

"She's barely three weeks old."

"Exactly," she says, looking up. "When I brought you home, your grandmother told me what her mother said to her when I was born: 'That baby needs to learn early on that the world does not revolve around what she wants. And never will.'"

She wants food, I think to myself, not the Hope diamond. While my mother goes back to her magazine, I look down at Aislynn, partly because I could look at my daughter all day, but mostly so my mother won't see my face if she happens to glance up.

As I watch the tiny mouth draw in its fill, I suddenly wonder what it was my mother wanted that she never got, from the world and from her mother. And aren't the two the same? At least to a small child.

Chapter 42

THE BOOK IS EASY TO FIND on the shelves in Aislynn's room because it is small and cream with pretty red lettering on the spine, *Lullabies for Babies*. When Patricia gave it to me at my shower with a card saying, "Here's to get y'all singing until she learns our Red Bird songs," I thought it was sweet, but something that would be unused. Until yesterday, when I realized that I can't remember the verses to any songs other than "Swing Low, Sweet Chariot," which Neil thinks is a funeral dirge, and maybe it is, or should be.

I take the book down, and am looking through its pages for the words to Brahms's "Lullaby and Goodnight" when something falls to the floor. I reach down for it. The paper is shiny and thin, and I already know what I'll find on the other side before I turn it over.

Chapter 43

THE FIRST THING MY MOTHER SAID TO ME when she picked me up after my first Red Birds meeting was "Where are your socks? And what are those things you're wearing?"

I knew she was going to ask, so all day I'd been trying to figure out something to say that would keep her from punishing me.

"They got wet."

"Wet? It hasn't rained in a week."

"In the bathroom, there was this puddle, and—" I let my mother think yucky things about puddles in bathrooms.

She looked at me to decide whether she believed me.

"Sister Dolores let me use these." I knew my mother didn't think I'd lie about a nun.

"Well," my mother said, looking at me over her large sunglasses. "Just be sure to give the Red Bird socks to Louise to wash before your meeting next week. You do have the socks, don't you?"

I nodded and looked out the window, glad that my book bag that my Red Bird socks should be in was under my legs.

"And you'll need to take those back to Sister Dolores. I

guess they came from the lost and found. Not that anyone would ever want those again. My God, they must be ten years old. Well, as long as you have yours."

Then she turned on the radio and began singing along.

For the rest of the week at school, I kept hoping that Patricia would give me back my socks. When she didn't the first couple of days, I figured her momma just hadn't washed them yet. But as the week came to an end, I knew I wasn't going to get them back. I thought about just saying to her, "I need my socks or my momma's gonna get real mad at me." But I didn't. Because every time I started to, Patricia would think up some fun new game, or we would have just pooled our money to share a cinnamon roll and chocolate milk during little recess, and I'd forget all about Momma and how mad she was gonna get—until I got off the bus, and walked into our house.

I didn't sleep the night before the next Red Birds meeting. I lay in bed, trying to figure out some way to get out of the house without my mother's seeing me, or wishing the fairies and pixies would come and knit another pair of Red Bird socks for me, so Momma would never know that I had given mine to my new best friend.

That morning, after Momma put her head in my room to tell me to get up and get dressed, I dragged myself into my Red Birds uniform, then looked down at my bare feet. The fairies and pixies hadn't left any socks for me, so I opened my sock drawer, took out a pair of dressy white ones that were only for parties or Mass, and put them on. For a second, I thought about taking them off and drawing Red Birds on them, but I knew they wouldn't look right, and then Momma would be even more mad that I had ruined these socks, too. I waited until the last possible minute that I could, then went down the stairs and into the kitchen.

Louise was at the stove, making pancakes and bacon. My father was at the breakfast table, hidden behind his newspaper; only his hand coming out to take his coffee cup and putting it back showed any bit of him. My mother was standing next to the phone on the wall, changing a tennis lesson for that afternoon. She watched me, as I walked to my chair and sidled in.

It was the second of silence after she put down the phone that scared me.

"Fiona, where are your Red Bird socks?"

Louise's hand hesitated for a moment over the skillet she was pouring batter into. I looked down at the place mat that my parents had bought me on a business trip they went on in Miami.

"Answer me, young lady; where are those socks?"

My stomach felt as if the knife and fork at my place were cutting it up. Louise put fresh bacon in the skillet and began softly humming a hymn from her church that she sang me sometimes. My father turned a page of his newspaper with a loud rustle and snap.

"Louise," my mother said, whirling around to her. "Did you see Fiona's Red Bird socks in the wash this week? I told her to put them in there."

Louise flipped the three pancakes, pushed the bacon around in their pan, then slowly turned around. "Those socks done got ruined, Mizz M."

"Ruined?" My mother looked at me, triumphant in her victory of catching my lie.

"Those little bird things on them just come right off in the wash. Threads everywhere. Dinky things they was. No good for even one wearin'." Then she turned back to her skillet, scooped up the pancakes, settled them on a plate, and flipped the bacon in the pan.

"Huh." My mother fixed her gaze on me.

Louise started humming one of her church songs again. My father cleared his throat.

"Well," my mother said, then looked around, but Louise was filling the breakfast plates and my father was still hidden behind the paper.

I picked up my orange juice and took a small sip. Inside, I was flying as if Red Birds were sewn all over me.

Louise walked to the table and put down my plate. "Hurry up and eat, child. You gots to be gettin' to school."

But I knew there was a smile under her words.

Chapter 44

I PUT THE BOOK OF LULLABIES BACK ON THE SHELF in Aislynn's room and carry the photograph over to the windows where the bright day is pouring in. Vicky took the picture when she came to pick up Patricia after the last Red Birds meeting of our first-grade year. I had always wanted this picture but knew I couldn't keep it at my house.

Patricia and I are standing outside our classroom in our Red Birds uniforms, me in my plain white socks and her in my special Red Bird socks. Our broad smiles show tooth-fairy grins, and our arms are around each other, bodies pressed close, as if we are one person. And then, for a moment, I can feel the uniform on me, can hear the school sounds around me, and can imagine Patricia next to me.

"Now we're just alike," Patricia's voice says from so long ago.

And I suddenly understand that the socks on her are also on me, and what happened to me also happened to her.

I look out the window of my daughter's room, my view framed by the fairy toile curtains, as if the world out there is only as real as a play.

I walk out of the room, go downstairs, check on Aislynn

asleep in her basket, sit down on the couch, pick up the phone, and dial the number.

"Hello?"

"I think the L.A. chapter of Red Birds is overdue for a meeting."

There is a small pause, then Patricia says, "Way overdue."

A+

AUTHOR
INSIGHTS,
EXTRAS, &
MORE...

FROM

**DELAUNÉ
MICHEL**

AND

AVON A

Reading Group Guide

1. Lifelong friendships are treasured for the great joy that they bring. But they also bring great pain. Do you find yourself choosing sides with either Fiona or Patricia?

2. Fiona says that ending her friendship with Patricia would be "Like divorcing a sister. No, worse, a part of my self. Because without Patricia in my life, where would all those memories and experiences that we shared and lived through go?" (Chapter 15) Are those strong enough reasons for Fiona to stay friends with Patricia?

3. Why do you think Patricia is drawn to Fiona? And why does Patricia remain friends with Fiona?

4. When Fiona finds out that she is pregnant, she goes to Patricia's home to tell her. She then lies to Neil that she didn't tell Patricia the news. Fiona justifies this by telling herself that "It's almost like she [Patricia] was here first, in terms of loyalty." (Chapter 3) Is Fiona's loyalty with Patricia appropriate? Does this loyalty justify Fiona's lying?

5. When Fiona first sees her mother's new haircut, she immediately wants it, too. "A pixie cut! The name alone was a ticket to join the land of fairies. I wanted to be a pixie." (Chapter 5) But

it isn't until years later that she is finally able to get the haircut, long after she has stopped believing in pixies. Why does she cut her hair? To defy her mother or something else?

6. Before Fiona cut her hair, kids at school were already teasing her about her red hair. After she cuts it, she is even more afraid of what they will say. Should Patricia have tried to stop Fiona from getting it cut?

7. Why does Fiona's mother become so enraged when she gets her haircut? Is it only because Fiona broke her rule or is it something else?

8. How does the punishment that Fiona's mother comes up with set Fiona up for what happens to her at the end of the summer? Or does it?

9. Once Fiona is visibly pregnant, the way she is perceived in the world changes. She feels that "My entire old self has become invisible, and I wonder if I'll ever see it again." (Chapter 23) How much of that is a reality and how much is her own thinking? Did her experience after the haircut make her more sensitive to this?

10. Fiona struggles with how she sees herself once she is pregnant and motherhood is looming. How does her relationship with her mother play into that?

11. Fiona knows that her mother eavesdrops on Fiona's phone calls with her father. "Though I doubt my father would be pleased if he ever figured it out. Or if I told him. But I won't. Which my mother counts on. Colluding on the secret of her breaking my privacy." (Chapter 10) Did Fiona learn to keep secrets as a way to get through life from her mother or did she learn it as a defense from her mother?

12. After Fiona's mother punishes her, Fiona's father "never mentioned the clothes. As if they weren't there. As if what I looked like wasn't there. I wondered if I would ever be seen by him again." (Chapter 24) Why doesn't Fiona's father ever intervene?

13. Patricia defends telling their secret by telling Fiona that "It came out. I didn't plan for it to, it just did. But it's not like anyone knew it was you." (Chapter 36) How much ownership did Patricia have of that secret? Was it her right to tell it when she wanted to?

14. Patricia asks Fiona the one question that Fiona has never wanted to face since that eventful summer. "Why didn't you?" (Chapter 36) Was that the best thing for Fiona to hear or the worst?

15. After Fiona confronts her mother, her mother goes back to being the way she was before. But later, Fiona has a new understanding. "I suddenly wonder what it was my mother wanted that she never got. From the world and from her mother. And aren't the two the same? At least to a small child." What enabled Fiona to see her mother in that way?

16. Fiona and Patricia both came from abusive homes: Fiona emotionally and Patricia physically. How did each of their personalities develop in relation to those environments? And how did their careers and lives in Hollywood change who they are?

17. What does *The Safety of Secrets* reveal about the strength and fragility of human relationships?

Questions for DeLauné Michel
by Mark Sarvas

Mark Sarvas's debut novel, *HARRY, REVISED*, will be published by Bloomsbury in May 2008. He is best known as the host of the popular and controversial literary Web blog "The Elegant Variation" which has been covered by the *Los Angeles Times*, the *New York Times*, the *Guardian* (A Top 10 Literary Blog), *Forbes* (Best of the Web), *Los Angeles Magazine* (A Top L.A. Blog), the *Scotsman, Salon*, the *Christian Science Monitor, Slate*, the *Denver Post*, the *Village Voice*, the *New York Sun*, *NPR*, and numerous other fine publications. His book reviews and criticism have appeared in the *New York Times Book Review*, the *Threepenny Review*, the *Philadelphia Inquirer, Truthdig*, the *Modern Word, Boldtype*, and the *Los Angeles Review*. He is a member of the National Book Critics Circle.

1) As the title suggests, *The Safety of Secrets* looks at the costs exacted by secrets—the innocent (or seemingly innocent) ones and the more insidious. And L.A.—and the film business, in particular, in which this story is set—is, in its way, a city of secrets, both manufactured and organic. Can you talk about what drew you to this rich theme?

I wanted to explore betrayal in a lifelong friendship. And it occurred to me that one currency of intimacy in a best friendship is shared secrets, so I wanted to see what would happen to that relationship when its most powerful secret is given away, and given away thoughtlessly, like so many pennies dropped on the floor. I was interested in the way that secrets are used to ally and/or alienate ourselves from those that we love. There is such stark and deep knowledge of one another in an ages-old friendship that I wondered about how some secrets are used as a mask to hide and protect ourselves, or are used to continue to be that person that we think our best friend needs, or to try not to be that person anymore, even when we still are. I felt there was a mirroring of Fiona and Patricia's friendship's emotional landscape with their careers in Hollywood. All of that layering and hiding are essential tools in Hollywood. I think one trait that distinguishes stars from other actors is their ability to appear completely exposed while in fact they are presenting only and exactly what they want us to see.

2) Among many other things, *The Safety of Secrets* casts a light onto that unofficial Hollywood caste system that's not talked about much, namely friends who fare differently, who land at different squares of the game board of success. Can you talk about how this informs your characters' relationships and how it informs life in this city?

What I found fascinating about that caste system while writing this book is how much easier it can sometimes be to be comfortable with the enormous success of a new friend as opposed to that of an old. The difference in success is the same, the difference in bank accounts is the same, and yet none of that seems to matter. I wanted to see what, if anything, could hold Fiona and Patricia's friendship together in the face of that. And it isn't only worldly success that wreaks havoc with relationships, but also a great marriage or the birth of a child, all of those life markers that should be the happiest times in our lives, yet sometimes are accompanied by the withdrawing of someone dear.

As far as how that plays out in L.A. I think that caste system is one of the reasons the industry can be so addictive: every move one makes is a point gained or lost. It is impossible not to get caught up in the constant scoring, like some giant video game that never ends.

3) Both of your books draw on your experiences in L.A., and although it's the mistake of the amateur to confuse the character for the author, you write with the firsthand immediacy of one who has lived it. How have you managed to navigate the thorny journey of writing a work that is fiction even as it's informed by fact?

I write about the worlds that I know, and I write stories that would keep me up at night if I didn't write them. Some of my work is more fictive than the rest. My first novel, *Aftermath of Dreaming*, was loosely based on a relationship I had with Warren Beatty. I visited a lot of book clubs with that novel, in person here in New York, and over the phone with groups in L.A. and elsewhere. One thing I found interesting was that all the L.A. book clubs knew exactly whom the book was about, while not all the other groups did. But finally, the characters in that novel are characters—it isn't a memoir. As this book isn't either.

Because of all the writers in my family (my mother, Elizabeth Nell Dubus, my uncle Andre Dubus, my cousins Andre Dubus and James Lee Burke, and more), this question has been one I have dealt with my whole life even before I started writing. It was sometimes hard to read my relatives' work and not wonder what was true or who was who. But as a result of that, I learned early on that those questions are not only a waste of time, but also a road that leads nowhere. To try to answer it feels like trying to separate grains of sand: this grain of sand is "true," while this grain of sand next to it is not. What matters is the whole picture and that is a creative work of fiction.

4) Your books embrace L.A. as a literary setting, and you write expertly about local scenes from Fred 62 to the Bel-Air Hotel. How does L.A. as a setting work its inspiration on you and what are the greatest challenges and greatest joys in capturing this unique city in prose?

I went to L.A. from New York in my early twenties with a boyfriend and meant to stay only a few months. At that time, I couldn't imagine not living in New York. But I fell completely and deeply in love with L.A. It was everything the West is held up to be: open and expansive and raw. Just standing in the sun, in that silver-tipped light, with the desert winds moving around, made me feel transformed. I needed to write about L.A. the way a child might write about a parent. That city made my adult self. It is an endless trove for me and it can't help but continue to be prominent in my work. But the biggest challenge when one's real estate is well-tread, so to speak, is to write with a fresh view. My answer to that has been to write about the city the way I know it to be, which is to say a wonderful and terrible god that happens to be comprised of people and nature and architecture.

5) You're a creator of strong women characters who cross traditions of Southern gentility and urban sensibility. What's the source of this interest and ability?

I grew up in an area that is basically almost its own country. South Louisiana has its own traditions and history that are very separate from, not only the rest of America, and the rest of the South, but even the rest of the state. I have always identified myself first as coming from that particular world. My father's family has been in New Orleans since the 1600s. My mother's family—my namesake, in fact, Hélene DeLauné and her husband Jules André—arrived in South Louisiana during the French Revolution. Marie Antoinette gave my namesake jewels to help her leave to escape the guillotine. So, I have a deep connection there. And yet, I moved to points north and west where I had to, and continue to, seek out other ex-patriots who understand why my one-word answers are three pages long, and why when I apologize for anything from terrible traffic to the Saints losing again that I don't think I'm responsible. It was impossible, and would have been foolhardy, to live in New York City and L.A. without taking on some of their mores, and I wanted to. But my core cannot change, thank God. It is where I draw my strength. There have been many times in my life when I have thought that whatever hardship I was enduring was nothing compared to my namesake's leaving the court of France for the wilds of South Louisiana, and that has helped.

6) Please tell us something about what sparked the wonderful Spoken Interludes series, and how it's faring as a bicoastal affair?

The series initially grew out of my love for parties. Where I grew up in South Louisiana, the year is governed by the Catholic Church's calendar, so starting with Advent season, life just becomes a long series of parties that build in scale and intensity until their culmination in Mardi Gras. I always get terribly homesick during that season. So, one year, when I couldn't get home, I decided to have those parties myself. This was in L.A., so the Catholic rituals and aspect were a bit diminished, but still. So, I had all these parties, and friends came and brought friends, then those people came to the next ones and brought friends, so the parties got quite large.

A few weeks later, I went to the post office after a theater audition, and I was waiting in line, thinking about my parties and my audition when suddenly I realized that if my parties had been a play, it would have had great audiences. So I thought, "Why not let a performance be in the middle of a party?" Then I decided that I wanted the performance to be stories, since storytelling is the original form of theater, and because it is what we do when we go to parties—we break into little groups and tell each other stories about ourselves. I wanted it to be as if someone at a party got up and told a story, but instead of a small group of people hearing it, the entire room listened.

At that point, I had already written my first two short stories, which had won recognition, and I wanted to write more, but frankly, I do better with deadlines, so I figured scheduling myself to read them in public would be a pretty good deadline. And I had so many friends, including a sister, who were writing that I decided to make it written stories. At that time in L.A. in 1996, there were many places to read poetry, but very few to read short fiction or essays, so I felt it might be filling a need. I also thought it would be a way for writers to connect with their audience without having to wait for publication. The first show was in May 1996 and, to my great surprise, it sold out. The series has been going strong ever since.

In the years since, Spoken Interludes has been heard on National Public Radio, and has had special shows in conjunction with other organizations including the Getty Museum. Writers such as Ann Packer, Mona Simpson, Bruce Wagner, Alice Sebold, Michael Korda, Arthur Phillips, Arianna Huffington, and Michael Connelly, including newer voices, have come to read their work.

In early 2001, I made Spoken Interludes a nonprofit arts organization so I could develop an outreach writing program for at-risk teenagers. My formal education was cut short at the end of eleventh grade due to family matters, so reaching out to teenagers in that way is very important to me. The Spoken Interludes Next writing program is an eight to ten week writing course where students, in small groups of six to eight, work with professional writers to learn how to write their own short story. The program ends with a graduation reading for the students that family, friends, and the public all attend. The first session was that spring in a downtown L.A. high school. The following year, we brought the program to a high school in the L.A. Juvenile detention system. The program continues to teach eleventh graders in both of those schools and is in the process of going into four to ten more high schools in the L.A. area. Spoken Interludes Next has served homeless and gay teenagers in other facilities. We also had a literacy program for fourth graders, Spoken Interludes Read, in a downtown L.A. grammar school.

In 2004, I moved to the New York City area with my family, and started the Spoken Interludes reading series here in the spring of 2005. The reception was immediate, warm and welcoming, and I feel the same sort of family connection with the audiences here that I felt in L.A. I am looking forward to starting Spoken Interludes Next here, as well.

7) Speaking of bicoastal, you've now had a chance to live in two literary milieus, New York and L.A. How would you compare life in the two literary scenes—and might there be a literary *roman à clef* in your future?

Novelists are a small herd in L.A. Ever since I started producing Spoken Interludes there, I felt an immediate sense of community with the writers who were part of the series. I think, and hope, that Spoken Interludes became a home to many of them. I meant for it to. A number of writers developed work there, or came to read chapters of novels while they were writing them, such as Yeardley Smith's upcoming book, *I, Lorelie: The Mud Letters*, Harry Shearer's *Not Enough Indians*, and Christopher Rice read the story that his first novel, *A Density of Souls*, was launched from after he read it at Spoken Interludes. Writers aren't glorified in L.A. the way actors, or even directors, are. I wanted Spoken Interludes to be one place that they could go where their work on the page was more important than an actor's (eventual and possible) interpretation of it up on the screen.

New York is a different story. I don't get the sense that writers feel that they are coming in from the cold when they read at Spoken Interludes here. And that makes sense because there are so many more places for them to read, and there are lots and lots more fiction writers, but the warmth and connection and passion for the written word is just as strong, and that really is the common bond. In the twelve plus years that I have been producing the series, I can count on three fingers the number of writers who were anything less than wonderful, and I'll never tell who they are. So if I were to write a literary *roman à clef*, about the reading series at least, I'm afraid it would be quite sunny, and with not enough sex.

8) Who are you reading these days and who are the authors you most admire and feel influenced by?

I'm reading lots of John Banville, including *Christina Falls* that he wrote under the pen name Benjamin Black. I recently finished re-reading *The Habit of Being—the Letters of Flannery O'Connor*. *The Emperor's Children* by Claire Messud was a great read. I loved Dani Shapiro's *Black and White*. Ha Jin's *Waiting* is a new favorite. And I turn to P.D. James, Michael Connelly, Robert Crais, and T. Jefferson Parker for my ideal indulgence—murder mysteries.

In my teens and early twenties, some of the writers whose work taught me that literature can live inside me were: Joan Didion, Walker Percy, my mother, J.D. Salinger, Fitzgerald, Milan Kundera, Steinbeck, Gabriel Garcia Marquez, Edith Wharton, DH Lawrence, Eudora Welty, and Shakespeare.

But I learned how to live the life of a writer from my mother. She first started writing when I was in grade school, but she needed a place to work, so she shoved aside the clothes in her closet (and my mother loves her clothes), and my father built her a desk and she wrote there. Then when I was fifteen, my parents separated, and my mother and I moved into a small house. She used to get up every morning at 5 or 6 a.m. and write for an hour before she got me up for school and then went to her 9 to 5 to keep a roof over our heads. And from the beginning, she was prolific. She had her own newspaper column, she published five books, she wrote plays, and stories, and musicals, and basically everything except poetry, though I'm sure she has a box of it somewhere and has just never told me.

What I saw early on was that one makes the time and space to write, no matter what. It isn't life's job to make it easy to write. One just writes. And that has been the most important lesson I could have learned. And it was made all the more valuable since I could see firsthand how writing transformed her life and gave her to herself.

In terms of the technical aspects of the work, I have learned the most from Chekhov, particularly his plays. He once said, in regards to his play *Ivanoff*, that if a gun is shown in the first act, it must be fired in the third. But he was a master at creating worlds where anything is possible, and where one keeps questioning the outcome until the very end even though the inevitable finally does happen. I was also influenced by Tennessee Williams because he portrayed the South the way it was, at least the corner I recognize.

9) Your career stands as something of a rebuttal to the notion that only MFAs are getting book deals these days. What, if anything, would you consider as the value of writing from "The School of Life"?

My education has never been rooted in academia, even when I was in school. I started modeling when I was fourteen (okay, this was Baton Rouge, but still), then at fifteen began teaching modeling to women older than myself and to residences in a home for battered women to raise their self-esteem. In what would have been my senior year of high school, I was living on my own and was the manager and buyer of a clothing store. I basically was living like a thirty-year-old at eighteen. Then I moved to New York City, had an unexceptional fling as a model there and in Europe, then returned to New York City, and settled down to what I really wanted to do and began studying acting.

I was fortunate to have great teachers from such places as the

Actor's Studio, the Neighborhood Playhouse, and Juilliard. I learned about such things as character development, building an arc, when to start a scene, themes. I just had no idea that I would eventually use all of that in my writing. And acting classes are tough. There is such a stripping down that happens, but finally in a good way. It taught me to hear criticism, but to balance it against what I know to be true. And one of the great gifts that studying and working as an actor gave me for my writing was that for all those years, I was one of many people all working together to tell a story, and the story had to be (or should have been) more important than any one person involved. That still gives me great perspective when I'm working; I try to make the story that I am writing more important than how I feel about writing it.

Coming to writing from the background of an actor having read and worked on scripts and plays taught me to view the work theatrically, or at least, cinematically. I see the scenes playing out and I hear the characters in them. Many times, they surprise me. It feels a bit like watching my novels unfold in front of me.

I am grateful that I had to and did all those different things which were like a slow unraveling of the outside person that I thought I was or wanted to be only to have this life revealed. There are many times when I think about some of those lives, and the different ways that my life could have gone, and I look forward to writing about what that could have been.

10) With the understanding that most mothers would consider their proudest accomplishment the raising of their children, what would you—an actress, award-winning author, impresario, advocate of children at risk—consider your proudest nonparental achievement?

Without a doubt, it is creating and teaching in the writing program for at-risk teenagers. It was joyous and heartbreaking and awe-inspiring to work with those kids. They are in such a fragile stage of life, and some of the things they were having to deal with would be completely overwhelming for adults, much less for them. What I learned from teaching them is that everyone has an essential need for their stories to be heard, and that great transformation can happen when they are. I was honored and humbled to be part of what enabled that to happen.

And watching them grow and discover parts of themselves and skills that they have is a true blessing. Many of them discover a love for reading for the first time because they are no longer viewing stories and novels as something "other," but suddenly a thing they have done themselves. One of my students from the very first session sent me an e-mail last week with a new story he wrote for a writing course, and I was so happy to read it. But all of the students I taught have had a huge impact on me. It is such a precarious time, that in between right before they go out to the world from high school. It was my mission that the writing program give them the time and space for their stories—and what stories—to be heard.

I am thrilled that Spoken Interludes Next is continuing in L.A. I am looking forward to starting it here in New York, so I that can work with kids again. As full and happy as my life is today, I miss that part of it.

Delauné Michel

DELAUNÉ MICHEL was raised in south Louisiana in a literary family that includes her mother, Elizabeth Nell Dubus, her uncle André Dubus, and her cousin James Lee Burke. She has worked as an actor in theater, television, and film.

In 1996, Ms. Michel created Spoken Interludes, a critically-acclaimed reading series where award-winning, bestselling, and upcoming writers read their own work. In 2001, she made it a nonprofit arts organization through which she has developed, has taught in, and continues to run outreach writing programs for at-risk teenagers in the Los Angeles public high schools and detention halls. The Spoken Interludes reading series has been heard on

National Public Radio and continues to have readings in Los Angeles and New York. Please visit www.spokeninterludes.com.

The first two stories Ms. Michel wrote won recognition by the Thomas Wolf Short Fiction Award, and later work won the Pacificus Foundation Literary Award. She has written nonfiction for many publications, and has performed her own work on NPR. Her first novel, *Aftermath of Dreaming*, was published by William Morrow in 2006. She lives in Westchester County, New York, with her family, and is currently working on her third novel. For more information, please visit www.delaunemichel.com.